Nothing But
the Truth

Nothing But the Truth

A NOVEL

HOLLY JAMES

DUTTON

DUTTON

An imprint of Penguin Random House LLC

penguinrandomhouse.com

LIBRARY OF CONGRESS CATALOGING-IN-PUBLICATION DATA has been applied for.

ISBN 9780593186503 (paperback)
ISBN 9780593186510 (ebook)

Printed in the United States of America
1 3 5 7 9 10 8 6 4 2

BOOK DESIGN BY KATY RIEGEL

*For everyone who lost or found
something in 2020*

CHAPTER

1

Lucy Green stood on a precipice.

Really, she sat on a barstool contemplating her drink while she waited for her boyfriend, Caleb, who was working late again. If he didn't cancel altogether, they'd order another round, talk about their routine days, go back to his place and have mediocre sex, and she'd fall asleep listening to him grind his teeth because he refused to wear a mouth guard. And that would be how she spent the final night of her twenties.

But it was fine. *She* was fine. Everything was *fine*.

"Would you like something different?" the bartender asked her.

"Hmm?" She looked up and found a handsome face hovering before her. She'd paid no attention to him when she came in, ordered her drink, and immediately proceeded to check her email, because it had been twenty minutes since she left her office and literally anything could have happened in the world of celebrity publicity.

He looked like most bartenders in L.A.: tall, chiseled, probably an actor. Except in place of vain indifference was an interested warmth that made Lucy sit up and pay attention. He wadded a rag in his big hands then pointed to her glass. "Your drink. You don't seem to be enjoying it. Would you like something else?"

She looked down at her martini and saw two olives staring back at her like skewered eyeballs. Her boss, Joanna, favored the drink, and Lucy found herself aspiring to such sophistication. "I like it just fine, thanks."

He snorted a laugh. "That's a lie. You've taken two sips." He leaned in and whispered like he was telling her a secret. "And I make really good martinis."

Lucy's lips quirked, and she realized that she actually didn't care for a martini. Though she aimed to someday be as classy as Joanna, a woman she greatly admired, perhaps her beverage choices were not the means to that end. She didn't want to get drunk. She couldn't. She had too big of a day tomorrow, with a promotion on the line. But maybe something different would be nice.

She pushed the glass across the bar toward him. "All right, then; pour me something else."

He took the carefully crafted cocktail and dumped it into a sink beneath the bar with a flick of his wrist. "As you wish." He gave her a smile that could have easily landed him a role on a streaming series. He flipped his rag over his shoulder and turned around.

Lucy swiveled on her stool to face the door, watching for Caleb.

The bar had a beach-chic vibe with a big glass wall, white

marble bar with copper finishing, and pops of teal and apricot on the walls, the stools, the chairs. It was more inviting than depressing, which was how Lucy found most bars. Open and airy, it didn't hide secrets in the dark.

No sign of Caleb.

She checked her phone again but only saw his last message from twenty minutes earlier.

Running late.

She scrolled up in their chat to see the selfie of the two of them standing in front of the condo they had just signed a lease on. They were two weeks from moving in together, and Lucy was counting down the days until she could stop tripping over all the boxes in her apartment and live with her boyfriend. Caleb was smart, kind, ambitious but not heartless; sometimes she couldn't believe he checked so many boxes. He was the guy she could see herself marrying and moving to the suburbs with to watch their two kids chase a labradoodle around a pool someday. After two years of dating, she was ready for him to drop to a knee and present her with the emerald cut of her dreams, and if Hollywood was to be believed, he would do it tomorrow, on her birthday.

If only he could show up for drinks on time.

She distracted herself from waiting by scanning social media to make sure everyone was behaving. It was the best source for any breaking client drama. At the top of her search was her own problem child client, Leo Ash, whom she'd inherited when she made junior publicist at her firm, J&J Public. Leo was a rock star in his late twenties who got famous as a teenager and had a celebrity scandal rap sheet a hundred miles long. Next was one of her boss's star clients, Ms. Ma, a female rapper releasing a music video the next morning that was sure to set the music world on fire.

No scandals on either front.

"Here you are," the bartender said. "Something different." He slid a martini glass filled with lavender-colored liquid over the marble. Tiny bubbles spiraled from its center like it might have champagne in it. A lemon wedge clung to its rim.

Lucy huffed a laugh. "What is this?" She pulled it close and got a whiff of sugar. "It looks like something a sorority girl would order on her twenty-first birthday."

The bartender grinned. "Perhaps. But it'll cheer you up."

"Who says I'm unhappy?"

"You do. With the way you're checking your phone, watching the door, and ordering drinks you don't like."

Heat flushed her cheeks. She felt totally exposed. Naked in front of a stranger. But in his hazel eyes, she saw that he wasn't being cruel. Just observant.

Lucy smirked at him. "Aren't you keen."

"That's why they pay me the big bucks." He swung his rag over his shoulder again. "That, and making life-changing cocktails." A dimple popped in his cheek, and Lucy could easily see him on a red carpet, looking dashing in a tux.

She looked at her glass, and the playful swirl of purple inspired her to make a wish. It seemed appropriate on the eve of such a milestone birthday. Not to mention, she could use all the good luck she could get for her big day.

She tilted the glass toward the bartender with a smile. "Well, tomorrow *is* my birthday, so. Cheers."

As the tiny bubbles fizzed her tongue and the smooth liquid

poured down her throat, she silently wished for the next day to be perfect.

"How is it?" the bartender asked.

"Life-changing."

He nodded in approval. "My work here is done. I hope you have a happy birthday tomorrow."

Though she expected some kind of tectonic shift, perhaps cosmic acknowledgment that there was now a three in front of her age—a sore hip, a chin whisker, a wave of suffocating Millennial guilt that she hadn't accomplished *anything* despite her achievements—Lucy's birthday began like any other day.

She woke in her bed, alone because Caleb had in fact not shown up for drinks. Sorry, babe. I have to cancel. I'll see you tomorrow night. Although not surprised, she had been disappointed. She stared up at her powder blue ceiling, which she'd painted in a fit of freshening up her small living space the previous summer—she'd found the tip in an article called "How to Freshen Up Your Small Living Space"—and took a deep breath. It was a big day. Yes, her thirtieth birthday, but also the day she would secure her promotion at J&J Public, a Hollywood institution, and best the insufferable Chase McMillan, her workplace archnemesis.

His rise in rank right alongside her—intern, junior assistant, assistant, junior publicist—had earned him the nickname

Chase McMillan the Supervillain in Lucy's innermost circle. Admittedly, he was excellent at his job, but he was also callous and often handed things Lucy deserved. They were both vying for a seat at the table with the senior publicists that had been left vacant by a recent departure, and Lucy would be damned if he beat her to it.

She wanted it so badly she could taste it. She could taste it like a champagne toast on the rooftop at Perch, the exact restaurant where she'd be holding her birthday party later that night.

After she got her promotion.

First, she had to nail her lunch date with Joanna and Lily Chu, the hottest new starlet in Hollywood, who was already generating Oscar buzz for her breakout role in an indie film. Lucy was no stranger to lunch with celebrities—it was literally in her job description. Like half of Hollywood, J&J Public was competing to reel in Lily, and Lucy was going to be the one to land her. Lily & Lucy: she already liked the way their names sounded together. She would win her over, she knew it. And Lily Chu as a client was the exact edge she needed to land that promotion.

All in a day's work.

1. Lock down Lily Chu.
2. Secure promotion.
3. Gracefully ascend into the divine decade of her thirties.
4. Have one hell of a birthday bash on a rooftop in downtown L.A. where her boyfriend would finally propose to her.

She was ready. She was *ready*. All she had to do was get out of bed and start her day.

She stretched her arms over her head. Her elbows popped, but that was normal, definitely not a sign of age. She threw back her duvet, swung her legs over the bed, and saw that her mother was calling her.

In fact, she saw that she had a missed call and two texts from her mother already—alerts she didn't hear because she gave herself the birthday gift of sleeping with her phone on silent.

She lifted her phone from her nightstand and looked at her mother's name on her screen. She considered giving herself another gift by not answering. Without a doubt, the phone call would include a birthday wish coupled with a reminder that Lucy was now in her thirties, not married, and had no children—things Maryellen Green had accomplished by the time she was twenty-seven.

Lucy was an only child, so her mother put all her reproduction stock in her, which meant things like publicly noting that her left hand was still void of a diamond and stockpiling hand-knitted baby clothes and blankets. If she listened closely enough, Lucy was sure she'd hear knitting needles clicking in the background while her mother pinched her phone between her ear and shoulder, refusing to acknowledge that speaker-phone made life much easier.

She marveled at her mother's ability to instill guilt at the mere sight of her name, and surrendered.

"Hi, Mom," she answered.

Click, click, click. Right on schedule.

"Lucy, sweetheart. Happy birthday."

"Thanks."

Needing to get her day going, Lucy sidestepped a moving box full of books and headed toward her bathroom. Always one to be prepared, she had started packing belongings that could stand not being used in the coming two weeks until she moved. Boxes littered her small apartment like bins at a rummage sale, half full of a random assortment of art, dishes, seasonal shoes. Her efficiency would pay off in the long run, but the early preparation made her daily routine a bit of an obstacle course.

"I assume you're preparing for your big day today? You know, I saw that movie with Lily, and she is just *fantastic*. I hope you make a good impression on her," her mother said.

Annoyance prickled Lucy's scalp. Her mother fancied herself a coconspirator in her life, always knowing what was going on if she wasn't trying to orchestrate it herself. Lucy didn't even remember telling her about Lily, and Maryellen had remembered the date of their meeting. She even called her by her first name like they were acquainted.

"That's the plan, Mom."

Click, click, click.

The sound of the knitting needles was like a little bomb counting down to detonation. Lucy loved her mother, she really did, but she knew where their conversation was heading, and she quite honestly didn't have the patience for it on her big day.

"Good. And what about you and Caleb? You know, you better get married soon if you're going to have ch—"

"I don't even know if I want kids, Mom!" she snapped, shocking herself. She wasn't surprised they'd gone from happy birthday to discussing children in ten seconds flat, but she was surprised about what came out of her mouth. Even though she'd been the one to say the words, the confession felt like a slap in the face; she even flinched. Kids had always been at the back of her mind, an assumption, a future expectation, but she had never given it an honest moment's thought because honestly, she hadn't had a moment to think about it.

The world told her she wanted kids, starting way back with the toys she played with as a little girl: baby dolls, dollhouses. And then every plotline from bedtime stories all the way through award-winning films about the formidable and undying strength of a mother's love. It was supposed to be her purpose in life according to just about everyone. Otherwise there had to be something wrong with her; she was defective, selfish, she'd change her mind someday—she'd heard all the rhetoric.

"That's ridiculous, Lucy, of course you want kids," her mother cut in as if on cue. "And you're thirty now, so—"

"So, what? I've hit some kind of threshold?" She felt something take hold of her. Something invisible that was both binding and freeing at once. Before she could stop herself, feelings she'd never expressed came spilling out. "It's pretty unfair, you know. You spend all of your twenties trying *not* to get pregnant, then right when your career is taking off, the clock starts ticking and you're pressured to have kids before you're thirty-five because all the risks set in and suddenly, you're too old! It's a ridiculously small window for such a major life decision. And it's just *expected* that I want kids—that all women want kids! Maybe I do, eventually, but can I at least get a minute *to think about it*?" Her voice crescendoed into a shout that bounced sharply off her bathroom mirror. She blinked at the flushed woman she saw in the reflection, wondering where the hell she had come from.

Her mother, on the other end of the phone, was speechless.

Lucy didn't know what else to say, so she said, "I've got to get ready to go to spin class, Mom."

She ended the call and stared at her reflection. Despite that outburst feeling like it came from a stranger, she saw what she always saw: blue eyes, blond hair in need of a root touch-up, California sun-kissed tan. Tiny dark circles puffed beneath her eyes, but those had been there since she made junior publicist. She wore them like a badge of honor. And then caked them in layers of Bobbi Brown every morning so no one else could see her exhaustion.

She was staring at herself, Lucy Green, in the mirror, not some impostor. And those were her honest thoughts. She didn't know if she wanted children, not now anyway. And did she need to have an answer on her big day with everything else on her plate?

No, she decided, and was relieved when Maryellen didn't immediately call her back and demand one.

She gripped the sink's edge to steady herself after shouting at her mother. She realized with an exhilarating rush that reminded her of breaking curfew in high school that she'd never spoken to her that way.

It made her a little dizzy.

Her glossy white bathroom sparkled around her. Her succulents hung from their copper cages on the walls. She climbed into the bathtub, thinking some fresh air might help. By L.A. standards, Santa Monica was fresh. She slid open the window. The gritty air, smelling like orange blossoms, salt, and a hint of exhaust, curled in her small bathroom, and she took a centering gulp. But she didn't linger in the tub. Her best friend, Nina, was due over shortly to head to their spin class together.

She went into her closet, skirting a collection of boxes already housing her winter wardrobe, given it was nearing the end of spring, and reached for her maximum-support sports bra. Her collection ranged from mesh loungewear to the strait-jacket with underwire and a front zipper that left her skin criss-crossed with angry red indents but kept her chest from bouncing around. Most would agree it was a toss-up between which was more uncomfortable: the bouncing or the constriction. But knowing their spin instructor, Troy, would have them sweating until their quads burst into flames, she opted for the tightest bra she had.

She dug her fingers into the cups, straightening out the removable pads and wondering why they moved at all considering her nipples stayed in one place. She looped the harness over her arms and pulled it snug to fasten in the front. The underwire dug into her ribs as she clasped it. She took a breath in preparation to zip herself all the way in, and the zipper caught halfway up.

"Oh no," she whispered, fearing a dreaded stuck-zipper scenario that required patience and time she did not have if she was sticking to her strict schedule of spin class, shower, breakfast, commute in order to make it to work on time. She cautiously tugged, easing the little plastic tag along like she was chancing fate, and the already zipped part split and curled like a leaf, leaving the zipper jammed in the middle, refusing to go up or down.

She stared down at it, at a loss. Given how tight the whole contraption was, she was stuck in a crooked mess that would look ridiculous under her shirt. She considered scissors but decided to ask Nina for help; she was due over any minute. Having been inseparable since college, they'd held each other's hair while they puked, mended broken hearts, and rescued each other from plenty a dressing room wardrobe malfunction, including the time Lucy was stuck in a dress with her arms straight over her head, unable to see a thing.

After pulling on her leggings and socks, she went in search of her spin shoes. She kept them in her gym bag by the closet door, but the black nylon tote was empty. Perhaps they'd accidentally been scooped into a box in her most recent round of packing, she thought, and pawed through the nearby one labeled *Scarves*. All she found was a fluffy mass of neck drapery suited for Southern California; rayon and silk that added a slouchy burst of color more than any sort of warmth. She scanned her shoe rack but only found colorful tiers of heels and flats. She was reaching for her *Coats* box just as the doorbell rang.

She frowned. Nina never rang the doorbell; she always knocked.

She crossed her small apartment, dodging more boxes and thinking of her new condo with Caleb, to look out her peephole.

A billowing bouquet of flowers waited on the other side, hovering at eye level.

She swung open the door to the scent of fresh lilies and roses. "Happy birthday!" Nina sang from behind the bouquet.

Lucy stepped aside to let her in. "You got me flowers?" she asked, not able to think of a single instance in their twelve-year friendship when Nina had brought her flowers. Maybe it was something people in their thirties did.

"I did not," Nina said. She passed inside and set the vase on Lucy's dining table, mere feet inside the front door. The small room instantly filled with fragrance. "I was just at the door the same time the delivery guy was."

Lucy searched for a card.

Happy birthday! Sorry about last night. —Caleb

She read the note and felt her annoyance with her boyfriend ease but not erase. She appreciated the gesture, but she had to wonder: If things went according to plan, was she sentencing herself to a workaholic husband who sent flowers in place of himself?

"From Caleb?" Nina asked.

"Mm-hmm."

Nina ran her finger along the underside of a lily petal. "Apologizing for missing another date?"

Lucy did not miss the judgment in her voice.

"He's wishing me happy birthday."

Nina snatched the card. "Then why does it say *Sorry about last night*?"

Lucy snatched it back. "He's just busy."

Nina shrugged. "You're busy and you make time for him."

Lucy could not argue that.

Nina arched a brow at her and finally took note of her outfit. "What's going on here?" She waved a hand over Lucy's spandex and half-clasped sports bra.

"I got stuck. It's too tight to pull over my head. Can you help?" She thrust her chest at her friend, and Nina stepped in without question.

Nina tugged and pinched, working the stubborn zipper from top and bottom, biting her lip and mumbling.

"Pull it down," Lucy instructed.

"I am."

"No, like at an angle."

"I *am*."

Nina's dark brow furrowed. She wore her hair in matching braids over her shoulders, and Lucy could smell her freshly laundered spandex and minty deodorant, they were standing so close. She was all long limbs and willowy frame and had a good four inches on Lucy. "Hold the bottom," she told her.

Lucy did as she was instructed, marveling at the fact that it took two people to free her from an undergarment.

Nina went in, aggressively, from the top. She got a solid grip and yanked. The zipper gave way, and the force of her tug sent her hand straight into Lucy's nose with a sharp whack.

"*Ow!*"

"*Oh!*"

Lucy threw a hand to her face and felt a warm trickle. Her eyes instantly swam with tears.

"Oh god, I'm so sorry!" Nina rushed off to the kitchen and left Lucy dazed.

Tiny stars sparkled in her blurry, wet vision. She moved her hand to see blood spotting her palm, and for some reason, it made her laugh.

"You just gave me a bloody nose! Because of a bra!"

Nina rushed back in with a wad of tissues and a handful of ice cubes wrapped in a towel. She shoved both at Lucy's face and guided her into a dining chair. "Hold this and pinch."

"Thanks," Lucy mumbled in a nasally hum, grateful her friend was a nurse and knew exactly what to do, even if she had caused the injury herself.

Lucy sat still until the coppery taste of blood left her throat. She'd had bloody noses before, but always from dry air or altitude or a really, really bad cold. Never from being hit in the face.

Another laugh shook her shoulders. "I can't believe you gave me a bloody nose! On my birthday!"

Nina cringed in shame, but she too was laughing. "That's not your present, promise."

Lucy set the ice and tissues near the little terrarium center-piece she'd made on a wine-and-art date night with Nina when Caleb had bailed on her, and sniffled. She checked the time. "Maybe this is all a sign I'm not supposed to go to spin class today."

"What's a sign, me punching you in the face?"

"That, and the fact I got stuck in my bra and can't find my spin shoes."

"They're right there."

Lucy followed Nina's pointing finger and saw her shoes, in plain sight, sitting beside her couch next to a box labeled *Living Room Books*. She had walked past them twice and managed not to see them. The realization made her wonder if her signs were less signs and more some subconscious effort to avoid class.

She found herself contemplating spin class as a whole. She woke up early for it, felt like she wanted to die during it, and convinced herself after that she enjoyed it. Sure, it was great exercise, but did she really need someone shouting at her first thing in the morning? Did she *really* need to punish her body into a mold that wasn't its natural state, that honestly hurt sometimes, and that she had to fight tooth and nail to main-tain mainly for aesthetics?

Really, the only benefit of spin class was that she got to see Nina every morning, and they could just as easily go for a gen-tle jog instead. She suddenly saw it with such clarity.

"I don't want to do spin class anymore," she announced.

Nina laughed like she'd said something sacrilegious. "What? We go every day."

"I know, and I hate it. I'm always sore, and it's loud, and Troy is kind of intense."

"*What?* I thought you loved Troy!"

A vision of the Ken Doll come to life who led their class, Troy with his cut arms and legs, movie-star smile, flip of sun-bleached blond hair, filled Lucy's mind. The guy was intense, obsessed, and had barked at her for slacking more than once.

"Do *you* love Troy?"

Nina hesitated, pinching another lily petal with her long fingers. "Well, I mean, he *is* a little intense, but that's part of it. It's motivating."

"Is it though?"

They silently stared at each other, the truth hanging between them.

Lucy's stomach rumbled, and she thought about the thimble of Greek yogurt she was going to eat after her workout and decided that the place down the street that served eggs and bacon sandwiched between fresh, hot bagels gooey with cheese sounded much better.

"Want to get breakfast instead?" she asked.

Nina suspiciously eyed her but, ever easygoing, shrugged. "It's your birthday."

They got a table on the sidewalk, just inside the railing lined with planter boxes and petunias. Thursday morning was slow for breakfast. When they came for weekend brunch, they always ended up wandering the garden shop next door while waiting an hour for a table. It was the precise reason Lucy owned so many succulents. They dined with other Westsiders in workout gear, people reading books and sipping coffee, the occasional mom with a stroller.

Nina nibbled tiny spoonfuls from her yogurt and granola bowl, abiding by the self-imposed rules of low-calorie breakfast. Lucy took a bite of the most gorgeous bagel sandwich she'd ever seen in her life: layers of melted jalapeño cheddar, bacon, fluffy scrambled eggs. She normally joined Nina in what they deemed careful eating: dining on clean food, juice cleanses, keto this, no-carb that. Foods that often tasted like dirt or cardboard and left literal hunger pangs stabbing at her belly and mood all day, all so she could fit some standard that was a tight dress, a toned body, a bikini in the summertime. So she could be the *slender woman* the world demanded she be when sometimes all she wanted was a goddamned bagel sandwich.

It suddenly struck her as insane, cruel even, to deny herself something as delicious as the bagel she sank her teeth into. A glob of cheese strung from her chin. She swiped it into her mouth and let out a little moan of satisfaction. She thought of offering Nina a bite, but she knew she wouldn't take it, and she wanted it all to herself anyway.

Nina scooped a single blueberry onto her spoon and ate it like a bird. "Do you think Caleb is going to propose tonight?"

"No."

Lucy startled. Not at her friend's blunt question—Nina had permission to ask things like that—but at her own response. And more importantly, how easily it rolled off her tongue.

She silently asked herself the question again, just in case she hadn't heard Nina and answered the wrong thing.

Do I think Caleb is going to propose tonight?

And the answer popped up just the same.

No.

For so long, she'd been telling herself *yes, yes, yes* and that *tonight's the night.* He'd had so many opportunities—beach sunsets, Michelin restaurants, even that one time at Disneyland that would have topped the clichés, but Lucy wouldn't have cared—and he still hadn't asked. And somehow, even though she knew he'd have the opportunity of a lifetime that night—her birthday, the day of her promotion, a rooftop in downtown L.A.—she somehow knew that night still wouldn't be the night.

She let the answer sit, not really sure how it made her feel. Disappointed, maybe, because she'd been waiting for so long. But maybe also relieved? She'd been waiting for so long, and knowing that the *will he, won't he* distress would be missing felt kind of . . . great?

There was something freeing in it, the certainty. Where it came from, she didn't know, but she suddenly felt like a bug struggling on its back, legs flailing, that had finally been flipped over.

"No, I don't think he will propose tonight," she told Nina, and buried her face back in her bagel.

Nina watched her with a raised brow, no stranger to her *tonight's the night* mantra.

When Lucy first whispered her suspicion to Nina last fall, after a perfect day in Palm Springs where the guys golfed and the girls hit the spa; when Lucy and Caleb snuck back to their room and had midday sex before joining everyone at the pool; when Lucy was so caught up in the sun and the drinks and the warm fuzzy vacation vibes, she was absolutely *sure* Caleb was going to ask her to marry him that night, Nina joined her in delighted squeals and freshly manicured hand clapping. But then he didn't ask. And then he didn't ask again and again, and the novelty wore off. Nina's squeals simmered down to smiles and encouraging nods, the occasional thumbs-up, despite Lucy still insisting *tonight's the night.*

That was why Nina stared at her with no small amount of skepticism.

"You sound remarkably . . . okay with that."

Lucy studied her glorious bagel sandwich, sad to see she only had a few bites left, and shrugged. "Maybe I am okay with that."

Nina didn't argue or point out the hypocrisy in her sudden change of heart after all the times *tonight's the night* resulted in pints of ice cream, sweatpants, and *Grey's Anatomy* reruns on her couch. Instead, she nodded, albeit with a confused look on her face. "Okay, then."

They let their breakfast span the same length of time spin class would have, enjoying the pale sunlight on the sidewalk, the sounds of Los Angeles coming to life for another day, and started their walk to their respective apartments. They lived together through college and for a few years after but had expanded into personal space once their careers took off.

But not too personal; they still lived three blocks from each other.

Lucy took a deep breath of morning air just as a man across the street whistled at them.

Living in a big city, Lucy had tried, hard, to train herself not to look when someone whistled, called, sucked their lips like they were summoning a cat, or made an otherwise lewd sound, but most of the time, reflex won out and she turned her head toward the noise.

The man looked like he'd seeped out of a crack where dark things went to hide during the daylight. His grungy clothes sagged, his backpack hung near his thighs, and Lucy wondered, as always, why he thought he had the right to harass them while they were just walking down the sidewalk.

"Hey, ladies. Where you heading?" he called, and suggestively grabbed his crotch.

"Oh god," Nina mumbled with a sigh.

Lucy knew what to do in the everyday situation: ignore him and keep walking. *Do not engage* was rule number one for staying safe as a female out in the world, even if she wanted to turn and give him a piece of her mind—especially in that case. Who knew if he had a weapon or wanted to hurt them in other ways? And that exact uncertainty was what gave him and others like him all the power. Lucy and Nina knew they were the ones with something to lose, whether it be their sense of security, their dignity, or something far worse. And because people like the strange, vulgar man on the street existed, they'd been trained to walk away or risk endangering themselves.

Just another day.

The unjustness of it all suddenly struck Lucy like a gong ringing too loudly to ignore. *How dare he* infringe on their pleasant morning, on her big day. On her birthday! Compelled by an invisible force that she couldn't name or even locate, she couldn't pretend to ignore him anymore.

She pivoted toward his side of the street but didn't cross, knowing she shouldn't actually approach him even though the thought of slapping him in the face made her palm twitch with pleasure. She would verbally slap him instead.

"Hey!" she yelled.

"Oh my god, Lucy, what are you doing?" Nina whispered.

She ignored her.

"Hey! Asshole! I'm so sick of having to put up with shit from men like you! We don't *want* your attention, we don't *need* your attention, and frankly the fact that you think we owe you something is *embarrassing*. Whatever power you think you have only exists because women keep quiet, but I'm saying shut the hell up and leave us alone!" Her voice rang up and down the street. The people eating egg sandwiches all the way back at the restaurant probably heard her. She didn't care about that as much as she cared about the shock on the man's face.

From the looks of it, he wasn't used to his victims fighting back.

Lucy threw up a middle finger for good measure just as

Nina grabbed her arm and dragged her around the corner. They ran half a block like teenagers stealing their parents' liquor and stomped to a stop outside of a hat boutique.

"Oh my god, Lucy! You are insane," Nina gushed, unable to fight her smile.

Lucy's heart hammered in her chest. She felt lighter than air even though she was shaking. How many times had she wanted to do that? She couldn't even count—which was testament to just how rampant harassment really was. He was only one guy on the street, but she felt like she'd just stuck it to all the men who thought it was their right to solicit women in public. She wanted to jump in the air and do a superhero kick. *Pow!*

She smiled at Nina and laughed. "That felt *amazing*. Now let's get out of here before that guy comes back and murders us."

Lucy jumped in the shower as soon as she was home. She and Nina took an alternate route in case the man on the street did in fact try to follow them, which left her a few minutes behind schedule. But she was fine with those minutes if they spared her life from a psycho killer.

Nina left her with strict instructions to text her after her meeting with Lily Chu and have a great day, and promised she'd see her on the roof at Perch later, ready to celebrate.

After her shower, Lucy dug through her underwear drawer. Her outfit for the day had been picked out two weeks in advance; she'd bought a new dress for Lily Chu. J&J Public had a high standard for dress code. Joanna swanned around in ready-to-wear runway, her Jimmy Choos clicking on the floors like little hammers. Jonathan, Joanna's brother and the company CEO, set the standard for the men, wearing laser-cut suits and Ferragamos. There was no such thing as casual Friday at J&J.

Lucy had splurged on a Max Mara sheath dress that required shapewear, but she squeezed into Spanx most days of the week anyway. Of course, the Spanx would be tighter thanks to the pleasant fullness in her belly from breakfast, but at least she wouldn't be counting down the minutes until she could have a handful of almonds for her midmorning snack.

She reached in her drawer and laughed out loud at the sight of her Spanx, suddenly seeing them for what they were: a torture device. The silky beige shorts looked fit for a child, and Lucy was expected to shove her adult body into them like sausage and deal with the tight band limiting her air supply all day and spend an extra minute to peel herself out of them every time she visited the restroom.

"That's stupid," she said to no one in particular. Or maybe to everyone, she wasn't sure. Either way, she decided to skip the shapewear.

She reached next for a lacy thong, and the tiny scrap of fabric suddenly struck her as absurd. Times had long since changed from the trendy neon string peeking out above low-rise jeans, so what was the point? Sure, thongs meant no panty lines, but was it supposed to be a secret that women wore underwear? Because someone, probably a man, decided a visible seam was offensive, she had to walk around with a wedge of fabric stuck up her butt all day? And on that note, weren't wedgies the ultimate middle school threat for boys?

She suddenly saw it all: a misogynist who'd been bullied in school sought his revenge by convincing society that uncomfortable women's undergarments were fashionable.

Just to spite the lunacy, Lucy reached for a pair of cotton briefs from her comfortable undies collection—the soft, stretchy ones in fun colors that she wore under sweats and sundresses with flowy skirts. The ones she changed into as soon as she got home from work, when she ditched the shapewear and lacy floss. The ones she sometimes ate ice cream and watched TV in because she was over wearing pants altogether.

Her intimate region thanked her immediately.

She headed back into the bathroom to do her hair. She lined up her tools for the necessary punishment: blow dryer, flatiron, balms, and styling sprays, ready to set to work.

Except it all suddenly seemed as absurd as the uncomfortable underwear.

Left to its own devices, her hair really was fine, albeit a bit poofy on a humid day. Somewhere around puberty, she bought into the need for her first flatiron and clouds of sticky hair spray. She didn't hit the hard stuff until college, going from box dyes to triple-figure salon visits every five weeks, and she'd been investing in hair maintenance ever since.

She shuddered at the thought of what a decade of being bottle blond cost her.

And why? she wondered as she unplugged the flatiron, whose ceramic plates had begun to chip from overuse. The heat and the chemicals and the *time*, when she could just embrace what naturally grew out of her head and spare herself the physical and financial damage?

It *was* her birthday, and maybe that was reason to wear the hair she was born with.

She removed most of the moisture with a gentle blow drying, then ran some smoothing balm through the loose waves. When she finished, she noted, pleasantly, that she was not sweating as she was most mornings from blasting her hair dry then ironing it into shape and effectively undoing the shower she had just taken.

She eyed the clock and saw that she was ahead of schedule. What a pleasant surprise when her mornings were usually wall-to-wall with her fitness and beauty routines.

Speaking of beauty, she prepared to put on her face.

Lucy enjoyed makeup, but she had to admit, it came with a price. Litcrally, the steep one she paid across several retail chains that amassed her an embarrassing number of rewards points. But also the price that meant she couldn't touch her face, sweat, cry, blow her nose, wear sunglasses, or even blink too hard without messing any of it up. Making up her face was a form of artwork, except art held still and didn't perspire, sneeze, get a watery eye, or occasionally itch. Even with the best setting spray, scratching her cheek meant coming away with a fingernail full of foundation. The slightest sniffle meant erasing all the hard work off the tip of her nose with a tissue. Forget wiping her brow if she got sweaty; she'd leave a streak on her sleeve. Summertime heat left her eyes smudged with melting mascara and liner like a raccoon.

Why do I put up with it? she wondered as she opened her tacklebox of pencils, powders, creams, wands, and brushes. She'd been wearing makeup long enough—since her mother finally caved when she started high school—to feel naked without it. She'd lost track of the line between makeup being her choice and something society expected of her, and maybe it was both, honestly, but she suddenly had perfect clarity on the ridiculous expectation that she was supposed to just put up with the inconvenience of layering her face in an untouchable, sweaty mask every day—even if it was pretty.

She stared at her makeup and saw the same thing she saw when staring at her hair tools: time, effort, and a small mint worth of products designed to make her look like someone else.

She picked up her primer and had a sudden and overwhelming urge not to use it. Same went for her eyeliner and mascara. She considered her go-to tube of rose lipstick and decided lip color was the least egregious of the options, and she actually did not mind the tinted moisturizer.

As she painted her lips soft pink, liking the way she looked, she wondered how she would be received at her company, which held very high standards for physical appearance. But did she need to, for all intents and purposes, put on a costume to prove she was competent at her job?

The thought took her into her bedroom, where she had laid out her outfit.

She considered her dress, the one she picked out specifically for Lily Chu. It was beautiful, but the maintenance required to wear it was not. It would constrict her arms, and she'd have to squat instead of bend over to reach for anything below her knees. Without her shapewear, she'd be sucking it in all day because the sky-blue slip left no room for mystery, and just the thought gave her a backache.

She decided, definitively, the dress was not worth the hassle.

She returned to her closet and scanned her options. She'd wanted something special for her big day, something her coworkers hadn't seen her in before. A statement piece for her birthday and promotion. But suddenly, making a statement seemed far less important than wearing something functional. Her favorite little black dress caught her eye, a bodycon scoop neck with cap sleeves, but even that felt too restrictive. She considered a respectable emerald green number of a similar cut, but when her eyes landed on her favorite non-work dress, a midi-length floral print that reminded her of Sunday brunch with Nina, a summer concert at the Hollywood Bowl, the decision to wear it was so obvious, she wondered why she even shopped for different options in the first place.

When she looked at her rack of heels, she laughed a little hysterically, like it was a joke that she'd even consider stepping into one of the toe-crushing stilts. Instead, she slid her feet into soft, suede d'orsays.

Thanks to her low-maintenance morning, she was ready to leave for work a whole fifteen minutes early. The slack in her normally frantic morning struck her as a welcome surprise. She might even have time to get a coffee.

She grabbed her work tote, noticing the easy flow of loose fabric around her legs, something markedly different than the constricted dresses and skirts she normally walked out of the house wearing. Her feet didn't click down the hall but pleasantly whispered. She noted how much faster she could walk as well and wondered why she didn't dress so comfortably every day.

Lucy checked social media on the way to her car, knowing there would be a barrage of birthday posts. She smiled at the old photos friends tagged her in and the well-wishes. She was pleasantly surprised to see that Leo Ash, the bane of her professional existence, posted a picture of them together behind the scenes at an event, Lucy with a lanyard press pass around her neck and Leo looking like the tousled, tatted-up rock star he was, with a caption quite bluntly thanking her for putting up with his shit.

When she inherited Leo, she initially thought it was a form of playful hazing but had since realized it was a test that she'd passed with flying colors. It was sink or swim with a client whose romantic flings, wardrobe-as-political-statement stunts, late-night talk show confessions, leaked nudes, and arrest record landed him all over the internet in the worst way possible. But he never started a fire Lucy couldn't put out with her quick maneuvering before anyone got too badly burned. She deftly recast his eccentricities as endearing and made sure everyone kept loving him. Like that time she framed his Vegas drive-thru chapel wedding and subsequent annulment to a super-model he'd known for two weeks as the soul-searching inspiration for his fourth and arguably best studio album. And that time he had demanded to have a live lion in a music video, and she researched a reputable rescue sanctuary to find one and wove a heartwarming story around Leo and his new five-hundred-pound feline friend. She topped it off by directing fans to a website in the video's credits where they could donate to protecting endangered and vulnerable species. She person-ally cut him a little slack considering fame had rerouted his life at a young age and left him living in a near-alternate reality. Despite his flaws and extremely high-maintenance nature, she'd grown a soft spot for him over the years. It also didn't hurt that his voice sounded like black velvet wrapped in barbed wire and he had the brooding-bad-boy thing locked down well enough to give lessons.

She took a moment to reply to his post with a kiss emoji blowing a little heart.

And then she prayed he wouldn't cause any drama on her big day.

Her phone chimed several times with happy birthday texts as she climbed into her car. Her commute to work was only three miles but it took thirty minutes in the faithful gridlock. Traffic crawled slowly enough for her to pull up the texts on her dash console. She noted the one from Caleb: Happy birthday! with a heart emoji. The other messages were from cousins, old friends who texted her precisely once per year on her birthday, and her dad.

By the time she parked in the cool concrete tomb beneath her office building, she had her game face on and was ready to conquer her day, despite the morning's mishaps. She touched her fingertips to her nose to make extra sure it was done bleeding before she crowded into the garage elevator with a handful of anonymous building coworkers. Though she knew no one by name, they'd all seen each other in passing enough to recognize one another, and she couldn't ignore the curious eyes on her outfit, the fleeting glances at her mostly bare face. The confidence she felt in her bedroom, the certainty she could pull off her appearance, slowly slipped away with each floor they climbed.

She arrived on the sixth floor and entered the lobby of her own office suite. J&J Public's creamy white-and-teal lobby with its rounded reception desk, fresh flowers, and black leather furniture perfectly combined Joanna's and Jonathan's feminine and masculine energies. Lucy caught two of her junior coworkers chatting.

Mikayla sat behind the reception desk, manning her workstation, and Annie, the newest in a long line of young, leggy assistants to serve Jonathan Jenkins, casually leaned over, balancing on the balls of her skyscraper heels, which hurt Lucy's feet just to look at. They paused their conversation and stared at Lucy with a mix of emotion clouding their heavily made-up faces: confusion, mainly, but also an ingrained and reflexive judgment, followed by a hint of fear that maybe turning thirty dashed your beauty standards overnight.

"Lucy! Happy birthday?" Mikayla greeted her, probably not intending it to come out as a question but unable to shield her confusion over Lucy's appearance. Annie eyed her from head to toe.

"Good morning," Lucy said, ready to get to the safety of her own office. "And thank you for the birthday wish."

"Of course." Mikayla, who usually beamed at everyone who

walked in J&J's door, gave her a wary smile. "Is everything all right this morning?"

Lucy flushed. They were used to seeing her in the same heels and tight dresses that they wore every day. A sundress and minimal makeup had to mean something went wrong. That her electricity went out, or she was wallowing in despair after breaking up with her boyfriend, or maybe it was even some bizarre walk-of-shame scenario. They couldn't fathom that it was her *choice* to leave home looking like she did.

She realized she couldn't blame them for their concern because, like her, they had been trained from a very young age to equate a woman's appearance with her competence, intelligence, kindness, status—her *value* as a person.

The list made Lucy angry, so she stopped making it in her head. The point was, they didn't know any better, and it wasn't their fault.

"I just felt like changing things up today," she assured her younger colleagues.

They blinked at her like two glass-eyed does, and Lucy knew defending her appearance all day would be an uphill battle.

Annie pushed up off her elbow and drummed her nails on the desktop. "Jonathan wants to meet with you today, Lucy. Just a heads-up."

That gorgeous bagel sandwich she had for breakfast did a backflip in her belly.

She did not want a private meeting with Jonathan for a multitude of reasons, but she especially didn't want one on her big day. Not at all.

"I don't want to meet with Jonathan," she blurted. "He makes me uncomfortable."

The words slipped out of her mouth and shocked all three of them. Mikayla gaped, Annie flinched, and Lucy felt her face fill with a hot rush.

"Um, oh . . . okay," Annie said, like Lucy had spoken a language she didn't understand. "I can tell him—"

"No!" Lucy shouted, making them both flinch this time. "I mean, no; please don't tell him that."

She couldn't understand what possessed her to confess. She had tolerated the light touching, the discreet advances, the inappropriate comments for years, but she'd never said anything on record because she liked her job too much to risk losing it. There were only two people on the planet who knew how she felt about Jonathan, and neither of them were currently staring at her like she'd gone senile. Of all the people she could have confessed to, she opened her mouth to Mikayla, the all-seeing front-desk eye, and Annie, Jonathan's personal assistant.

She wanted to melt through the floor.

"I have to go," she said, and whisked off, leaving them stunned.

She walked down the hall, past the gridwork of cubicles in the office belly, and toward her office, three down from Joanna's corner suite. Jonathan's office anchored the floor's other corner, behind wooden doors Lucy didn't care to visit.

She made it into her office, a neatly appointed cubby with a view of West L.A. Like her apartment, she kept it clean and decorated with succulents and colorful art. As a junior publicist, she had room only for a desk, her computer, a bookshelf, and a chair for a visitor. Joanna's office had a couch, a palm, a sideboard with fresh flowers, and a TV. She wasn't gunning for all that just yet, but the senior publicists had room for two chairs, maybe a fern.

Lucy deposited her tote and sat at her desk. She pressed her hands to her face and took a deep breath.

She had just confessed she didn't like the CEO on the day she was hoping for a promotion. That did not bode well at all. Not to mention the looks Annie and Mikayla gave her reminded her of her early teen years, before she was allowed to wear makeup. When all the older girls flaunted their glitter eyeshadow and sticky lip gloss and made her feel left out and judged. Such strong emotions during her formative years had a lasting impact, and those looks in the lobby woke a dormant adolescent insecurity that made her wonder if she'd made a mistake.

Luckily, she kept a stash of emergency makeup in her desk. Sample sizes, demos, castaway colors she didn't love but couldn't bring herself to throw out because she'd paid for them. She opened her second drawer and reached behind a pack of Post-its and an extra mouse to grab the little pouch. She unzipped it and fished out a tube of mascara just as someone entered her doorway.

Oliver, her favorite person at J&J and other favorite person in the world along with Nina, smiled, holding an extravagant chocolate cupcake in his hands. A mile of white frosting dusted in gold flakes teetered on top of it; a gold candle stuck out like an exclamation point.

"Hap—" He stopped in his tracks when he saw her, his boyish face collapsing into concern.

Oliver wore his emotions like a picture book: everything exaggerated and obvious, as if to get the point across to less perceptive minds. He claimed it was left over from his days as a theater kid, when he used his booming voice and overstated gesturing to be seen onstage.

It was ironic, then, that he worked at a publicity firm. A good publicist was a master of chaos management, which included the ability to keep a straight face—a reassuring face—when a client landed in hot water. *Everything is fine; I'll take care of it.* Words Lucy had said more times than she could count, and almost every time, nothing was fine, and taking care of it gave her three more gray hairs and one fewer year of life. Oliver struggled with the subtlety required by such unremitting composure. He preferred passing judgment via screenshots and DMs, sending Lucy scandalous updates on the latest celebrity mishaps with captions like *Good luck spinning this* and *#canceled.* He once told Lucy he could never make it as a publicist because if his client crashed his Lamborghini and puked in the gutter in front of ten cameramen, like Leo Ash once did, he'd have told him to stop acting like a dick and grow up. As such, he remained on the periphery of the chaos as Joanna's assistant. His candor kept Lucy's feet on the ground. At work, he was the sane albeit crass and judgmental voice in her ear reminding her that celebrity publicity, although a cog in the mighty wheel of global commerce, was in fact not saving any lives.

Oliver cut off his birthday wish mid-breath. "Are you okay?"

Just like the girls in the lobby, he assumed something was wrong. And there were actually a few things wrong: she had yelled at her mother, gotten a bloody nose from a bra, confessed her dislike of Jonathan, and had her self-esteem mowed down by two twentysomethings all before nine in the morning. But Oliver didn't know about any of that. His question was based solely on her appearance and, unlike Mikayla and Annie, she felt comfortable confronting him about it.

Their friendship spanned years; they'd seen each other drunk, slept on each other's couches, shared a Netflix password. He was completely safe. And he was a guy, which Lucy had to admit somehow felt more appropriate to be taking the brunt of her frustration.

She set the mascara down and rounded her desk. She reached for the cupcake. "Thank you. Why do you ask if I'm okay?" She was going to make him say it. She sank her teeth into the creamy frosting without hesitation. Normally, she wouldn't eat such a thing. In any other circumstance, she would have politely accepted the gift from Oliver, left it on her desk, maybe swiped a finger into the frosting, and then buried it in the trash when no one was looking. But the sugary blob looked like the cure to her strange morning. With ten times her strength, she couldn't have resisted it.

Oliver frowned at her, bewildered. "I was going to light that and maybe even sing."

She plucked out the candle and sucked the frosting from it. "This is delicious." She set the remaining half of it on her desk before she choked on the rich cake, and went in search of water. She felt Oliver's eyes on her outfit; her flats made her a good five inches shorter than him.

"What are you wearing?" he asked, and there it was. The real question she was waiting for.

"Something comfortable, for a change."

Oliver arched a brow. He wore glasses and had supple cheeks that were faintly flushed at all times. He reminded Lucy of one of Michelangelo's cherubs if they were man-size and lived in West L.A.

"You realize the stuff I walk around in every day here gives me blisters and makes my back hurt and leaves huge red indents in my skin, right? That it's seriously a toss-up between what I most look forward to taking off as soon as I get home: my makeup or my clothes? I don't know who decided I have to look a certain way to be taken seriously, especially at work, but I think it's unfair. In fact, I'd probably be *more* competent at my job if I didn't have to worry about nylons and shapewear and heels and all of this crap." She overturned her makeup pouch, having changed her mind on using any of it, and let the contents rain down on her desk.

Oliver watched the tubes roll and a pot of goes-with-everything gold eyeshadow flip open and crack with a furious little fault line. A hint of alarm shaded his face, but of the men in Lucy's life, he was most sensitive to the frustrations plaguing the female existence.

"That seems reasonable," he agreed.

"Of course it's reasonable. I just need to get other people to agree with me so they stop assuming something is wrong if I'm not dressed like Barbie with a full face on at all hours. You should have seen the way you looked at me. And the way Annie and Mikayla looked at me in the lobby. Oh *god*, I said something to them that I shouldn't have." She remembered their encounter, and the other half of her cupcake suddenly needed to be eaten. She sat back in her chair and stuffed it in her mouth.

Oliver snapped into action like a first responder. He shoved her door closed with the tips of his long fingers and rounded her desk. He pivoted her chair and knelt in front of her. His voice softened to a downy whisper. "Lucy, are you having your period?"

She swallowed her chocolatey bite and glared at him. "Oh my god, Oliver. No!"

"Okay! Okay. You don't have to yell at me. It's just, you

seem distressed and you're wearing weird clothes and shoving chocolate in your face, so I just—"

She silenced him with another glare. "You brought me the chocolate."

"You're right! I did. And I'm . . . sorry?"

She grumbled and folded her arms, suddenly annoyed. "Don't apologize; it was delicious. But you know, it's ridiculously unfair that if my period were the explanation for my mood—which it's *not*—I'd have to hide it."

He blinked at her, confused, with the caution of a soldier crossing a minefield.

"Oliver, you literally shut my door to ask me about a physiological process my body goes through on a regular basis like it's something to be ashamed of. Like it's a secret my uterine lining makes a slow escape once a month that feels like being stabbed by hot, twisting knives and all I want to do is curl in a ball and cry."

He gaped in horror. "That's what it feels like?"

"To put it mildly, yes. And we're just supposed to power through like nothing is wrong." She stretched her arm like it was riding a wave. "We're not supposed to talk about how much our boobs hurt or that we have to rearrange our wardrobes to accommodate underwear that fits maxi pads for a week each month. We have to smuggle tampons to the bathroom like contraband because heaven forbid anyone know we're bleeding. We don't talk about pee string either. I bet you don't even know what that is." She narrowed her eyes at him with an accusatory finger, and he leaned back, mouthing *pee string?* in fright. "If *your* kind menstruated, I bet we'd only work three weeks out of the month. Cramps would be valid reason for paid sick days—hell, we'd probably have *cramp days*. You've never had a beach vacation ruined or had to sleep in biker shorts so you don't stain your sheets. You've never counted days and panicked when your period was a few late or wondered what you did to deserve it when it lasted twice as long. You've never had your mood swing so high and low it feels like there's no more middle. You are not at the mercy of a cycle you get no say in."

Her voice faded out, and Lucy realized that she apparently had many thoughts about her period.

Oliver sat back on his heels and smoothed his palms against his pants. "Sorry. I . . . I didn't know it was like that."

"Of course you didn't! Because we never talk about it!" She flailed her arms for emphasis. "Literally half the planet goes through this on a regular basis, and it's more hush-hush than what goes on in the Pentagon. And I have to say, it's equally unfair that you assumed that's what was going on with me this morning. *Woman acting strange; must be hormones.* Maybe I'm just having a bad day!"

He looked at her like he couldn't win.

Maybe he couldn't. And maybe, for once, that was fine.

Someone knocked on the door and pushed it open without waiting for a response. It was the last person on the planet Lucy wanted to see.

"Good morning," Chase McMillan said with the iciness he reserved only for Lucy.

On a good day, she found him as pleasant as a papercut.

He stood in her doorway, and a question flitted across his face as to why she wasn't dressed in something the same caliber as his suit and tie. Why her hair didn't have half the product in it that the sculpted brown wave atop his head did. His confusion gave way to a smug grin as he, like everyone else that morning, interpreted her appearance to mean something was wrong, and in his case, he clearly thought it meant he had pulled ahead in their race for the promotion.

Lucy's instinct was to dive under her desk and hide, but she would not let him get the best of her, not with what was at stake. She stood from her chair and felt a swell of courage.

"Can I help you, Chase?"

His grin widened. "I was just dropping by to wish you good luck with Lily Chu today."

"No, you weren't," Lucy said, rounding her desk with her hands on her hips. "You were coming by to intimidate me."

The words slipped out before she even realized they'd been waiting on her tongue. Oliver snorted a laugh, and Chase paled.

"Excuse me?"

Lucy scanned her brain for what to say next because she had *no* idea where that had come from, and she found she didn't have to search far. The rest of the truth was right there waiting.

"You didn't come by to sincerely wish me luck. You came by under the pretense of wishing me luck but really meant to plant a seed of doubt because you think you can get to me. We both know Lily Chu is key to my getting the promotion we both want, and you're trying to throw me off my game. But guess what? You can't." She poked him in the chest for emphasis.

They each took a step back, shocked.

She could not believe she had poked Chase McMillan in the chest.

Chase stared at her, keeping his face smooth and calm, but she saw the confusion in his eyes. The struggle. She'd called him out, and they both knew it. The next move was his.

He went straight for a reminder of why he held sworn-enemy status. The smug grin returned. "Well, I hope you fired your dry cleaner for destroying your clothes and leaving you with only *that* to wear on such an important day. I'm sure that's the only explanation for your . . . appearance." His eyes traveled from her head to her toes as he drew out the last word.

The urge to smack him made Lucy's hand twitch.

Oliver intervened before she could. "Aren't there asses you should be kissing somewhere, Chase?"

Chase shot Oliver a glare and stepped backward out of the door. "Best of luck with Lily, Lucy, and have a great birthday!" he said loudly enough for everyone to hear. It was all for show, and it made Lucy's skin crawl.

"God, he drives me insane," she said once he was gone.

"That was pretty great what you said to him though. Calling him out like that," Oliver said.

A rush of warmth rose up in Lucy's chest. She smiled. "It was pretty great, wasn't it?"

"Yep. Especially since you had frosting on your face while you said it." He used his thumb to swipe her cheek.

Embarrassment consumed her like a flame. She slapped her hands over her mouth and wanted to die.

Oliver laughed. "Relax. It was only completely noticeable. I'm sure he saw it."

She punched him in the shoulder and spun back to her desk. She grabbed the small mirror that tumbled from her makeup pouch and checked her reflection. Her face was still bare, though flushed, and her hair had dried into relaxed waves that, while not smooth and glossy, were not the unsightly mess she expected based on Chase's reaction.

She dropped the mirror and looked to Oliver.

"Oliver, did I make a mistake? *Do* I need makeup and a tight dress to be taken seriously?"

He flattened his lips and glanced toward the door. "By guys like Chase, probably, but not by anyone who knows your value." He softened. "But even for those of us who know and love you, it might take a little time. We're not exactly used to weekend-casual Lucy at the office, you know? But if you want to lead the charge in freeing the modern career woman's wardrobe from the grip of the patriarchy, I'm here for it."

He squeezed her arm and she laughed, feeling better.

"While you confront the injustice, may I offer a suggestion? Be right back." He spun out of the room on his heel and left Lucy alone.

She took a deep breath and assured herself her appearance was fine.

"Lucy?" yet another visitor called from the doorway. It was a bright, confident, commanding voice she knew well enough to set her nerves on edge.

Joanna.

Her boss, her mentor. The most stylish woman in the building—the person Lucy needed to impress above everyone else—was standing in the doorway.

She summoned every ounce of her training—skills Joanna herself taught her—to keep calm, to keep an assuring face.

"Joanna! Good morning."

Joanna stepped inside the office and unconsciously reached for the necklace resting against her collarbone. The simple act showed her nerves. Lucy had picked up on the tell years before. It was the only way Joanna, strong-willed, powerful, confident Joanna, showed her vulnerability. She could level a boardroom with a gaze, tell an award-winning Hollywood director to get his shit together or else, hold her ground in big-time negotiations, but she couldn't hide her nervous tic. She always touched her necklace when she was nervous.

Lucy had to assume she was nervous because of her unexpected appearance, whether she was aware of it or not.

"I was just dropping by to say happy birthday," she said, though her eyes said more.

"Thank you."

Before either of them could say another word, Oliver came sweeping back in the door with a colorful scarf fluttering from his hand. "Okay, I haven't had the chance to wrap this, and I was going to give it to you at your party tonight, but I think it might give a little something extra to this bohemian look you've got going on. Oh. Joanna. Good morning." He startled when he saw her, nearly jumping sideways.

"Good morning, Oliver."

The three of them started at one another as awkward silence crowded into the small room. Lucy could see curiosity painted all over Joanna's face as to why she was wearing what she was wearing and why Oliver was providing her assistance with her look.

"Everything all right?" Joanna asked.

They both looked at Lucy.

Lecturing Oliver was fine, but she didn't really want to lecture the woman wearing Chanel and holding her promotion in her hands about the finer points of unjust wardrobe standards set for women.

She tried to make an excuse for her appearance, she really did, but her mouth wouldn't work. She reached for the excuse Chase served up—*dry cleaning accident; all my clothes were destroyed*—but she couldn't grab it. There was a tongue-shaped wall between the words in her mind and their form in her mouth.

But she had to say *something* because her boss was staring at her, waiting.

She threw caution to the wind and went for it.

What resulted was a gurgled *nngrahup* sound that only confused them all more.

Oliver played it off with a laugh. "Plumbing mishap; her apartment flooded, poor thing. The crew is there cleaning it up right now, but she didn't want to be late since today is so important."

Lucy threw him a glance so heavy with gratitude, it could have knocked him down. Then she looked at Joanna and shrugged for lack of a better idea.

"Sorry to hear that," Joanna said as she checked her watch. "I hope it doesn't spoil your birthday. See you in a bit." She slipped out the door with the efficiency of someone on borrowed time.

"What the hell was that?" Oliver demanded as soon as she was gone. "You just stood there gaping like a fish. I get *screw the patriarchy* and all, but you couldn't have come up with something?" He began folding the scarf in on itself to make it into a headband.

"Sorry. The words were in my mouth; I was going to say something about dry cleaning, but nothing would come out. It was like I couldn't—"

A thought struck her. A thought so crystal-clear and simultaneously irrational, she didn't know what to do with it. She held it up in her mind like a puzzle piece, overlaying it on every bizarre thing that had happened that morning. And every time, it fit.

"Oh my god," she muttered.

Oliver raised his arms above her head and pulled the scarf against her hair. He was no stranger to aiding in emergencies. At Joanna's behest he had delivered replacement wardrobes to shoots, fixed busted stilettos, and surely found a spare headband to remedy a client's bad hair day. It didn't surprise Lucy in the least that he was ready to assist. "What? Lift," he instructed.

She wadded her hair in her hands and lifted it from her neck. Oliver reached around and deftly tied the scarf taut against her skull. He yanked it tight so it wouldn't slip, and the small rattling of her brain made her certain of a wild truth.

"Oliver, I can't lie."

She dropped her hair, and he set about tugging strands and adjusting the scarf. "What? Of course you can. Everyone can lie. And you're a publicist; it's literally part of your job . . ." His voice trailed off into a laugh, but Lucy swallowed a hard lump in her throat.

So far, the lies she couldn't tell had all been personal—confessing to her mother about children, spin class, breakfast, what she said to her coworkers. She hadn't thought about needing to lie for her job. She wasn't a *liar*, but sometimes she needed to bend the truth to let people hear what they wanted to hear. People like celebrities who paid her to keep their public image pleasant.

As soon as she thought about her predicament, she realized just how many lies she told for her job: *that dress looks great; you will bounce back; don't worry, everything is fine.* That last was the publicist gospel—telling eccentric public figures everything was fine. What would happen to her career if she had to tell every celebrity she worked for just how big the messes they made were and that everything was in fact not fine?

The thought made her knees weak. She collapsed into her chair.

"Oliver, this is serious. I think I'm in trouble."

"What are you talking about?"

She knew she could be honest with him even if she sounded completely insane. He was the friend she'd run to if she ever traveled back in time and had to convince someone she was from the future. Nina was too logical to buy into things like that, but Oliver—Oliver would follow her into the time machine without question.

Still, she could see he was struggling with what she was telling him.

She knew it sounded crazy, but every word coming out of her mouth made her surer that she was right. It was all coming together. All making confusing, terrifying, but perfect sense.

"I mean, I can't lie. When I tried to tell Joanna some excuse about my clothes, I literally couldn't. *Physically* couldn't. And it's not only verbal lies—it's like I have to tell the truth in all ways. I have to . . . *act* the truth." She gasped and threw a hand over her lips. "Oliver! That explains it!" She popped from her chair and started pacing. "I didn't go to spin class because I hate spin class; I just *pretend* that I like it. *Lie.* At breakfast, I ordered this bagel sandwich because it sounded delicious and I didn't want yogurt and three blueberries like I normally eat. *Lie.* And then that guy on the street! I told off some guy harassing me and Nina when I normally would keep quiet even though I was upset. *Lie.* Not to mention what I said to my mother about the future grandchildren she may never have, and the things I've said to Annie, Mikayla, and Chase this morning. And when I was getting ready for work, I had this overwhelming urge *not* to do my hair, make up my whole face, or wear anything I stuff my body into each day because it's a lie. The . . . *costume* I put on every day. It's not *me*. It's not the truth!"

Oliver stared at her, looking less like he'd follow her to that hypothetical time machine and more like he was going to ask if she was on drugs.

The pieces were still clicking in her head, coming together like frightening little mosaic tiles, and she needed someone on her side. Someone to believe her.

She reached for his arms. "Oliver, I know this sounds nuts, but I think this is really happening. I need you to help me prove it. Ask me something I'd normally lie about."

His face moved from stunned disbelief to consideration to temptation faster than Lucy was comfortable with. The devilish glint in his eye made her hold up a finger.

"*Don't.*"

He hummed a teasing laugh like he was toying with all sorts of cringeworthy options: the number of times she'd watched the *Fifty Shades* trilogy; what Caleb was like in bed; what she thought about his last boyfriend, but he kept it tame. "Fine. What color is my shirt?"

Pink, pink, pink. It was pink. Though Oliver would probably scold her for saying pink when it should have been salmon or blush. Whatever the color, it matched his socks like always. But that was beside the point. She knew what she had to do.

Green. Just say the word *green*.

She focused as hard as she could, fearing and somehow already knowing what was going to come out of her mouth.

"Your shirt is gre—"

She couldn't do it. Although she could think it, the word wouldn't come.

She cleared her throat and tried again.

"The shirt you are wearing is gr—" She clutched at her throat, feeling like her tongue was trying to strangle her.

Oliver's mouth fell open. "Holy shit. You can't lie."

Lucy pressed her hands to her cheeks. "Oliver, this is not good."

He checked his watch. "No, it doesn't seem like it. But we've gotta go right now. Just keep your mouth shut at the stand-up, and we'll reconvene after."

She nervously nodded, trusting him to help her because she needed something to hold on to. She felt her hair and found the scarf snugly in place. "Thanks for the gift. How do I look?"

He tugged on a tendril. "You've kinda got a Lily James Cinderella thing going on now. It works. Let's go."

CHAPTER
5

Twice a week at J&J the whole company gathered for a stand-up meeting. The twenty or so minutes consisted of Joanna and Jonathan leaning out of their respective office doorways at either corner of the floor, senior and junior publicists crowding the walkway between, and all the assistants and interns getting to sit at their desks in the cubicles, which Lucy found unfair. The people with the lowest status at the company got to be the most comfortable for the whole ordeal. She couldn't help wondering if the setup was left over from Joanna and Jonathan's childhood, if their sibling squabbles took place from their bedroom doorways.

Lucy assumed her usual position at Oliver's cubicle outside Joanna's office, but instead of leaning against the little gray wall like normal, she slipped inside to avoid more questions about her well-being due to her appearance. Oliver made no comment about her taking up his space. She was nearly sitting on his lap.

She noticed Chase in his usual spot outside Jonathan's office, looking like a puppy begging for a treat. He handed Jonathan a cup of coffee and said something about being in the kitchen already and that it was no big deal.

Lucy didn't even try to disguise her eye roll, and she hoped he saw it.

She cast her gaze to where Joanna held her spot against her own doorframe. She leaned into the building like she was holding it up on her own, and really, everyone knew she was.

Jonathan and Joanna's father, Jonathan Senior, founded J&J in the seventies. He named it after his two children in an illusion of equality that was in fact just a middle finger to Joanna. If there was a rightful heir to the throne, it was Joanna by about a thousand miles. More like by a communications degree, an MBA, and leadership experience that eclipsed her younger brother's. But as fate would have it, when their father retired some twenty years before, he passed the helm to Jonathan despite Joanna being a better candidate. While she had gone to school and prepared herself to take over the company, all smooth-talking, grad-school-dropout, penchant-for-partying Jonathan had to do was rub elbows with the old boys' club and he was a shoo-in for the position.

Lucy resented that fact on Joanna's behalf as fiercely as she stood in awe of her ability to keep her cool as second-in-command when everyone knew she deserved to be CEO.

True to form, she took charge of the morning's meeting.

"Good morning, everyone," she called over the din. The room immediately fell quiet. "Not much of an update today since everyone's got their work cut out with summer season on the horizon, but just a few things to highlight . . ."

Lucy felt a tug on her skirt. Reluctantly, she turned to Oliver at his desk, keeping one ear on Joanna.

Oliver pointed at his computer screen with a comically sober look on his face. It showed a picture of a candle in a bowl of water surrounded by lemons under the words *Reverse the Curse*.

Lucy scowled at him, and he smiled with a shrug, as if to say, *It was worth a shot.*

And maybe it was?

Joanna was still talking, giving an update on her client Ms. Ma's music video, which was already making waves since its release that morning. The song blatantly embraced female sexuality and pleasure—in the same way male artists had been doing for decades—and critics were quick to call it vulgar and inappropriate. In perhaps the grandest missing of the point, some called it demeaning to women. Already exhausted by the hypocrisy, Lucy tuned out and took a half step closer to Oliver's screen. From the corner of her eye, she saw the rest of his search results: *How to Undo a Voodoo Curse*; *Reverse a Curse Spell*; *Hex Removal—Learn How To.*

She felt insane for even thinking it, but . . . maybe?

Oliver discreetly clicked on the *Hex Removal* option, and it took him to a website selling protection amulets.

Lucy stifled a laugh. Of course she could buy something to solve her problem. People found a way to cash in on literally everything, mysterious maybe-curses included.

She shook her head, wondering who would curse her.

As if in response to her silent question, Chase McMillan opened his pretentious mouth.

"We've been negotiating with the Lakers' front office," he said. "I've got a lunch with Shawn Stevens today, and I expect a signature soon."

Lucy tore her eyes from the hex magic website and looked

from Chase to Jonathan to Joanna so quickly, she got dizzy. The fact that they were all smiling made her feel sick.

Oliver tugged on her skirt again, and she swatted his hand away because she definitely needed to pay attention.

The *Lakers*? Chase was talking to the *Los Angeles Lakers*? And he was having lunch with Shawn Stevens, the superstar basketball rookie with a three-year, twenty-million-dollar contract, on the same day she was having lunch with Lily Chu?

How did she not know this?

She knew by the smug grin on Chase's face that her shock was obvious. He had the swagger of a teenager who just pulled off the best prank in high school history.

Dammit, Chase McMillan.

She thought back to their encounter in her office not twenty minutes before, when she called him out on trying to intimidate her. Little did she know what he had in his back pocket. He could have told her right then, but that wasn't his style. No. He wanted to wait until they were in a room full of people to break the news, because watching her squirm in public was better than a private show.

"Terrific news, Chase," Jonathan said. "That will be a huge win for the firm, and you personally." He clapped Chase on the back. Lucy felt eyes searching her out from all over the room. It was no secret she and Chase were vying for the same position, but apparently it was a secret that Chase had a lunch date with a megastar too. Some of the eyes were sympathetic, and she knew exactly why.

Lily Chu could win three Oscars and she still wouldn't be as cool as an NBA star in the court of public opinion—and J&J subsisted on public opinion. Everyone knew the fight was unfair.

"Yes, definitely a boost for our sports division," Joanna chimed in. "But let's not forget our stage and screen division represents some of the industry's biggest names, which we plan to add to in the very near future." She looked right at Lucy with eyes that all at once said, *Screw these boys, I'm counting on you*, and *I've got your back*. It both inspired and petrified Lucy in one complex surge of emotion.

She gave Joanna a tiny nod.

"Great," Jonathan countered with the air of a bratty sibling. "We'll all look forward to major announcements later this afternoon."

No one needed to say it, but everyone knew.

The bosses just put their best fighters in the ring, and it was time for them to duke it out. On any other day, Lucy would rise to the challenge, but she could only speak the truth while Chase was a silver-tongued devil in a three-piece suit.

In that moment, Lucy knew, without a doubt, that she was completely screwed.

"Have a great day, everyone," Joanna said in dismissal. "Oh, and happy birthday to Lucy." She shot her a smile that put a tiny ounce of wind back in her sails.

A chorus of *happy birthdays* struck up around her. She dutifully accepted the attention, though all she wanted to do was run back to her office and look up how to put a hex on Chase McMillan.

Chase glided by with a conceited grin, leaning in as he passed. "See you at the Palm later."

If she wasn't still standing in Oliver's cubicle, she would have stuck out a foot and tripped him.

How dare he.

He was taking Shawn Stevens to the same restaurant for

lunch where she'd be having her date with Lily. Of course he was. If he was trying to get in her head, he just walked right in the front door.

"I hope you choke on your steak!" she hissed at his back, unable to stop herself.

To her horror, he heard her and stopped. He whipped around and shot her an icy glare. "I'm vegetarian."

She squeezed her fists so she didn't punch his self-righteous face. "Then why are you going to a steakhouse?"

He opened his mouth to say something else, but his lips closed into an unexpected smile. "Jonathan," he said, before nodding and turning away.

Lucy froze, knowing the CEO was standing behind her and praying he hadn't heard their childish exchange.

Jonathan cleared his throat, and Lucy slowly turned around.

He was tall and handsome with dark eyes and flecks of gray at his temples. He had a Clark Kent dimple in his chin, but the similarities stopped there. He stood in front of Lucy with all the confidence of someone who always got what he wanted, and the thought of what Jonathan wanted made Lucy take a step back. His eyes traveled the length of her body, which they would have done even if she weren't wearing a sundress and minimal makeup. She felt her pulse pick up that familiar flutter like a rabbit caught in a trap. He smiled, and the thing about Jonathan was that he wasn't blatantly slimy. He was sly and charming, and before you knew it, he was standing close, pressing a hand into your back, complimenting your perfume. His wife was an ex–soap opera star with Dolly Parton proportions, and they had two kids in middle school.

It was a common misconception that men with families— daughters in particular—were exempt from misbehaving.

"Good morning, Jonathan," Lucy said, thankful the wall of Oliver's cubicle stood between them.

He leaned on it, resting his arms along the top. His suit jacket sleeve slid back to reveal a Rolex that cost as much as Lucy's car. "Happy birthday," he said with a smile. "Joanna tells me you have a big day today."

"I do."

"Well, I wish you the best with that, though I know you don't need any luck. Listen, if you've got a few minutes, I'd like to have a word with you in my office. Swing by at nine thirty?" He knocked his knuckles on the cubicle wall and walked off before she could respond.

A stream of profanity ran through her mind. Even though Annie had warned her it was coming, the invitation was not pleasant.

She turned to a wearied look on Oliver's face. He was well-versed in Jonathan's ways, and he knew just how powerless Lucy felt. Most women had to put up with some form or another of office bullshit. A slick, overly familiar boss was hers.

And that was another reason she didn't want a private meeting with Jonathan. With her sudden inability to keep her mouth shut on matters of personal integrity, she wasn't sure she wouldn't tell him off and lose her job on the spot.

She returned Oliver's look with a sigh.

He checked his watch. "Well, fifteen minutes to reverse this curse, right?"

She weakly laughed, not completely dismissing her hope that they'd be able to figure it out with some internet magic.

He looked back at his computer screen and pointed to the picture of the candle in the water bowl. "Still got that cupcake candle?"

They hurried back to Lucy's office, stopping by the kitchen on the way to grab a drinking glass, a lighter, and salt.

"This is insane," Lucy said.

"Yeah, well, so is you telling Chase McMillan to choke on a steak and die."

"I didn't say *die*."

"It was heavily implied. Damn, the candle is supposed to be black." Oliver had transferred the curse-breaking instructions to his phone. He set the half-filled drinking glass on Lucy's desk and scrolled his screen with his thumb.

"How is a tiny birthday candle going to stand up in there anyway?" Lucy leaned down level with her desk, and Oliver lowered the candle into the glass. As expected, it floated to the surface like a toothpick.

Oliver frowned. "Let's hope it's not an exact science." He fished out the candle and handed it to her, then reached for the salt-shaker. He sprinkled a shower of tiny white crystals into the water and scrolled farther down his phone's screen. "Okay, now it says you're supposed to visualize white light going into the water."

Lucy arched a brow at him.

He waved his hands, telling her to get on with it. "Take deep breaths while you do it too."

Lucy rolled her eyes before closing them and pictured a beam of white light passing through the glass like a spear. She breathed in her nose and out her mouth three times.

"Okay." Oliver's voice broke into her concentration. "Now light it and say your spell."

"My *spell*?"

"Lucy, I'm open to other suggestions if you've got any."

She grumbled and picked up the lighter. The flame licked close to her pink nails, and she thought, not for the first time, about how flammable nail polish was. "What am I supposed to say?"

"Dunno. Just ask it to go away, I guess."

She took a deep breath and held the candle over the glass of salt water. "Please, Curse, please go away. I need to be free of you so I can make it through this very important day. Thank you."

She met Oliver's eyes, and he shrugged in approval.

"You're supposed to let it burn down until the water puts it out, but—"

Lucy dropped the candle into the glass, and the flame snapped out with a hiss.

"Or you could do it that way."

They stared at each other, unsure.

"Did it work?" Lucy asked.

Oliver pursed his lips. "What color is my shirt?"

"Gr—" She sighed in defeat. "Still pink."

"Damn."

She leaned back in her chair, surprised by how disappointed she felt considering how absurd it was that they just tried to cast a spell.

"Well, the next option is burning sage. And then things escalate pretty quickly to animal sacrifice."

"Oliver!"

"I'm just reading what the internet says!"

She buried her face in her hands and leaned on her desk. "Why is this happening to me *today* of all days? What did I do to deserve this?"

"Actually," Oliver said, interrupting her rapid descent into self-pity, "what *did* you do?"

She dropped her hands and glared at him. "You think I deserve this?"

"No! Of course not. What I'm saying is, what did you do between last night and this morning that may have caused this? I don't know if we're dealing with a curse or some hex magic, or if you seriously pissed off the universe, but *something* had to have happened, right?"

She thought about what he said, and the word *universe* rang louder than the rest.

Was the universe doing something to her? Was some cosmic force intervening in her life on a milestone birthday to teach her a lesson about the value of honesty?

A giggle burst from her lips. "Oliver, I think I'm going insane."

"Maybe, but work with me here. What did you do after work yesterday?"

She sighed a weary breath, thinking yesterday felt a million miles away after the morning she'd had. "I went to meet Caleb for drinks and he didn't show—"

"Typical."

She glared at him, and he shrugged, unapologetic. "*Like I was saying*, he didn't show, so I ordered a round and—"

She stopped like she hit a wall.

"The wish."

"The what?"

She slapped a hand to her forehead and felt clarity rush in. *Of course.* "Last night at the bar, the bartender made me this drink, and I made a wish that today would be perfect. I don't know what the drink was; it was off menu. But he called it a *life-changing* cocktail. I thought he was joking, but maybe . . . ?"

She looked up at Oliver, hopeful.

He waved his hands and frowned. "Wait, hang on. You made a *wish* that today would be perfect and now you can't lie? How does that make any sense?"

Hearing him say it, she recognized the flaw in her theory.

"I don't know. Maybe some signal got crossed somewhere."

"Where, between Aladdin's lamp and Neverland?"

"Oliver! This is serious!"

He laughed. "I know, and I'm sorry. I guess it makes as much sense as anything else."

Lucy thought about her wish and how not a single thing about her day had been perfect, except maybe that bagel sandwich she had for breakfast. Were wishes even real? Could they come true, or, in what appeared to be happening in her case, *un*true? Even more important—could wishes be undone?

She didn't know, but she knew she needed to go back to the scene of the crime and see if she could fix her problem.

She popped up from her desk and grabbed her tote.

"Where are you going?"

"Back to the bar," she said, like it was obvious.

Oliver checked his watch. "You've got that meeting with Jonathan in three minutes."

Oh.

Her heart sank for multiple reasons.

"But I'm sure you can squeeze in a trip to the bar before you go to lunch with Lily." He gave her a reassuring smile, and she knew how lucky she was to have a friend like him. One who'd conduct impromptu curse-reversal rituals in her office, entertain ideas of wishing gone wrong, and reassure her everything would be all right.

She just had to make it through a surprise meeting with the boss she didn't like on the day she couldn't control what came out of her mouth. No big deal.

Jonathan's office could not have been more different from Joanna's. Where hers was pastel, calm, feminine, his was sharp edges, black leather, an obscenely large TV. Again, it made Lucy wonder what their childhood bedrooms looked like.

She took a breath before she knocked on his open door.

He sat at his desk, a sweeping onyx thing shiny enough that she could see her reflection. "Lucy, right on time." He welcomed her with a smile and said what he always said, the four words that made Lucy's rabbit-trap heart kick up a gear: "Get the door, please."

Dutifully, she shut it behind her. Her palms were slicked with sweat. She wiped them on her dress's skirt and hoped he just wanted a quick chat and she'd be back at her desk in minutes, but she knew better.

"Have a seat." He gestured to the chairs opposite his desk.

Lucy sank into one, hearing the soft leather hiss under her weight, and focused on the view out his window. Joanna's window looked west: a straight shot to the ocean on a clear day and an angle that bathed the welcoming space in golden afternoon light. Jonathan's looked east, toward smoggy downtown and the San Gabriel Mountains, which hovered like distant, pale ghosts. The view was yet another reason she didn't like visiting his office.

"Lucy, I understand today is a big day for you, for multiple reasons—happy birthday again—and I wanted to take the opportunity to speak with you." He leaned back in his chair and steepled his fingers. He wore a simple wedding band, and she knew he got regular manicures at a place in Beverly Hills. Not only because she could plainly see his buffed fingernails and trimmed cuticles, but because Annie had told her before that he couldn't take a meeting because he was out getting a manicure.

"Thank you," she murmured, unsure where he was heading.

"You're welcome." He held her gaze for longer than necessary, and she knew it was a power move. If he wanted awkward silences, he'd have them. "So, I know you're up for a well-deserved promotion, and I'd like to know if it's truly what you want."

She blinked at him, wondering if it was some kind of test.

"Of course it is," she said, and she knew it was true despite the fact that she couldn't lie.

"I figured you'd say that." He rose from his desk and buttoned his jacket. He was lean and toned and in fantastic shape for someone nearing fifty. "You know, you are one of the most talented publicists we have here. Watching you develop and succeed has been a pleasure." He paused mid-step and faced her like he expected her to thank him for the compliment.

"Thank you."

He circled to her side, unbuttoned the button he'd just done, and leaned back on the desk. His knee came within inches of hers. She couldn't help but adjust her posture and smooth her skirt. He drummed his fingers on the desk's lip, drawing out another silence that made Lucy itch.

"You're the one I should be thanking for your commitment to the company," he said. "I'm wondering though, with your promotion on the line and some stiff competition for the same position, just how committed you might be to advancing your career."

She watched his jaw muscle twitch, his eyes held steady on her. A surge of dread lurched up her throat, and she hoped he wasn't implying what she thought he was implying; that this was some thinly veiled solicitation, and normally, she wouldn't dare ask. She wouldn't let him know he'd cornered her conversationally because that would give him reason to doubt her, to question her intelligence. Normally, she'd use her own cunning to navigate to the heart of the matter. She'd correctly frame her response so that he heard her but wasn't put off.

But because of her damned honest mouth, she came out and said, "I'm sorry, but I'm not sure what you mean."

The efficiency of cutting to the chase felt like a blast of fresh air on a muggy day. For once, the mental tax she usually paid for doing verbal gymnastics stayed in her bank. Her brain wasn't analyzing permutations of optimal word choice to get her point across. She wasn't trying to interpret what he'd said and making her best guess at how to respond.

Lucy found it remarkably easy to say what she meant and wondered why she hadn't been doing it all along.

Jonathan chuckled and took the opportunity to playfully knock his knee against her leg. "I've always admired your boldness, Lucy," he said, confirming that cutting to the chase was in fact seen as bold. "Since we're being honest here, let me make myself clear." He reached over and squeezed her knee. "I'd like to know how *committed* you are to advancing your career."

It wasn't the first time he'd touched her, but it was the first time she shoved him away.

Before she could even consider the practiced shift to make

his hand fall, the friendly palm on top of his and gentle removal—any of the things she'd been trained to do to thwart unwanted advances but not come off as defensive—she pushed him away and stood up.

Her rabbit heart pounded like a jackhammer, but she felt the beats slowing into something steadier, stronger. She clenched her fists and took a breath to aid the calm.

He stood from his desk, his face full of fake concern. "What's wrong?"

The urge to deflect, to excuse his behavior and apologize, flailed inside her, but the freight train of honesty plowing through her day leveled it dead.

"*What's wrong?* The fact that you even asked that question is what's wrong, Jonathan. You know exactly what you did and what you've done—to me and other women here. And I'm sick of it."

The calculated calm slipped from his face. He watched her with a look of startled horror.

Tears welled in Lucy's eyes, years of frustration threatening to spill over. Just because she was on an honesty train didn't mean it wasn't scary.

And the train wasn't stopping.

She swallowed a fiery gulp of anger and glared at him. "I want my promotion because I've *earned* it, not in exchange for god only knows what you're offering. And I'm not the only one who knows the truth about you, Jonathan; the things you do and say to women in this office. You think you have control over us, but you're too arrogant to see that we're the ones with all the power." She spun on her flat heel and marched to the door. Her hand shook as she reached for the knob, and she wasn't sure her knees weren't going to give out. The terror of what she'd just said rattled every last one of her nerves, but the brazen streak of honesty keeping her spine straight kept her on her feet. She turned and cast one last glare at him. "Your sister is twice the leader you are, and everyone knows she deserves to be in charge of this company."

She slipped out the door and closed it behind her with enough force to make the nearby assistants jump. Eyes blinked at her from the cubicles like a dozen spiders in a boxy web. She was suddenly center stage under a glaring spotlight.

And she couldn't stop the tears she'd been damming back.

She held a hand to her face and turned for the bathroom. She felt Oliver's eyes on her the hottest, probing with concern. He popped from his chair like a prairie dog and watched her all but run down the hall. He'd let her cry into his crisp, pink-not-green shirt no question. He'd console her and condemn their boss with a litany of swear words in a soothing mother-hen voice until she calmed—they'd been through it before.

But she needed to be alone. She needed to get her head straight after what she'd just done.

She'd probably gotten herself fired.

She shoved open the women's bathroom door and knew it would stop Oliver like a roadblock. He'd barge into her office, sure, but not the women's bathroom.

J&J kept impeccable bathrooms with shiny granite counters, spotless sinks, a fresh bouquet each day. She'd taken refuge in the fluorescent room with lavender walls on more than one occasion, but to her dismay, it wasn't empty in that moment.

Annie stood at the sink. She smiled at Lucy in the mirror as she flicked water into the basin from her manicured hands. Her face fell when she registered Lucy's dismay.

"Are you okay?" she asked with all the concern of a sister-in-arms. Crying in the bathroom was an open invitation to offer a hug, a tampon, maybe to go kick some guy in the balls.

Unlike when they had met in the lobby that morning, Lucy clearly wasn't okay. She swiped a wad of tissues from the wall and sniffled. "I think I just lost my job by standing up to Jonathan."

She didn't mean to say it, but the words came out in a stream like they'd been doing all day, except they were water-logged and weepy. The ability to try to stop them—the urge to, even—had diminished almost completely, she realized, and it made her wonder if the honesty was getting stronger. If maybe the filter was off, and the truth would just burst out of her body in whatever way it pleased for the rest of the day.

Annie studied her with a guarded gaze. "What do you mean, 'standing up to Jonathan'?"

Lucy flapped a tissue like a tiny flag of surrender. "Well, he just propositioned me in his most aggressive attempt to date. I shoved him away when he touched me this time." She took a shuddering breath, thinking that move was the nail in her career coffin. She might as well apply for a job waitressing because no one in Hollywood was going to hire the girl who shoved Jonathan Jenkins.

She looked in the mirror to adjust her eye makeup out of reflex and remembered she wasn't wearing any. Where she expected twin streaks of mascara, all she saw were puffy pink eyes. She noticed the tense silence beside her. Annie had gone rigid.

She turned and caught the frightened look on her face. She was pale as a sheet.

"Are *you* okay?"

Annie tucked her hair behind her ear and stared at the floor. She bobbed her head, and Lucy wasn't sure who she was trying to convince. "I'm fine."

She thought about what she knew about Annie. She was an ambitious twenty-three, fresh from college, and had been Jonathan's assistant for just shy of a year. She had lasted longer than most in her position, and Lucy wondered if she knew some magic trick for dealing with unpleasant men.

She reconsidered when she noted the way Annie's thin shoulders hunched, her eyes cast down; how she looked like a Ted Baker–clad building collapsing in on itself. Lucy had figured she wasn't the only one on the receiving end of Jonathan's advances. In truth, her comment about *other women* when she confronted him was mostly a hunch, and confirmation she was right wasn't satisfying at all.

She reached for Annie's arm. "Hey. Fuck that guy, right?"

Annie's eyes snapped up. She blinked her impossibly full lashes, startled.

Lucy had startled herself, but she meant what she said. She squeezed Annie's arm. "You don't deserve to be mistreated. There's a lot of bullshit out there, and you're early enough in your career to decide you aren't going to take it." She huffed a soggy laugh, thinking of her own career and how she'd probably just ended it. "You can make a change before you get to the point of telling off the CEO of your company on the day you're supposed to get a huge promotion."

Annie gave her a sad smile, and Lucy wondered if their age difference really warranted sounding like such an old sage. But then, thirty probably seemed ancient to a college grad.

Annie sniffled. She was crying too, but somehow doing it very prettily with just a sheen to her big brown eyes. Lucy wondered if crying, like collagen, got less graceful with age. "You're right," Annie said, confidence restored. She threw her shoulders back and nodded. "We don't deserve this, and we shouldn't have to stand for it."

Lucy nodded back, feeling a sweet feminist fire light inside her. At the same time, she was terrified of what would happen. What sense of urgency she woke in Annie and how it might get them both fired.

But maybe she should just go down with the ship, since it was surely sinking anyway.

Annie turned for the door with a click-clack on the marble floor. She stopped and looked back. "Thanks, Lucy."

When she left, Lucy sighed and pulled her phone from her pocket. A major perk of her sundress: pockets burrowed in the skirt to squirrel away necessities. None of that shoving-her-phone-between-her-boobs-while-she-peed nonsense. She dialed Nina's number because she needed an outside party's perspective. She'd hash it out with Oliver, of course, but she wanted to talk to someone who didn't witness the scene.

"You okay?" Nina immediately answered, and Lucy was thankful. Trying to reach Nina at work during the day was always a gamble.

Lucy heard hospital sounds in the background: squeaking shoes, an intercom paging Dr. Someone, Nina chewing a granola bar, likely between patients.

"Well, I probably just lost my job, but I don't have another bloody nose or anything."

"What? Lost your job? What happened?"

Lucy sighed and turned around to lean on the sink. "Something very strange has happened to me, Nina, and I figured out what's going on. It's totally nuts, but I swear, it's real."

A pause while she chewed. "I'm listening."

"I can't lie."

"Okay, then tell me the truth."

"No, that's it. That's what's going on: I can't lie."

"I'm lost."

Lucy knew Nina would struggle with the logic, mainly because there was none to be had, and Nina's brain thrived on rational things like equations and common sense.

"Look, ever since I woke up this morning, I've been unable to be dishonest about anything."

"And that's a bad thing?"

"Yes! Well, in some aspects, I guess not, but for the most part, yes."

Another pause. "Does *the most part* have to do with you losing your job?"

Lucy studied her face in the mirror. Her complexion actually looked fresh and supple. Sure, her eyes were smaller without the drama of flared lashes and liner, but with her pink lips and the rosy glow of natural skin, she looked more like a relaxed day at the beach than the wearied hag she expected.

She sighed. "Yes. I just had a meeting with Jonathan, and he asked me how *committed* I am to getting my promotion and touched my knee."

"Gross."

"Yeah. And then I basically told him he sucks and I hate him."

"Again, that's a bad thing?"

Lucy grumbled. "*Ugh*, Nina. He's my *boss*. I don't know how things work in the medical field, but in publicity, it's generally not a good idea to threaten your superiors."

"Yeah, but, Lucy, he *does* suck. You've been putting up with shit from him for years. Maybe what you did was a good thing."

"I doubt it."

"Are you still having lunch with Lily?"

"As far as I know, though I haven't been back to my desk yet to check for *you're fired* emails. I came straight from Jonathan's office to the bathroom to cry like a true pillar of feminist bravada."

"You're too hard on yourself. That guy's a dick, and he totally deserved whatever you said to him."

Lucy let the reassurance of a best friend's unconditional support warmly fizz in her heart. It was the exact reason she'd called Nina, whether she was aware of it or not.

"Where's Oliver?" Nina asked, knowing full well Oliver filled her role during business hours. They got along famously, and Lucy couldn't have been more thankful for their little trio.

"Probably waiting outside the door."

"As he should be if you're hiding in the bathroom crying."

"I'm not crying. Not anymore."

"Then my job here is done."

She smiled, thankful Nina knew what to do, like always. She hadn't gotten very deep into the whole *can't tell a lie* thing, and she decided that was best. In the time it would take her to convince Nina that the honesty plight was real, she and Oliver could try at least ten other internet remedies for curse reversal.

"Thanks, Nina. I have to get back to my desk."

"Chin up, girl. It's your birthday."

She heard the smile in Nina's voice before she hung up. She took a deep breath, nodded at her reflection, and turned for the door, ready to take on whatever trouble she'd caused by opening her mouth.

She nearly ran into Oliver as he was, in fact, waiting outside the door.

"Are you okay? What happened?"

"The meeting didn't go well."

"Yeah, no kidding. Everyone just saw you run out of Jonathan's office and into the bathroom." He fell into step beside her as they marched toward her office.

She spent two seconds panicking over the gossip she surely started before a calendar reminder went off on her phone.

In all the Lily Chu anticipation, she completely forgot that Zeke Davidson, an eccentric, rising darling of the local theater scene, was coming in for a meeting. He'd be in her office in ten minutes.

Though flustered and still able to feel the hot imprint of Jonathan's hand on her knee, she was thankful she could take her mind off it with work.

Oliver chattered like a chipmunk as they approached her office, questioning her about what transpired behind Jonathan's closed door and tossing out theories about her no-lying predicament. Lucy tried to digest his words, but her mind strayed to Zeke. Not to mention the fact that Jonathan or Joanna could appear at any second and throw her out on her ear. They were less likely to do that while she sat in a meeting with a client, so the protection of her office was paramount.

". . . made a wish, then maybe you have to unwish it," Oliver blabbed.

"What?"

"Are you even listening?"

"Of course! I have to unwish my wish so I can lie again."

"Yes, that's what I'm saying. I did some research, and the web says the curse reversal didn't work because a wish and a curse are different things."

Lucy considered his theory as they turned the final bend toward her office, ignoring how absurd it sounded. "Interesting."

"I know. The logic doesn't make total sense, but none of this makes sense anyway, so maybe there's hope for getting you in shape for lunch with Lily."

"That's assuming I don't get fired before lunch."

"Fired?" He stopped walking for half a second.

She let out an exasperated breath. "Yes. Long story short, Jonathan propositioned me and I told him off. That's why I ran to the bathroom. I'll tell you the whole story later."

A flurry of swear words slipped from Oliver's lips and quietly dissolved on the air behind her.

They were ten steps from her office, and she didn't see one of the Js waiting outside the door or charging at her like a raging bull, so she at least had a job for the next hour while she met with Zeke.

"Do you still have time to go to the bar before lunch?" Oliver asked. "You said you had a weird drink, and the internet says maybe—"

"Oh!" Lucy said, having forgotten about her plan to visit the bartender who had probably spiked her drink with truth serum the night before, which she had to admit, though still absurd, was slightly more plausible than the wish theory. "Yes, I will most definitely be going to the bar before lunch."

"Okay, I'll—"

Lucy cut him off with a gasp when they arrived at her office. "Zeke! You're early."

They froze in the doorway and gaped at the man standing on the chair opposite her desk. Zeke Davidson posed like an explorer, fists punched into hips, one foot raised on the chair's arm.

"Once more unto the breach, dear friends, once more," he said.

Lucy was baffled both by why Zeke was standing on her furniture and why he spoke in a British accent when he had grown up in Long Beach.

Oliver shot Lucy wide eyes. "Have fun with that," he murmured, and headed for his desk.

Lucy politely smiled and entered her office. "Zeke, I wasn't expecting you for a few more minutes."

"All is forgiven, m'lady," he said, continuing with the British accent as he, thankfully, hopped down from the chair.

Ezekiel Davidson stood over six feet tall and dressed like a brooding thespian: a cardigan, a light scarf that served the sole purpose of draping his neck in stereotype, a shaved head. He was the most hyperbolic client Lucy had; everything was *fabulous* and *stupendous* or would *absolutely be the death of him*. His flair for drama left no moment dull, and with a client list that included demanding divas and playboys who landed themselves in the tabloids, lovably zany Zeke reminded her that working in the land of make-believe could be a delightful privilege.

"What do you think of my British accent?" he asked.

She was glad it was good because she'd have been forced to tell him if it wasn't. "It's fantastic."

"Fabulous," he trilled in his normal voice. "Your opinion means absolutely everything to me, Lucy. I would be devastated if you didn't like it."

"No pressure." She winked at him. "May I ask what it's for?"

He sat sideways in her chair, draping his grasshopper legs over the arm. His feet still touched the floor. "A new role. I'm taking the crown in a modern take on *Henry V*, which the writers dubbed *Five*"—he held up his hands like the word was an exploding firecracker—"and the geniuses in marketing decided to brand it as just the Roman numeral five, so everyone has taken to calling it *V* like the letter. It's a complete disaster."

His voice betrayed no concern over the disaster, and it made Lucy smile.

"Sounds interesting."

"Indeed. Rehearsals for the next month, opening this summer." He waved a bored hand, then suddenly sat straight up, feet on the floor in front of him, and pressed his hands to his knees. His penchant for languid, graceful movement coupled with explosive action made him exciting to watch. Lucy had seen him onstage several times, and it was for that exact reason that she couldn't take her eyes off him. "I'll have a pair of tickets with your name on them ready and waiting."

"I look forward to it."

Zeke's charming energy, his larger-than-life presence, and the thought of him onstage portraying a fifteenth-century king made her marvel at her own suspension of disbelief. How actors convinced her to trust what they were saying and doing—that they were someone else.

A glance at the clock said she had under two hours to fix her problem before she met Lily, and heading into negotiations with an A-lister was not something one did under the influence of strict morality. She wasn't going to *lie* to Lily, of course not. But she might need to make some promises, dangle a few exaggerations, to get her to take the bait. And she couldn't do that with her tongue tripping over every untruth. She suddenly wondered that if maybe she pretended to *be* someone else, if *that* person could bend the truth.

It was farfetched, but so was every single thing that had happened to her since she woke that morning.

"Zeke, can I ask you something?"

"Anything. I'm yours to read like a book."

"When you're acting, how do you get in the head of someone else and make their will come out of your mouth?"

His brow flicked. He seemed to search internally for the answer, and Lucy wondered if she'd ignorantly asked him to give away the ultimate trade secret. "Well, you let your own thoughts go," he said. "You let the character fill your mind and body. You think like them, move like them. You forget how *you* would react in any given situation, and suddenly, you are them."

It sounded like a simple recipe.

"That sounds easy enough." She smiled.

His face flattened into a stare so lethal, Lucy almost hid under her desk. "Darling, if it were easy, everyone would have three Emmys and an Oscar."

"Sorry, I didn't mean—"

He waved his hands with an embellished sigh. "It's all right. I'm sure if being a publicist were easy, we'd all swan around in skirt suits with raging ulcers and phones attached to our heads too. I like the casual look today, by the way. Very *La Bohème*."

Heat blossomed on her cheeks, but she couldn't help smiling.

"Why do you ask? Are you thinking of a career change?"

The thought that she might need to change careers after what went down with Jonathan cooled her smile. "No."

"Good. I couldn't bear to lose you on my team. You are my single most favorite person alive on this planet." He kicked an ankle onto his knee and waggled his fingers away from his face like he was opening a curtain. "Now, I've come to discuss getting this gorgeous mug on everyone's obsession list, so let's talk strategy."

Lucy settled into the business at hand, discussing social

media tactics, appearances, an interview with the city's theater guild. They drew up plans and picked who, what, and where would best make Zeke Davidson's star shine brighter. She didn't stumble over any lies because she didn't have to tell any with Zeke. He always wanted it straight. When they finished, he kissed both her cheeks and whisked out the door with a promise to wave at her in the audience on opening night of *Five/V*, whichever she wanted to call it.

As soon as he left, she checked her email. She'd ignored it while they met, and not only was an hour more than sufficient time for the world of celebrity gossip to implode, but there was also a non-zero chance she had a summons from a J—or, even worse, HR. To her relief, her inbox held nothing of the sort. Still, she couldn't resist peeking out at the two corner offices.

Both Js had their doors closed, and her heart settled into a more normal rhythm, figuring her job was secure at least until lunch. She leaned farther out her door and caught Oliver's ever-watchful eye. She tilted her head as a sign she wanted to chat, and he held up a finger.

Knowing he'd be a minute, Lucy turned back into her office, ready to test out her new theory. *Let your own thoughts go*, Zeke said. *Let the character fill your mind and body.*

She was going to pretend to be someone else. How hard could it be? Apparently, with all the lies the universe had informed her she told on a daily basis, she was pretending to be someone else every single day.

That thought felt very significant, but she didn't have time to dwell on it. Not when she had to hightail it to the bar for Plan B before lunch if Plan A—become a character—failed. She vowed to return to the thought later and analyze its importance. She would do it even if she fixed her problem because surely there was a lesson to be learned from it all.

Become a character.

She knew exactly who to be: Daphne. Her night-out alter ego when she didn't want to give her real name. Daphne was born along with Nina's alter ego, Claire, in the carefree era of college parties. When inhibition blurred into transient lust they didn't want following them home. The names only grew handier when frat parties morphed into bar hopping, the club scene, eventually industry events. The boys from college became men with delusions of entitlement, and the alter egos endured out of necessity. Daphne had changed interests and professions over the years. She'd been pre-med, a marine biologist, oddly into taxidermy once, even a lawyer for a cool ten minutes.

Lucy was ready to have her play the part of a publicist who needed to pull it together for a very important lunch so she didn't blow her promotion, assuming it was still on the table.

Daphne, Daphne, Daphne.

Daphne could lie, of course she could. Daphne could do anything.

She let her mind settle into this woman she'd created over a decade before. She fit like an old glove, and Lucy's hopes soared for the first time since she woke up ready to conquer her day.

Oliver knocked on her doorframe, and she whirled to face him, ready to declare in all her Daphne glory that his shirt was *green!*

"You look like you're going to be sick," Oliver greeted.

"What?"

He came in the door and reached for her. "You should

definitely sit down. You look like you're about to collapse." He shoved her into the chair still warm from Zeke.

"Oliver! W-what are you doing?"

As she said it, that telltale clammy rise of panic that gripped her body right before she threw up took hold of her, and the room spun.

"Are you going to puke? What did Zeke do to you?"

She held a hand to her forehead and felt it blistering with heat. "Nothing. He just told me how to become a character, so I got the idea that I'd pretend to be someone else, and maybe *she'd* be able to lie. I feel like I have a fever."

"And you look like death, so this ain't it. I think the universe is saying no."

She went to roll her eyes but realized they'd left the plane of reason. Oliver's theory made as much sense as anything, so she might as well take it seriously.

Hoping the truth would cure her sudden sickness, she pushed herself from the chair and announced, "I'm not pretending to be anyone else. I am me, Lucy Green."

The nausea vanished; the fever broke. The room stopped spinning.

She locked eyes with Oliver, and they silently agreed neither of them was insane; they had been witness to something inexplicable but real.

Oliver timidly cleared his throat. "Still got time to make it to that bar?"

"I—"

An email alert sounded from her computer. She was ready to sprint to the bar if it would fix her day, but she couldn't leave without checking anything urgent.

She rounded her desk, and that wave of nausea came hauling back—but not from an attempted lie.

An email from Jonathan stared her in the face.

"Oh god."

"What? You look like you're about to puke again."

"Jonathan wants to see me in his office. Right now."

Oliver's mouth rounded into an O, but no sound came out.

Lucy grasped for any scenario where this development was not bad news, and she came up with precisely zero.

"Want me to come with you?" Oliver asked.

"Yes."

He waved his hands and flushed. "Well, we both know I can't *actually* do that."

"Then why did you offer?"

"I don't know! I'm just trying to be supportive!"

Lucy grumbled, knowing full well it would be frowned upon to bring an emotional support friend to her meeting with the CEO but wanting to do it anyway.

"This is bad, Oliver."

He gave her a sad smile. "I believe in you."

She grabbed her phone and headed for the door.

"Good luck!" he softly called behind her, sounding as defeated as she felt.

For the second time that morning, Lucy found herself in Jonathan's office with its disagreeable eastern view. He lorded over his keep from his onyx desk. His workspace was clear of anything other than his computer and a piece of his personal letterhead with a fountain pen resting atop it.

"Lucy, have a seat," he greeted her.

The tension filling the room reminded Lucy of a horror film where something terrifying waited to jump out from the dark. She sat and felt her pulse fluttering in her wrists, in her throat. The hot imprint of his hand from only an hour before suddenly scorched her knee.

He sat across from her, confident as ever, as if nothing had happened, and it struck Lucy as wildly unfair that he could lie so freely about something so serious. He gave her a soft smile that she couldn't stand.

"Why am I here?"

He chuckled a sound Lucy would forever associate with contempt. "To the point, as usual. Lucy, after our discussion this morning and some time for reflection, I've decided it's best that our paths diverge going forward. I will ask HR to facilitate the termination paperwork. You will, of course, be provided with a generous severance package to accommodate the short notice."

The closest Lucy had ever come to an out-of-body experience was a regrettable night out in Hollywood that involved a questionable substance from the DJ Oliver was dating at the time. As she sat in Jonathan's posh office, the words *termination paperwork* suddenly gave her a bird's-eye view of herself. She circled around the ceiling for a few seconds before she came to and realized Jonathan was still talking.

"I'm sorry, what?" she said, cutting him off, and held out a hand. Though she half expected it after the morning's incident, the reality was sharper than a blade. "You're *actually firing me?*"

"Lucy, this doesn't have to be difficult. And like I said, your severance offer"—he flicked his wrist to reach for his pen—"is generous." He scratched out a number, the gold tip of his pen glinting in sharp licks, and slid the piece of paper toward her.

She picked it up, and moisture blurred her vision, whether from rage or fear, she wasn't sure. She blinked it away and looked at the J&J letterhead: *Jonathan Jenkins, CEO* printed beneath the logo. She did a double take at the number of zeros following the dollar amount. It was more than her annual salary.

Pieces snapped into place so quickly, Lucy almost flinched from understanding. She couldn't stop herself from standing up and calling it like she saw it.

"You're bribing me?"

Jonathan blanched. "I'm sorry?"

"Don't play dumb," she snapped, and almost threw her hands over her mouth. The truth curse was alive and well, and she was racking up points for saying inappropriate things to the CEO.

But even so, she couldn't stop.

"I have done *nothing* to deserve getting fired." She waved the form. "This is just an attempt to get rid of me before I say anything about being harassed."

He uncomfortably adjusted his posture, clearly not expecting her to speak so plainly again, but he had no idea what he was up against. He faltered for a moment and smoothed his hand over his tie, regaining his composure. He sternly cleared his throat. "I have no idea what you are talking about."

"Oh, come *on*," Lucy nearly groaned. "You know exactly—"

"*Ms.* Green!" He cut her off with a dark note in his voice that made her take a step back. He remained seated; another power play. He didn't have to stand, to tower over her, to intimidate her. He spoke in a cool, measured tone. "There seems to have been a misunderstanding. I know nothing about harassment claims. The severance package is in gratitude for your contributions to this company. I can revoke the offer and you can leave with nothing, if you would prefer. Either way, you no longer work for J&J Public, effective immediately."

The phrase was quite possibly the worst combination of words she had ever heard in her life.

Something tight clenched her throat like the sour pucker of lemonade. Except there was no refreshment along with it. Just fear. And anger.

She glanced down at the paper again, all those zeros. She felt sudden sympathy for all the women who had been pressured to accept money in exchange for silence. Was there a price high enough? Jonathan thought so. Clearly.

On another day, she may have joined the legions paid to keep their mouths shut. But since keeping her mouth shut was no longer something she could do, it seemed she had more options at her disposal.

"You can't fire me," she said, with an amount of conviction that shocked her.

A slow, sinister grin spread over Jonathan's face and turned her insides to jelly. "As CEO of this company, Ms. Green, I assure you I can do whatever I want."

"We'll see about that," Lucy hissed, and turned for the door, severance offer still in hand.

In the hall, she took a hard left toward the office she should have visited after he touched her earlier that morning—the office she should have visited years before, when it all started.

By the time she was standing in front of Joanna's desk, she was shaking. The cool, calm colors of the room and ocean shimmering in the distance did next to nothing for her nerves.

"Lucy? What's wrong?" Joanna asked. She sat at her desk, startled by Lucy's sudden appearance and authoritative closing of her boss's door like she owned the place.

A hot ball of emotion jammed Lucy's throat. She swallowed tears. She slapped the severance offer on the desk. "Your brother is trying to fire me."

Shock rearranged Joanna's face. She rapidly blinked and reached for the paper. "What?" Her eyes scanned, and Lucy began to breathe faster and faster.

"He just called me into his office and gave me this."

"I don't . . ." She blinked at the number. "I don't understand. Why would he fire you?"

The truth Lucy hadn't wanted to tell Joanna for several years sat on the tip of her tongue like a grenade. All the times she thought of confiding in her, the barrier of Jonathan being her brother stood in the way. How could she tell her mentor, her friend, something so awful? She had worried time and again that the act in itself would ruin her chance at advancement. The bind cost her many hours of lost sleep and several perfectly good manicures chewed to nubs.

But the time had come. She saw no other way. And she had no other choice.

"Joanna, Jonathan has been harassing me. This morning, he invited me into his office and asked how *committed* I am to my career. He touched my knee and insinuated there were things I could do to secure my promotion. I called him on it, and now he's firing me with this severance offer to keep me from talking."

Lucy had imagined the moment she shared this news with Joanna many times. In those scenarios, Joanna's reactions ranged from rage to tears to denial and shouting at Lucy to *get out.* The situation was complicated and sensitive, and now that she saw Joanna's reaction live in person, Lucy realized one of her scenarios should have included the sickly, pale sheen that washed over her face.

Despite that, the release of finally telling someone other than her two best friends the truth lifted a weight from Lucy so large, she felt untethered to the earth for a moment. And then she remembered her job was on the line, and the possibility that she really was fired suddenly felt too real, and it threatened to swallow her whole.

"I love this job," she said, her voice wobbly. "We're supposed to have lunch with Lily Chu today, and I'm going to sign her as a client. I can't get fired." Her words came out sounding numb and lost.

Joanna rose from her desk and rounded to Lucy's side. She reached out like she was going to hug her and hesitated before she gently patted her upper arms. There was so much to be said, but Joanna focused on the immediate matter. An emotion Lucy couldn't quite place nipped at her voice. "Lucy, I will take care of this. We are still going to lunch with Lily, so be ready in"—she flipped her wrist to check her watch—"an hour." She grabbed the severance offer from her desk and shuffled Lucy toward the door. "Don't worry," she told her with a smile.

Lucy knew Joanna was using her expert chaos management skills on her. The situation would not be helped by shouting and door slamming, even if it felt appropriate. As much as Jonathan wanted Lucy to go quietly, Joanna probably wanted record of Jonathan's quid pro quo to slide under the radar too. That didn't mean she wasn't going to go unleash big-sister wrath on him behind closed doors, and the thought lifted Lucy's heart a fraction.

As did the thought that Joanna really ran the ship at J&J. Even if she wasn't officially in charge, Lucy had to put her faith in Joanna coming to her aid.

She stood outside Joanna's door and caught Oliver's concerned eyes.

So? he silently asked.

Lucy didn't know how to respond, still stunned from it all. She held up a hand in a shrug.

Oliver narrowed his eyes and then used his hand to make a drinking motion with his thumb and pinky out.

Lucy thought for a second he was suggesting they ditch work and drown the morning's sorrows in booze, which didn't sound half bad, but then she realized his hand signal was a reminder that when Jonathan summoned her, she had been on her way to see the bartender to undo the wish that was ruining her life.

Lucy summoned a ride because no way was she going to navigate parking on a mad-dash mission she wasn't supposed to be taking time away from work to run anyway. Joanna said she would see her for lunch in an hour, and Lucy was ready to spend that hour doing just about anything to fix her problem.

She could not believe the things she had said to Jonathan, again, and she hoped Joanna really was going to take care of it.

And she hoped she wasn't actually fired.

And she hoped the bartender would help her resolve the lying issue because, according to Joanna, they were still having lunch with Lily Chu, and she wasn't about to walk into that with a curse weighing her down.

Her rideshare driver tried to make conversation along the way, awkward as it was, and for once, she plainly told him she wasn't interested in talking. She wondered as she checked emails, scanned social media, and fielded a few more *happy birthday* texts why she'd never been so direct about her conversation preferences before. Maybe it had something to do with being alone and at the mercy of a strange man behind the wheel.

It struck her that ridesharing was inherently terrifying.

She compensated for her dark thoughts about her driver—who was probably a perfectly decent human—by leaving a 20 percent tip when they arrived.

As she approached the bar's sunny front door, she wondered again if the honesty was growing in strength. If she'd lost the ability to resist it at all, and this confrontation with the bartender would be completely uncensored.

She shook the thought and swung open the door. The space looked almost the same as it had the night before: open, airy, except it was empty of mingling conversation and clinking glass. In fact, it was empty of everyone except the man behind the bar.

"We're closed!" he called, not unkindly, as Lucy stomped inside. She marched straight up to the stool she sat on the night before and watched him squat down to reach for something under the bar. When he popped back up to see her right in front of him, his face split into a grin. "Oh, hey, Birthday Girl."

"Hey, Hot Bartender—*I mean* . . ."

She wanted to drown herself in the bottle of tequila in his big hands. His brows jumped as the rest of his face lifted in a pleasant smile.

"Sorry." She tried to recover, though she was dying a slow, mortifying death. "I didn't catch your name last night."

He chuckled. "It's Adam, but I'll answer to Hot Bartender too."

Her face was on fire, she was sure of it.

He wiped down the bottle of tequila and set it on the bar. His hazel eyes were warm and keen just like they had been the night before. He watched Lucy with great interest. "What can I get you?"

"I thought you were closed."

"Right."

He sounded disappointed. Like maybe he wanted the unhappy woman from the night before to return midday and demand he woo her with another life-changing cocktail.

No time for that.

"I'm not here for a drink," Lucy said, harsher than she meant to. "I want to know what you put in my drink last night."

"I'm sorry?"

"The purple fizzy thing you served me, what was in it?"

His full lips bent into a sly grin that Lucy could *definitely* see in a leading role. This guy had the stuff. It was probably all there when she had met him the night before; she just wasn't being honest with herself about it. She bit her lip and tried to concentrate.

"Sorry, I can't share," he said. "That's my proprietary birthday special."

He was flirting with her, that much was clear, and on another day, she might have been in the mood. But not with her career hanging in the balance.

She stood up on the bar's footrest, making herself a few inches taller in her flats. She spread her palms on the marble top. To avoid sounding completely nuts, she held back confessing about her wish and kept it vague. "Listen, something strange has happened to me, and I can only trace it back to here—to *you*. I don't know what's going on, but I think it started with that drink, so I need you to tell me what was in it."

His face suddenly paled, and he looked ill. He leaned in. "Whoa, look, I don't know what may have happened after you left here last night, but I didn't put anything in your drink that would have . . . that might have made you . . ."

"Oh!" Lucy blurted. "No, no, I wasn't drugged or anything. Not in *that* sense anyway."

He pressed a hand to his chest, sighing a big breath. "Good. You scared me. I thought something bad happened to you."

"Sorry." Lucy tucked her hair behind her ear, impressed that Oliver's scarf job was still holding up, and felt chagrined. She hadn't meant to accuse him of slipping something dangerous into her drink. He still looked concerned despite her clarification, and she studied him studying her, which led her to notice how his agreeably tight olive tee shirt set off the green in his eyes.

"So, what's going on, then, if we're not talking beverage sabotage?"

Lucy shook herself from the grip of his gaze. Had it been that strong the previous night? Had she just not been paying attention, or had she been in unconscious denial about it?

It didn't matter. That wasn't why she'd come.

She leaned over the bar again and told him the truth. "We *are* talking about beverage sabotage. I made a wish when I had that drink, and ever since, I haven't been able to lie."

He stared at her like he was examining a piece of art. She felt as exposed as she did the night before when he told her she was unhappy. But this time, she couldn't be sure he wasn't about to burst out laughing.

"You wished you couldn't lie?"

"No! I wished for the perfect day today, and something went very, very wrong. Now I can't tell a lie."

His skepticism had nowhere to hide. "Okay, George Washington, what does that mean? You *can't tell a lie*."

He was being cute, and it was not the time.

"It means that ever since I drank that purple concoction—a drink *you* called life-changing—my life has been in chaos."

He wadded his rag in his hands, and Lucy tried to ignore how oddly appealing the motion was. "Chaos because you can't lie?"

"Yes. It's been a very rough morning, and I have a big, very important afternoon, so I need you to undo whatever you did." She fluttered her hands like the secret to his trick was hidden under the bar.

He kept staring at her, his eyes narrowing and his hands working the rag. "You," he said slowly, "can't . . . tell a lie?"

She nodded, and as heat curled up her neck and into her cheeks, she realized she'd walked straight into a trap—the same trap she'd set with Oliver, but he, being one of her best friends, had the decency not to humiliate her. There was no telling what this gorgeous stranger with a killer smile was capable of.

Adam the bartender leaned across the bar with mischief in his eyes. "What are you doing later tonight?"

Lucy swallowed against her dry throat. She had no choice but to tell him, but she didn't have to do it nicely.

"My birthday party at Perch."

"Classy."

"Yes, as long as I don't destroy my life beforehand because of whatever *you* put in my drink!"

"I didn't put anything in your drink!" He shrugged his bulky shoulders and held up his hands. "Listen, it was vodka, crème de violette, champagne, and lemon juice."

She eyed him suspiciously. "That's it?"

"Yes! Oh, and the truth serum, but I thought that was a given."

She snatched a cherry from the little black box of lime wedges, straws, and ruby red maraschinos and threw it at him.

He flinched and laughed. "I'm kidding! That's not even a real thing?"

"I think the CIA would disagree."

He leaned in on the bar, suddenly serious again. "You think I'm a spy?"

She reached for another cherry, but he moved the box away. "I think you're making fun of me when I came in here asking for help."

"This is how you ask people for help? By accusing them of causing your problems and throwing fruit at them?"

"I—"

She realized that was a completely fair observation, and she was annoyed with him for so readily making it. She folded her arms and glared at him. "Listen, if you didn't put anything in my drink, prove it. Make me another one. Right now."

"It's eleven a.m."

"Do I look like I care what time it is?"

"Okay!" He chuckled, backing away with a smile. "Coming right up."

She watched him work like a warden watching a prisoner. He carefully set each bottle on the bar, making a show of no funny business.

"What's your name, Birthday Girl?"

She realized she was captive, and he could ask her anything he wanted while she waited for her drink. But the question was harmless. And in all fairness, the least she could do was tell him her name considering she'd barged in on him outside of hours and demanded he fix her a drink.

"Lucy."

"Nice to meet you, Lucy." He smiled and poured the purple ingredient into the shaker. Watching him mesmerized her. She tried to focus on the reason she came—to undo whatever he'd done to her—but his fluid motion and warm, gravelly voice were distracting. He reached for the vodka and formed his mouth around another question.

"Don't abuse your power right now," she warned him.

He squeezed a lemon wedge over the shaker. "I wouldn't dream of it." He fastened the shaker's lid and shook it like a maraca. She looked away from his arm pumping up and down and the veins in his hand gripping the tumbler.

"How long have you worked here?" she asked for distraction. She gazed out the glass wall at the sunny day, thinking it would be nice to head down to the beach and forget everything else.

"Since I bought it," he said, and strained the purple liquid into a martini glass with a quiet hiss.

"You own this place?"

"Sure do. You sound surprised by that fact, Lucy."

She liked the way he said her name.

In truth, she was surprised. She assumed he was another actor moonlighting as a bartender to make rent.

And because that was the truth, she had to say it.

"I am surprised. I assumed this was a second job while you worked on a different career."

He reached for a fresh bottle of champagne. Lucy watched him unwind the little cage and twist the bottle back and forth until the cork burst out with a *pop* that made her jump.

"A career like acting?"

No sense in denying it, even if she could.

She shrugged a shoulder as he topped off her drink with a splash of bubbles. He took another lemon wedge and rubbed it around the glass's rim, squeezing gently, before leaving it hanging from the edge. He smoothly pushed the glass toward her over the marble bar top.

"I'll let you in on a secret, Lucy," he said quietly. "Not all hot bartenders in L.A. are actors. Some of us are just . . . bartenders."

She fought the wave of embarrassment, feeling foolish for making assumptions about him. "I noticed you left the *hot* part in there."

"Aren't you keen." He threw her line from the night before back at her, and she couldn't help but smile. "So, are you gonna drink that now? See if it'll reverse whatever honesty spell you're under?"

That was precisely what she was going to do. She didn't really want to be chugging booze right before her meeting with Lily Chu, but she also didn't want to spend the rest of the day navigating the treachery of total honesty.

She lifted it and tipped it toward him, the same as she'd done the first time. She scrambled for what to say—how to unwish her wish. *I wish I could lie* didn't feel very honorable. She settled on *I wish to reverse my wish* and sipped the same cool, delicious tonic as the night before. It went down just as smoothly. As impossibly blended into one flavor even though she knew all the ingredients.

Adam watched her sip until it was gone. "And?"

Lucy searched inside her head, her body, looking for a sign something had changed.

She felt exactly the same.

"Ask me another question." She braved the risk, hoping he'd go gentle on her.

He leaned on the bar, arms spread and elbows locked. He held her gaze with an intensity that made her glad she had sat on the stool. "Okay. Do you have a boyfriend?"

"Yes."

The look on his face said he hoped she was lying, and she realized he had no way of knowing that she was telling the truth.

"It didn't work," she said, just to make things clear. "I still can't lie."

But did that mean she *wanted* to lie about having a boyfriend? Did *he* want her to lie?

She shook away the confusing thoughts.

Adam frowned, and she couldn't tell what had disappointed him: the answer to his question or their failed experiment. "Maybe it's a midnight thing."

"A what?"

He began clearing bottles from the bar. "A midnight thing. You know, in fairy tales the spell lasts until midnight . . . That kind of thing."

"Huh," she mused. "I hadn't thought of that, but it could make sense. I mean, it *is* my birthday; maybe this is some kind of twenty-four-hour curse or something."

He shrugged with an ironic nod. "Sure. That definitely makes sense. Maybe you should consider the true-love's-kiss option too, if we're following fairy-tale logic here."

She pinched the lemon wedge that clung to her glass and threw it at him. "You're the one who brought it up."

"Yes, and you're the one knocking back hard liquor before

noon in the name of spell reversal. If you're going to keep throwing fruit at me, I'll have to ask you to leave."

"I— Sorry."

He smiled. "I'm kidding. See, *I* am perfectly capable of telling mistruths, and I am enjoying your company, as odd and demanding as it may be, so the last thing I want is for you to leave. But I am going to hide the watermelon wedges."

A smile warmed her face, and she couldn't be sure if it was Adam the bartender or the goblet of booze she'd just swallowed that was responsible for it. Maybe a little of both.

She found herself not wanting to leave either; something about his presence felt reassuring. Safe. But she knew she had to go if she was going to make it to lunch on time. She reached in her tote for her wallet, and Adam held up a hand.

"On the house."

She paused, elbow deep in her bag. "You sure?" She was happy to pay, but if he was giving her a pass on Westside drink prices, she was going to take it.

"Completely. I can't charge you for a drink that didn't work." His smile was both sweet and sarcastic, and she found the combination irresistible.

"Thank you." She pulled herself away before she thought of a reason to stay.

He waved as she walked away. "Thanks for stopping by, Birthday Girl. I hope you rediscover your sense of amorality. Good luck with your important afternoon!"

She shot him a glare and pushed back into the sunlight.

Outside, she checked the time and debated if she could make a pit stop before returning to her office to meet Joanna before lunch.

True love's kiss was suddenly wailing in her head like a siren, and she needed to see Caleb. Luckily, his office was nearby.

In a snap decision, she changed the destination in her ride-share app and texted her boyfriend.

I need to see you. Dropping by your office.

CHAPTER

8

On the ride to Caleb's office, a shiny wealth-management firm in Westwood, Lucy scrolled social media, making sure all of her clients were behaving.

So far, nothing scandalous for the day, though Leo's birthday post had a few hundred thousand likes. Which actually wasn't anything to get excited about since he could post a picture of a milk carton and the internet would go nuts. The more obscure the better, in fact.

Half of her job was babysitting, honestly, and Twitter and Instagram were twenty-four-hour baby monitors. More than once, a Google Alert woke her in the middle of the night with news that someone, usually Leo, had posted something worthy of trending and she had to run damage control in her PJs.

Thankfully, her brood was keeping it in line, maybe as a birthday treat, because she did not have time to manage anyone else's crises.

She took a peek at Ms. Ma's feed, and the video was blowing up just as expected. As were the hateful comments about how inappropriate and vulgar the lyrics and message were. Lucy had half a mind to reply with a row of middle-finger emojis to every negative comment, but she saw that hordes of fans had beaten her to it.

She also checked for any messages from Joanna or HR regarding the maybe-getting-fired incident. She hoped that the severance offer had gone through the shredder and Joanna put Jonathan in his place. Of course there would be follow-up over what she told Joanna about being harassed, and she wasn't sure what it would entail. But for the time being, she needed to have a very important conversation with her boyfriend.

Her driver stopped in front of Caleb's building, a mirrored rectangle with palm trees and a fountain. According to math and Westside traffic patterns, she had maximum fifteen minutes to make it in and out with enough time to get back to the office before lunch.

She'd only been to his office a few times: a few lunch dates, a night early on in their relationship when she found his working late sexy because it seemed so grown up and she brought him dinner, and that one time they did it in his new office when he got a promotion. It lasted under ten minutes because they were afraid they were going to get caught. It was a flurry of hands and rumpled clothing, and Caleb shuddering between her legs before she had the chance to really get going. Which, when she thought about it, was what most of their sex was.

She longed for the kind of lovemaking that stopped time and transcended physical bodies. But maybe that only existed in novels and films. Or maybe if it did exist in real life, she and Caleb just weren't compatible on that level.

Or maybe, she thought as she climbed the stone steps to the

building entrance, maybe she just never spoke up about what she really wanted.

A dark, intrigued laugh popped from her lips as she thought about her predicament playing out in bed. Being unable to lie during sex; what would *that* be like?

The thought sent a rush of blood swirling through her abdomen that made her press herself against the cool mirrored wall when she climbed in the elevator. She was suddenly hot and maybe even a little bit bothered. She took several deep breaths as the lift carried her up to the tenth floor.

Caleb had been promoted to VP of his division a year before. The title came with all the trimmings: bigger office, more pay, invitation to exclusive events. He managed money for rich people, and doing so earned him things like box seats at Dodger Stadium, booze cruises to Catalina Island, movie premiere tickets, and, of course, the perk no one wants: impossibly long hours. Their mutual career-driven lifestyles initially drew them together, and Lucy found it immeasurably comforting to have someone who understood late nights at the office, weekends lost to events, and answering emails from bed. They coexisted independently, together; each committed to their own goals, together.

But.

Lucy had largely ignored their relationship's backseat status and chalked it up to a part of how they functioned as a couple. The canceled dates, the apology flowers, the nights alone in her bed while the guy she thought she wanted to marry stayed more faithful to his job than to her. Were those idiosyncrasies or symptoms of something larger?

Her morning of honesty had shown her many things, including several ways in which she lied to herself. And as she rode the elevator to Caleb's office, she wondered if convincing herself she was happy in her relationship was one of the biggest.

The elevator dinged, and she stepped into the marble lobby on the tenth floor. Caleb's firm ran rampant with finance bros—guys from USC with Trojan license plate frames on their BMWs, mini basketball hoops in their offices, memberships to Equinox. She counted herself lucky that Caleb didn't partake in all the industry stereotypes, though she had been to a few stuffy USC alumni events because he was in fact a Trojan. Despite that, Caleb was more partial to sci-fi novels, museums, the occasional symphony—things his frat-boy colleagues would have shaved off his eyebrows for in college.

Lucy and Caleb met at a book launch one balmy L.A. summer night. One of Lucy's clients was signing copies of his newest novel, and she noticed the cute guy in the back, painfully looking like he didn't want to be seen at such an event. Turned out, he was a huge fan and knew everything about the book and the author. They dated exclusively from the moment they met. They vacationed together, spent holidays with each other's families. Moving in together was the obvious next step, or so she thought.

She threw a familiar wave at the reception desk, though she couldn't say for certain that the people sitting behind it knew who she was. Regardless, they didn't stop her from walking down the hall toward Caleb's office.

She found him at his desk, phone squeezed between ear and shoulder, hammering his keyboard, a frown for the ages on his face. He lifted his eyes and threw a look of surprise at her as she slipped inside. She knew he hadn't gotten her message about stopping by.

To let him know the urgency of her visit, she stayed standing in front of his desk instead of taking one of the tufted suede chairs across from it.

He kept typing and frowning, and she wondered why he was awkwardly pinching his neck instead of putting the caller on speaker. She gazed out his window while she waited, looking across the street at another high-rise glinting in the sun. Every time she looked out the window, she thought of the time they had sex in his office. They locked the door but did nothing about the floor-to-ceiling glass, and that was the thrill of it. A thrill that suddenly seemed like a desperate attempt to capture something that did not exist.

"That's not going to work," Caleb said to whomever he was talking to. "No. Call me back after closing." He hung up with no goodbye, and Lucy blinked in surprise, having had no idea she was dating a guy who hung up on people. He barely had the phone in the cradle before he directed his attention at her. "Hey. What are you doing here?"

"You didn't get my message?"

He moved a stack of papers teetering at the end of his desk and unearthed his cell phone. He thumbed at it with a frown. "Now I did. What's going on?"

By the time he looked up, she was standing right in front of him, having circled behind his desk. She grabbed his chair's arm and spun him so she stood between his knees. Without another word, she reached for his face and kissed him.

Caught off guard or not, like always, his lips stayed stiff and tight like he was playing the trumpet rather than kissing his girlfriend. Getting him to open his mouth was like a kid at the dentist. He usually kept any kind of unrestrained passion locked up behind a few drinks, and then it was a quick, sweaty-handed journey to sloppy. This kiss was no different than the hundreds they'd shared before.

True love's kiss.

Adam's words back in the bar sparked a realization. Not so much a solution to her honesty problem as the insatiable need to know the truth. She had come to see Caleb not to break the spell but rather to expose a lie.

Although, if a kiss really *was* going to fix her problem, she'd take the win because she still needed to make it through lunch with a movie star.

Except.

As she expected, the kiss wasn't doing anything. Where she half hoped to feel a shift, a rewind, an unraveling and respinning of the thread that held her life together, she felt a square peg and a round hole; shoes that didn't quite fit right; plaid with a floral print. And she realized it had *always* felt mismatched with Caleb, she had just never admitted it.

She abruptly pulled back and held his face in her hands. He had sharp eyes, a blade of a nose, and a jawline that would give their future children elfin features if combined with her own, but that scenario was looking less and less likely by the second.

"That wasn't good." Instead of surprising her, her declaration emboldened her. "It's never been good."

He blinked at her, confused. *"Okay."* He rubbed his wet lips together. "Have you been drinking?"

"Yes."

His brow flattened. "Lucy, what—?"

"Your shirt is bl—"

She tried her standard test, just to be sure it hadn't worked, and felt the familiar wall barricading the slightest dishonesty.

Caleb glanced down at his chest. "My shirt? What about it?"

She looked at him sitting there in his gray-not-blue shirt and knew that even if true love's kiss was the cure, she didn't love Caleb. She knew it with the same certainty she knew he wasn't going to propose to her that night. Or ever, for that matter. And she knew that she had been lying to herself about wanting him to all along.

"It's a nice shirt," she told him, her voice betraying a wobble.

"Lucy, what's going on? Why are you upset over my shirt?" He stood beside her and wrapped an arm around her shoulders like a soccer coach, not an empathetic significant other with spouse potential. The friendly shoulder squeeze was his go-to comfort move, sometimes a pat on the back. *Buck up, champ. You'll make it through.*

"I hate it when you do that," she said, and shrugged his arm away. "I'd rather have a real hug than whatever that is." She waved a hand. "I also don't like how kissing you feels like I'm kissing a shy middle schooler or a drunk frat boy, and there's nothing in between."

He stepped back. "Uh . . . what?"

She took a breath. She came to be honest, not cruel, and that was a bit harsh.

She sensed that she was about to humiliate herself, but ripping off the Band-Aid was better than continuing the charade.

"I thought you were going to propose to me tonight, Caleb."

His eyes went so wide, she could see the whites all the way around. "I— Propose?" Caleb rarely had trouble figuring out what to say; he always had an intelligent response on hand. But the stunned look on his face, his eyes darting like panicked pinballs, Lucy knew he was not on the same page she had been on about their future. "Lucy, I . . . That's not . . . I wasn't—"

"I know."

She was suddenly angry with herself for being so misguided. All the time and energy she spent waiting, telling herself it was what she wanted. She knew on some level that he wasn't ready, but seeing confirmation hurt.

Caleb ran a hand through his sandy hair and exhaled like he really couldn't believe what was going on. "You really thought . . . ?"

"Yes, Caleb, I did. I did because I thought it was the next step. We've been dating for two years; we're moving in together; our families love each other; we're both in our thirties. Every movie I've ever seen, book I've read, and Instagram post shoving wedding pictures down my throat says I'm supposed to walk down the aisle to Mr. Perfect at this stage in my life. But we're not perfect, Caleb. I've just been telling myself we are. And based on the look you just gave me when I mentioned proposing, marriage isn't even on your radar, which is entirely unfair since *I'm* made to feel like a failure if I'm not hitched by thirty, and *you* get to keep sending apology flowers and skipping out on dates like you've got all the time in the world!"

She didn't realize how much her voice had risen until she saw a smooth, tanned arm discreetly reach inside and close the door; Paige, Caleb's assistant. She waited for it to click and took the privacy as license to continue.

"Are we even in love, Caleb?"

The fact that he didn't rush to her, fold her in his arms, kiss her, and ask how she could even question such a thing was enough of an answer.

"That's what I thought."

His face flushed and his eyes widened like he'd been caught

doing something wrong. Then he held out his hands, looking like he was trying to catch his footing on mossy river rocks. "Lucy, what is even going on right now? You just show up out of nowhere and start talking about marriage, and now we're what, breaking up?"

The words stung, but Lucy could not deny their truth.

"Yes, I think we are breaking up, Caleb. I've realized I've spent all this time waiting for something I don't even want—*lying* to myself about it. Telling myself it's *fine* when you don't show up; it's *fine* that we're not physically compatible; another bouquet of flowers is *fine*. But it's *not* fine. And I don't even know if I *want* two kids, a labradoodle, and a house in the suburbs!"

He leaned back like she'd thrown something at him.

"Oh, get a clue, Caleb!" she snapped at his reaction, and paced toward the window. "You know women are pressured to have husbands and homes and kids; don't look so shocked."

"I—I'm not shocked," he said in what Lucy was sure was a lie. "I just didn't realize that . . . *you* were feeling that pressure."

She whirled on him, angrier than she thought she was. "Well, perhaps if you had paid closer attention you would have. I've been waiting for you to propose to me for six months. I've been telling myself *tonight's the night*, and it's never the night!"

He paused, looking half-affronted and half-concerned for her mental state. "Lucy, that's crazy."

"Is it?" She threw out her arms. "I don't know, Caleb. Maybe you'd be a little crazy too if society told you it was what you should expect. But I guess *guys* don't get that memo, which leaves us gals losing our minds holding out for something we never even wanted!"

Her voice cracked off the glass wall. Caleb flinched and looked like he would do anything to stop her from yelling.

"Do you . . . do you want to get married?"

"No!" she cried.

The word *yes* had sat spring-loaded on her tongue for months. And in the moment of truth, when it had the chance to launch from her mouth like a bride-to-be rocket, its opposite came exploding out.

"Caleb, you and I getting married would be a mistake."

He slowly nodded in agreement, as if what she said were the most obvious thing he'd heard. "Okay."

"*Okay?* That's it?"

"Lucy, what do you want from me? You show up here after apparently drinking in the middle of the day, telling me I'm a bad kisser, and mad at me for not proposing to you when I didn't even know marriage was on the table!"

"Don't judge me. You have no *idea* what kind of day I'm having, Caleb!"

"How could I if you haven't told me?!"

The harsh echo of his voice resounded around the room, hammering Lucy with another layer of realization.

She hadn't told him anything about her day. Not the curse, not the bloody nose—not even Jonathan. She'd never told him about Jonathan, in fact. The fact that she hadn't turned to him in any of her distress that day was perhaps a sign less of her independence and more of her indifference because she had told her friends. She even told Adam the bartender, to some extent.

"You're right. I haven't." But when she tried to picture telling him, she couldn't. "I guess I just never saw it."

"Saw what?"

"How little we have in common."

A silence settled between them. Lucy knew where they stood, but Caleb still looked thrown.

"So, just to be clear, we're breaking up because I didn't propose to you, but you *don't* want to get married."

"No, Caleb," she said patiently. "We're breaking up because we're not good together. We never have been. We were just too passively engaged in this relationship to notice."

After a moment, he nodded like he understood, and the fact that neither of them suggested they try being more actively engaged solidified their decision.

"I don't think we should move in together," Lucy said. It was a given, but she felt the need to say it anyway.

He gave her a pained look of agreement.

They stared at each other, neither sure what to say next. Was there anything left?

"So, I guess . . ."

"I guess so too," she said.

He gave her another nod, and that was it. It was over. It was swift and harsh, but she had gotten what she came for: the truth.

She didn't cry until she was in the elevator. Brutal honesty was more painful than she thought, a lesson she'd learned repeatedly throughout the day. Even if breaking up was the right thing to do, that didn't mean it didn't hurt. She sniffed boiling tears and felt simultaneous rage and relief. She couldn't tell who either emotion was directed at, but she knew Caleb wasn't the one for her.

Does the one even exist? she wondered as she crossed the ground-floor lobby. Maybe that was a made-up concept used to trick women into thinking they needed a partner to be complete. Maybe there was no rush to get married, get a dog, pop out kids, buy a house, and live happily ever after.

Ever after.

What about living in the moment?

Why was she making herself believe lies about the future that forced her to live her life on daily terms that didn't make her happy?

She stepped into the sunlight and walked down the stone steps. Lunchgoers crowded the small plaza, chatting on phones, waiting for cars, some sitting on the bench circling the fountain to eat. The buzz and clamor of it all made her feel alive. She was ready to move forward in the present and stop dwelling on the future, on made-up dreams and plans that weren't even really her own.

She heard Caleb call from behind her. "Lucy!"

His voice cut through the street noise like a chiming bell, and a vulnerable, post-breakup synapse in her brain convinced her she had been too harsh. She had made a mistake. She rescinded every thought she'd had between his office and the sidewalk. He was chasing after her, coming to apologize, and she'd take him back. They'd find a way.

She whirled around to let the real-life fantasy play out, and her skirt tangled around her legs. She didn't realize how close to the fountain she'd stopped, and when a pigeon launched itself into flight like a fat, flapping rat, she startled and felt its wing clip her chin. She flailed to swat it away, dropped her tote, stumbled, and fell headfirst into the fountain.

The splash cut off sounds of gasps and Caleb shouting her name a second time. The water was only two feet deep, but it was enough to submerge her in a sloshing bath of recycled chlorine, wishing pennies, and absolute humiliation. She almost opted to drown.

She surfaced, praying no one had pulled out their phone for a video, and pushed her sopping hair from her face. Caleb stood at the fountain's side looking horrified.

"Are you all right?"

She climbed out, heaving a wave of fountain water with her and splashing the concrete. Her dress plastered to her skin; her hair dripped down her back. Her new scarf from Oliver was probably ruined.

Everyone was staring. The poor people lunching on the fountain's rim grabbed their salads and jumped away from the woman in a soggy sundress. Even Caleb backed up to save his suit from getting wet.

Lucy wrung out her skirt and grasped for a speck of dignity. "Did you see that bird? It hit me in the face!"

Caleb looked over his shoulder as if searching for the guilty pigeon, but he was surely checking how many people were staring.

She squeezed water from her hair and tried for a smile because what else could she do? "Anyway. Did you need to tell me something?"

He reached in his pocket, and her heart almost burst out of her chest, thinking he really was chasing after her.

Except.

It wasn't an emerald cut in his pocket.

It was the key to their new condo, and she realized that grand gestures were nothing but Hollywood lies.

"Can you take this back to the leasing office? I won't have time." He held out the gold token like a spear straight to the heart of their dying relationship.

It was already dead; she'd just been in denial.

And she realized the fountain had to be the universe intervening again. Just like her sudden sickness in her office, the fountain was a means to stop her from lying, and in this case, the lie was running back into Caleb's arms.

"Sure." She took the key and reached for her thrown tote. Luckily no one had run off with it while she was underwater. She stepped around Caleb to grab it and wondered why he wasn't gathering it for her. He'd held her bag plenty of times before, but it looked like those days were officially over. All boyfriend duties relieved.

Bitterness filled her mouth like she'd swallowed the pennies from the fountain.

"Oh," he said, "I guess I won't be coming to your birthday party tonight. I think that would be kind of, well, *awkward* at this point, don't you?"

On a normal day, one where the universe wasn't conspiring to reveal truths to her in painful and humiliating ways, she would have acted like a grown-up, agreed with him, wished him the best, and walked away.

But today, instead of saying anything, she put her hands on her newly ex-boyfriend's chest and shoved him into the fountain.

She walked away to a splash, gasps, and clapping from an unacquainted but invested bystander.

Lucy noted the time and cursed under her breath. Her plan for dropping by Caleb's office and making it back to her own on time for lunch did not involve an unexpected plunge in a fountain. She needed to call for help if she had any hope of being presentable for her date with Lily.

She walked half a block, away from the scene of the crime, to order a ride and call her best bet for assistance. Given that Oliver's job entailed running errands for divas on Joanna's behalf, she knew he would take her demand in stride. He prided himself on his ability to deliver on the most impossible of tasks. If anyone could find her a dress in twenty minutes, he could.

He answered her call with no preamble. "Did it work? Can you lie again?"

"No. And I need your help, fast. I need a dress."

"A dress? What happened to *screw the patriarchy* and all that?"

"Yes, still that, but there's a difference between being comfortable and confident and looking like you fell into a fountain."

"You fell in a fountain?"

"Yes. I also broke up with Caleb. Long story for later. Now can you help me, please? I have to meet Joanna at the office to go to lunch, and I don't have time to go home and change first. I need you to find me something to wear."

"Uh, need I remind you that I'm *an* assistant, not *your* assistant?"

"Yes, and you're also my best friend, extremely good at your job, and you never let me down. Please?"

"That's more like it," he teased. "Of course I'll help. What do you need?"

"Thank you," she said, realizing she should have opened with flattery. "Something low-maintenance but classy. Maybe black because my bra is still wet, and it won't show through."

"Your bra is wet?"

"*Yes*. Fountain, remember?"

"What the hell is going on out there, Lucy? I thought you went to the bar."

"I *did*. I'll explain it all when you meet me in my office with something to wear to lunch."

"This better be a good story," he muttered. He sounded like he was displeased, but she knew he welcomed the challenge of finding a specific piece of clothing under pressure as if it were a game show. "So, you want something flashy, lots of leg, complicated straps, and at least four inches of cleavage. That right?"

"Only if you plan on wearing it for me." Her rideshare pulled to the curb, and she hoped the driver didn't notice just how soggy she was.

"Kidding. Budget?" Oliver asked.

"Use your judgment; this is an emergency."

"You got it, boss. See you soon."

Lucy kept her eye on the clock on her ride back to the office; it would be a whirlwind wardrobe change when she got there. As she sat in the back seat, she sent an email to the leasing office of her new condo informing them the lease would be broken and to please direct any costs incurred to Caleb Allman, Cc: Caleb Allman. She then texted Nina.

Caleb and I broke up.

She didn't expect a response given that Nina was surely starting an IV or filling a chart or perfectly positioning someone's pillow and rarely checked her phone during the day, but telling her made it feel even more official.

She was single.

And she was halfway dry by the time she made it to her

building. She grimaced at the wet butt print she left on her driver's back seat and decided it was worth a custom tip. Inside, she scurried past reception, head down, and made it to her office unscathed.

Oliver waited inside, not a hair out of place, like he'd been there with a garment bag all along.

"You are a wizard," she said with a smile, breathing a sigh of relief.

He looked her up and down and waved an open hand. "If I were, I'd wave a wand and undo whatever all this is. Tell me what happened again?"

She shut her door and kicked off her soggy shoes. She kept emergency flats in her file cabinet for days she just couldn't handle heels for another second. Who knew they'd also come in handy for freak fountain accidents.

"I went to talk to the bartender," she said as she crossed the commercial carpet that was more just a layer of stiff fuzz. She rattled open her bottom drawer and pulled out black slides with a hint of a block heel. "He made me another drink; I drank it and tried to undo my wish." She sat at her desk and opened her makeup stash drawer. She had a plan. She'd spent the morning with natural hair, but stringy, chlorinated hair wasn't going to fly. Not for lunch with a celebrity. A sleek topknot with a bold lip would do.

"And how did that lead to you falling in a fountain?" Oliver gave her a curious look as he unzipped the garment bag.

A black cap sleeve with a flared skirt. Perfect.

Lucy grabbed her brush from her drawer and attacked the damp tangles, whipping them up into a pony she then spun into a bun and stabbed with pins.

"When the drink and the wish didn't work," she said,

talking around the pins sticking from her mouth, "the bartender suggested I try true love's kiss to fix my problem."

Oliver circled behind her desk and hung the dress from her bookshelf. "Interesting. But again, how does the fountain come into play?"

Lucy found her hand mirror and tube of flaming-red lip color and set to work. "Because"—she spoke and painted at the same time—"*true love's kiss* made me think of Caleb and how our relationship might be a lie, that maybe we aren't that great together and I'm only telling myself we are. I went to see him, and thanks to all the honesty, we broke up." She rubbed her lips together and snapped the tube's cap back on.

Oliver couldn't hide his half smile. "I've always said you were settling for him and telling yourself he was the one."

"Thanks. I know that now," she said, smiling wryly.

He held up his hands. "I'm just saying."

She stood and shooed him toward the door, needing to get changed. "Yes, you've shared your piece, and I thank you. Now get out."

"You haven't told me about the fountain!"

She opened the door and pushed him out, knowing it was only a matter of seconds before Joanna came to collect her to leave for lunch. She looked side to side to make sure no one would hear and quietly muttered, "A pigeon attacked me, and I fell in the fountain outside Caleb's building."

Her closing door cut off the sound of his laugh.

Once alone, she peeled off her damp dress and reached for the new one, glimpsing the price tag as she pulled it off and silently thanking Oliver for not breaking the bank. The circle skirt fluttered around her hips with a vintage flair, and the bodice completely shielded her bra. She considered hiring Oliver as a personal shopper. By the time she stepped into her dry shoes, Joanna knocked on her door.

Lucy took a deep breath, preparing for the most important part of her day and doing her best to ignore the fact that she'd been injured, harassed, mutually dumped, and nearly drowned all before noon on a day she wished would be perfect.

Not to mention, there was a non-zero chance her boss was about to tell her she didn't have a job anymore either.

"Lucy, a quick word," Joanna greeted as she stepped inside her office. She eyed Lucy's new outfit with an efficient glance but didn't ask questions. "Cute dress. Before we go, I just wanted to assure you that everything is under control."

Lucy's heart leapt with relief. "You mean I'm not—?"

"No, you're not. I spoke to Jonathan and reminded him he can't run this place like his own personal club." She scoffed and rolled her eyes with an annoyance rooted in sibling rivalry, Lucy was sure. Her face then shifted into something much more serious. "We are going to have to address what you mentioned about his treatment of you, however. That is a very serious allegation."

Warmth spread over her cheeks in dread of the inevitable. "I know."

Joanna's eyes swept her office: her computer, her succulents, her makeup pouch, the damp dress hanging from her bookshelf. Her gaze lingered on the dress before she turned it back on Lucy. "It seems like you've had a bit of a difficult morning. Are you sure you're up for lunch?"

"Of course!"

Joanna smiled, but it was reserved. "I expected no less from you. Though I have to say, your impressive ability to perform under distress should not justify the distress. Too much expectation is put on women to adapt, when it is in fact the obstacles they face that need changing."

Lucy silently agreed.

Joanna leaned in with a conspiratorial glint in her eye. "What I'm saying is, just because you *can* put up with it doesn't mean you should have to. Now"—she took a sharp breath—"I hate to ask you to do this, but I know you are more than capable of compartmentalizing to make it through this very important lunch with Lily. We will see to this other issue when we return. Ready?"

Lucy had woken up ready that morning, and despite her day so far, she still was.

"Yes."

Joanna drove a silver Mercedes that made Lucy feel like Meryl Streep in *The Devil Wears Prada*. Except she sat in the passenger seat while Joanna drove, not in the back like the only person whose opinion mattered when it came to couture fashion.

The Palm was a stone's throw from Rodeo Drive in the heart of Beverly Hills. They passed glossy storefronts, cruising Ferraris, and manicured palms. Joanna kept the music low, tuned to some Zen meditation station. The whole car was rather Zen, closed off from street noise by triple-sealed luxury doors and the smoothest suspension that made it feel like they were flying in space. Lucy had been in Joanna's car once before, on a similar lunch date when they wooed one of the reigning queens of the pop charts. Lucy had just been along for the ride that time, a pupil under Joanna's wing to learn how it was done.

Joanna was discreet in her mentoring, never one to explicitly call out *pay attention to this, it's important*. But Lucy was keen enough to know when Joanna was demonstrating for her benefit.

She was also keen enough to know that Joanna reserved Lily Chu for her because she wanted to give her the opportunity. Everyone knew Lily was on the verge of superstardom, and the likes of such promise would normally go to a senior publicist at J&J, or even to Joanna herself. But Joanna had kept Lily behind a gate that only she and Lucy had the key to.

Her faith was both inspiring and intimidating.

Joanna slowed to a stop outside the restaurant and prepared to let the valet take over. She turned to Lucy and lowered her sunglasses. "Lucy, I don't have to express to you how significant this opportunity is. There's a reason you are here instead of anyone else."

Her chest warmed even as that inspiring intimidation lodged in her throat like a rock. For a second, she wavered on telling Joanna the truth—that she couldn't lie and it was bound to make lunch with Lily difficult. But she saw the faith in her eyes. The belief that she picked the right person, and Lucy had better not let her down.

"There's nowhere else I'd rather be, Joanna," she said, and found her own words reassuring.

She'd been preparing for this moment all month, since they first got word Lily was looking for a publicist. And the moment had finally arrived. The fact that she admitted there was nowhere else she wanted to be—and it had to be true—instilled confidence she was going to make it through lunch unscathed.

And then she got out of the car and saw Chase McMillan approaching the restaurant with Shawn Stevens. They were impossible to miss; Shawn was nearly seven feet tall and trailed closely by a man who could only be his agent, who was wearing a tee shirt under a suit jacket with his phone pressed to his ear.

Lucy caught Chase's eye and gave him the meanest glare she could.

He glared back, and she wondered if Joanna would look the other way if she went over and slapped him.

Vicious thoughts of sabotage danced in her head: poison his salad, trip Shawn Stevens and ruin his season, stand on a table and announce that Chase McMillan was a backstabbing suck-up who cared about no one but himself.

They had been friendly once, long ago. But then it became clear they were both very good at their jobs and they wanted the same thing. More than once, Chase won out on opportunities simply because he spoke up first or louder or more aggressively—behaviors that would have labeled Lucy as *shrewd* or *bossy*. He'd taken things from her without even trying, and she'd had to work twice as hard just to keep up. The sting of the inequality had faded with repetition, and she rarely complained to anyone but Oliver. Mostly, she was just tired from it all.

But that didn't mean seeing him try to take another opportunity from her didn't strike a match inside her that could grow into a raging wildfire if she let it.

She wanted to push him from her mind like she pushed Caleb in the fountain and focus on *her* lunch date, but to her horror, Chase waved at them.

"Joanna, Lucy!" He sounded like a long-lost friend thrilled to be seeing them again. The agent stepped aside, still on his phone, while Shawn stayed with Chase.

Of course they couldn't ignore him. Not only would it be rude, it would be bad for business.

Joanna took her ticket from the valet and approached them with a winning smile. "Chase, I didn't know we'd be running into each other here."

She was the supreme master of chaos control.

"Yes, it's quite a coincidence," Chase said, lying straight through his teeth. "This is Shawn Stevens of the L.A. Lakers." He gestured to the tree of a man beside him who needed no introduction. Lucy had to crane her neck to look in his eyes.

"Shawn, this is Joanna Jenkins, our VP. And this is Lucy, one of my fellow publicists." He gave her a smile laced with arsenic, and she shot one right back.

"Nice to meet you, Shawn. I'm a fan," Lucy recited.

Because of her job, she dabbled in what she and Oliver referred to as the sampler platter of sports and entertainment. She knew enough about each topic area to hold a conversation, recognize faces, know names, remember critical stats and figures. She was excellent at trivia night. She'd seen Shawn live on the court twice and on TV plenty of times. She knew he had an obscenely large rookie contract and a deal with Nike and that he averaged twenty points per game.

And he wasn't even her client.

"Hi, Lucy. Joanna," he said in a voice deep enough for someone with three-foot-long lungs. "Are we all having lunch together?"

"No!" Lucy and Chase blurted at the same time.

Good god, how awkward would that be?

They played it off with laughs, and Joanna cleared up the confusion. "No. Lucy and I are here to meet with another client, but it's very nice to meet you. You're in excellent hands with Chase."

Lucy took note of Joanna's tactic. Lily wasn't a client *yet*, but if Shawn saw them dining with one of Hollywood's It Girls, he'd know they meant business at J&J, and he'd want a piece of the pie.

As if on cue, a sleek car pulled up, and Lily Chu climbed out of the back seat looking like a star. Her black hair tumbled to her waist, setting off her white jumpsuit. Her heels were flaming red and her sunglasses gold. Her agent climbed out from the other side of the car, the fourth lunch guest and one of Joanna's personal friends—which had nothing to do with Lucy's chances of landing Lily as a client, Joanna assured her; you just had to work connections where you had them.

Lucy pivoted to greet them, making a point to overstep and mash her heel straight into Chase's toe. She saw him wince as she turned, which made her smile all the more genuine for welcoming Lily.

She let Joanna take the lead given the personal acquaintance, but soon she was shaking Lily's hand and entering the restaurant. They were seated three tables away from the booth Chase and Shawn took. The Palm emanated classy steakhouse: leather chairs, low light, an endless wine rack. A campy mural of Hollywood landmarks splashed across one wall and a glowing bar filled another.

They made small talk. Lily talked about moving to L.A. and how different it was from Northern California. She hinted at details about her new movie that would send anyone listening running to *Variety* with a spoiler scoop. She was young and a little green, but Lucy could tell that, with the right help, she'd radiate *star* with the wattage of a supernova. Not only that, she was charming and genuine and everything Lucy hoped she'd be. She wanted to be her friend as much as she wanted to be her publicist.

"I just feel like I have so much to learn," Lily said, her smokey voice incongruent with her fresh features and petite frame. She sounded like an old jazz singer and looked like she could easily play a convincing teenager despite being twenty-one. She twisted her wineglass's stem, showing off her ruby red nails. "That's why I'm surrounding myself with successful women in the industry. Bestow your collective wisdom, please." She waved her hands at herself like she was welcoming a tide and laughed.

How refreshing, Lucy thought. A young actor willing to learn. Most celebutantes just wanted ten million Instagram followers and the cover of *Vanity Fair*. Lucy could get both of those things for Lily, but she sensed an integrity she rarely saw in young stars coming up in Hollywood. And she wanted to nuture it.

"What's, like, the *biggest* thing you wish you knew when you were my age?" Lily asked, revealing her youth maybe more than she intended to. She directed the question at Joanna since she clearly had more years of wisdom to share, and Lucy tuned out, already having collected Joanna's pearls.

She eyed Chase's booth, where it looked like he and Shawn were already best friends, and felt a surge of rage. She realized she was so worried about having to lie that she was hardly participating in the conversation. And there was Chase, laughing it up with the Lakers' star rookie.

He was *not* going to take her promotion from her. She was *not* going to blow this lunch pitch for fear of opening her mouth.

She felt honesty surging up her throat, and before she could try to stop them, words came flying out. "Listen, Lily. This town is tough. There's someone waiting to take your place if you let up for even one second. Whatever you want to get out of your career, you have to want it with everything you've got, and you have to fight for it. And you need the right people on your team. You need people who share your vision and ethic, people who understand your value and will fight for you, because success doesn't just happen. You make it happen."

Lily blinked at her, shocked, and Lucy didn't even realize she'd cut off Joanna until she saw her mouth hanging open mid-sentence.

"Sorry," Lucy muttered, her face burning up. "That's . . . what I wish I knew when I was younger."

Their waiter, bless him, chose that moment to come and take their orders.

Joanna and Lily's agent, Francine, went with salads. And Lucy knew there was no reason to even pretend she would order anything other than the burger layered with three kinds of cheese.

What she didn't expect was Lily's gaze to follow her every move when she handed the waiter her menu, for Lily not to even glance at her own menu, and for her to smile at the waiter and say, "Same," when it came time for her to order.

Lily then turned her attention to Lucy, even rotating in her chair and propping her chin on her hand. "So, Lucy, who else is on your client list?"

Lucy tried to wipe the shock off her face. Never did she think a cheeseburger would be the way to a Hollywood starlet's heart, but she wasn't going to question it with Lily looking at her like she'd whipped Wonder Woman's lasso.

"Well, I work primarily in our stage and screen division, but I do represent a few authors and musicians."

"Cool," Lily gushed. "And what's your publicity strategy for them? Does it differ by industry?"

Lucy felt herself slide into the easy comfort of talking about work. For all intents and purposes, Lily was interviewing her, and she was nailing it. Words flowed effortlessly, and she had no need to lie about anything. She slipped eyes at Joanna a few times to make sure she wasn't angry about being cut off, and all she read on her face was pride. They casually worked their way through the strategy pitch, and it didn't feel like pitching at all. It was a comfortable conversation over lunch that happened to involve someone who'd soon be a multimillion-dollar movie star.

Lucy was halfway through the first cheeseburger she'd had in three years when Joanna excused herself to take a phone call. She took the opportunity to glance at Chase and Shawn.

She didn't even care that they were still chatting like old chums because she was absolutely killing her date with Lily.

May the best publicist win.

Her swelling optimism took a hit when Joanna came back to the table looking bilious. "Lucy, can I have a quick word, please?"

To see Joanna slip—at all—meant something serious had happened. Lucy could only imagine it was an A-list scandal of epic proportions. Whatever the drama, she was not about to make a scene in the fishbowl of industry power lunches. *Someone* was watching, she just knew it. She politely dabbed her lips with her napkin and excused herself.

Joanna walked her out of earshot, and Lucy couldn't help feeling Chase's eyes on their conversation. "Something has come up. A bit of an emergency. I have to head back to the office right now. I'm sorry to walk out, but I trust you to close this."

Lucy knew Joanna was being vague on purpose. If she

wanted to give her more details, she would have. "Sure, Joanna. I'll take care of it."

Joanna nodded before she marched back to the table, smile on her face, and apologized to Lily and Francine for having to leave. She promised them they were in good hands with Lucy and all but ran out the door like her skirt was on fire.

Lucy feared the worst, but she knew she had to wrap up lunch. She felt Chase probing her for answers, and she gave him the tiniest shrug before returning to her seat. There, she casually checked her phone for a heads-up from Oliver—he was her inside source on any pressing Joanna client news—but she saw nothing.

Lunch resumed with apologies from Lucy. She tactfully got them back on track, and they finished their food as they discussed plans for Lily's future. By the end of the meal, Lucy realized she hadn't needed to lie once. Either she was getting better at avoiding mistruths or Lily was the most genuine celebrity she'd ever met.

And then Lily said the words Lucy wanted to hear most.

"Lucy, I would love to work with you as my publicist."

The smile lifting Lucy's face was too big to contain. "That's the best news I've heard all day," she told Lily.

They hugged out on the sidewalk and exchanged phone numbers.

Lily disappeared into the back seat of her fancy car and Lucy allowed herself to pirouette in glee. Chase chose the perfect moment to exit the restaurant and see her dancing like a fool.

She quickly put both feet on the ground and hurried down the sidewalk, still smiling to herself. Her biggest goal for the day had a nice big check mark next to it. She couldn't wait to tell Oliver and Nina—even her mom—so they could all share in her excitement.

She pulled out her phone to start the flurry of texts when she heard a familiar voice.

"Birthday Girl? Is that you?"

She turned and felt her smile grow even bigger. "Hot Bartender. What are you doing here?"

Adam approached along the sidewalk, slim backpack swinging from his forearm and apple in his hand. She'd only ever seen him from the waist up standing behind a bar. He was midday casual in jeans and black Chucks.

He stopped in front of her and smiled. He looked happy to see her, and she had to admit, she felt the same. "I needed some fresh fruit because someone threw all of mine at me." He pointed behind himself at the nearby grocery store and bit into his apple with a loud crunch.

"You come all the way to Beverly Hills for fruit?"

He looked over his shoulder at the store's green awning like he just realized where he was. "Not usually, no. Something drew me here today though."

They watched each other with matching smiles playing at their lips.

"I see you've had a wardrobe change. How's your important afternoon going?"

She glanced down at her outfit and realized he had been the only one not to ask her if something was wrong when he saw her in a sundress with no makeup. "My afternoon is actually going well for the moment, all things considered."

"That's good to hear. You seemed a little stressed when you swung by the bar. Any luck on the lying front?"

"Afraid not." She frowned as he took another bite of his

apple. She noted how white his teeth were against the red skin. The way he licked his lips and how his throat moved when he swallowed. "Remember that question you asked me earlier?" she blurted without even thinking. His brows lifted. "Well, if you ask me again, you'll get a different answer."

He finished chewing a juicy bite that required him to press his wrist to his mouth. "The one about what you're doing tonight? I hope you didn't have to cancel your birthday party because of a lie you couldn't tell."

"No, the party's still on. And that's not the question I'm talking about."

He took another bite, drawing out the moment, and she knew he was doing it on purpose. He knew exactly which question she was talking about. "Ah, I see," he said, nodding. "The boyfriend is no more. Is this the same guy who left you sipping a martini alone last night?"

"The exact same. Your true-love's-kiss theory inspired me, and turns out, that was just a gateway to the end of our relationship."

"Yikes. I'm sorry."

"It's fine. It needed to happen. And the honesty actually helped."

He took another bite of his endless apple and slowly nodded like she said something profound.

"What."

He shrugged. "Maybe your problem is actually a solution."

She narrowed her gaze. "What does that mean?"

"You've spent all morning trying to fix something that seems to be making your life better. Maybe this wish going wrong is not a curse but a gift." He held her eyes for emphasis as he crunched the final bite of his apple.

She blinked in startled clarity.

A gift?

She didn't have time to get another thought in before her phone exploded with notifications. It chirped and rang and buzzed all at once with every form of alert she had: email, text, voicemail. Even an Instagram DM.

"Looks like someone wants your attention," Adam said.

"Um . . . sorry," she muttered, distracted, as she tried to triage the flood.

At the top of her email inbox was a message from HR that sent her heart to her toes and her lunch almost up her throat. She quickly scanned the message preview and noted that it was sent to the whole company.

> *Dear All, Allegations of misconduct have been brought to our attention, and we aim to take prompt action . . .*

And then below that, an email from Annie Ferguson, Jonathan's assistant, also sent to the whole company.

> *In my ten months with J&J I have experienced mistreatment at the hands of Jonathan Jenkins . . .*

And then below that, another email from Annie, sent only to her.

> *Hi Lucy, I thought about what we talked about and wanted to give you a heads-up . . .*

In the ten seconds she spent reading the message previews, Oliver sent her not one, but five text messages.

Holy shit. Check your email.

OMG.

Annie is burning this place down.

Come back to the office RIGHT NOW!

911 911 911

Panicked thoughts rushed in Lucy's head, crashing together and making her dizzy. *What has Annie done? Did she throw me under the bus too? Was this what Joanna got a call about at lunch? What is going to happen?*

She didn't have any answers, and the only thing that came out of her mouth was "Oh fuck."

Adam quietly laughed. She'd forgotten he was standing right in front of her. "You all right?"

"No. No, I have to go. *Shit.*"

She spun around like she'd parked her car somewhere close, then remembered she came with Joanna and was on her own for getting back to the office.

"*Oh no oh no oh no.* I have to get back to my office *now*, and I don't have a car." Panic spewed from her mouth. What had she done? She tried to remind herself she didn't have the full picture because she hadn't read the whole emails, but she knew. She'd set something serious in motion when she talked to Annie in the bathroom. And then she had gone and confessed to Joanna. Something she'd kept quiet for years was quickly becoming very loud.

"Do you need a ride?" Adam asked. He pointed over his

shoulder with a thumb. "I'm parked right here, and I don't mind at all."

"Yes!" she screamed at him without a moment's hesitation.

A woman loaded down with reusable grocery bags jumped sideways as she passed on the sidewalk.

Adam wasn't fazed by the screaming or the shopper looking at them like they were insane. "Okay, come on." He waved her toward the parking garage.

She hurried after him, nearly running to keep up with his long strides. They'd hardly made it into the shade of the parking garage when he slowed at the motorcycle parking section.

Lucy almost ran into his back when he stopped at a shiny black-and-chrome bike that looked like death on wheels.

"Are you kidding me?"

She didn't know who she was asking: herself, Adam, the universe. Maybe everyone. She had never been on a motorcycle in her life and counted the idea as one of her top fears. And there she was, staring at one as the solution to her current problem.

The cruel twist made her wonder if she was in fact being punished.

"Look, Birthday Girl, it's either me or you wait for an Uber and sit in traffic. And based on how you just looked at your phone like the world is about to end, I'm guessing you need to get back to work a-sap."

She really didn't have time to argue, though her whole body was already shaking at the mere thought of riding the thing.

Adam held out his backpack. "You're going to have to wear this if you're riding in back." Then he handed her a helmet.

She nervously nodded and took both. "Okay."

"Okay. Now, where are we going?" He threw a leg over the

bike, kicked something with his foot, and started walking it backward out of the parking spot.

Lucy was 80 percent sure she was about to die.

"Birthday Girl? I'm not a mind reader."

She blinked hard and shook her head, wondering if she was about to wake up and it would all go away.

Adam was still on his bike, looking hot as all holy hell, and she was still standing in a cool parking garage, wondering when her life had taken such a dramatic turn.

"Right, sorry. It's just a few blocks from your bar, actually. The Waterfield building."

"Got it. Let's go!"

He kicked the throttle or the engine or the motor or *whatever* sent the bike roaring like a dragon in the underground concrete cage.

"Where's your helmet?" Lucy shouted over the noise.

"In your hands! Get on!"

"But . . . but isn't it illegal to ride without one?"

He threw his eyes at the ceiling and half laughed, half grumbled. "Woman, you're kind of ruining my chivalrous rescue here. Can you please just get on the bike?"

Lucy hesitated, weighing the pros and cons of their plan.

On the one hand, she'd seen guys riding motorcycles in tee shirts and Chucks all over Southern California, usually with tatted-up arms that made her belly flip in a pleasant and unexpected way. They all had helmets though. And she was *sure* it was illegal to ride anything with a motor without a safety helmet. What the fine was for breaking the law, she didn't know, but chancing death was more of an issue than risking a pesky ticket.

On the other hand, Adam looked like he was made to ride

a motorcycle and knew exactly what he was doing. The way his big hands gripped the handlebars; how his shoulders strained against his tee shirt; how his brown hair was going to get all messed up in the wind . . .

Good *lord*, why was she hesitating? She had a chance to press her body up against *that* and go for a heart-pounding, we-might-die-together ride and she wasn't jumping on it?

Perhaps the day's most primitive rush of honesty kicked her like a horse, right in the vagina, and she came to her senses.

She unpinned her topknot to shove on the helmet and slipped the backpack over her shoulders. She lifted a leg, thankful Oliver nabbed her something with a loose skirt, and sat behind him.

He reached back and grabbed her ankle, pulling her foot onto a little rest. His hand on her bare skin felt like a lightning strike. "Put your feet here." He reached back for her arms and pulled them around his waist. "Arms here."

She scooted close and held tight, feeling her heart pound. She wondered if Adam could feel it against his back.

"Please don't kill us!" she shouted.

She felt him laugh more than she heard it. The muscles in his abdomen bounced against her arms. "I'll do my best."

She squeezed her eyes shut as they pulled out of the garage. She only chanced opening them when they slowed at a stoplight a few blocks down. She took stock of her body and found that she was in fact not dead, but very, very much alive.

The light turned green, and they shot off like a jet, zipping between cars. She leaned left and right with Adam, responding to his muscles tensing and shifting. The rumble of the bike vibrated up through her legs straight into the core of her like a high-voltage cable. All the while, she clung to his back like a limpet, feeling his breath expand his chest.

Forget sex in front of an office window. She'd take a motor-cycle ride with a hot bartender who'd come to her rescue any day.

They made it to her office far too quickly. When Adam stopped at the curb, she'd nearly forgotten the impending doom awaiting her. Her legs shook for more than one reason when she climbed off the bike. In a hurry to get inside, she yanked off the helmet, her hair a lost cause, and whirled around to hand it to him. She caught a flash of his wind-rumpled hair and devastating smile in the second before she misjudged the curb and her rubber legs buckled.

"Whoa!" Adam twisted sideways, still sitting on his bike, and threw out his arms. Lucy fell into them as if she had been shoved. And as if an invisible force were putting a point on the scene, she landed with her lips against his.

They both sharply inhaled, stunned.

Because of the odd angle and the fact that Adam's mouth felt like the breath of air she could never catch, Lucy stayed there, pressed up against him long enough for the accident to turn to intention.

With the thrill of the bike still coursing through her veins, the heat of his lips, and the feel of his big hands on her arms, she was suddenly quite sure she had wanted to kiss him ever since she met him, she just hadn't realized it. She could taste the apple on his lips and smell something light and fresh on his skin. The revelatory moment felt profoundly perfect.

He was the one to pull back because gravity had Lucy pinned on top of him with no leverage. He gently pried her off and held her in place while she got her footing back. They stared at each other in a state of shyness and shock, smiles teasing their bitten lips.

"Sounds like you need to go," he said, and nodded at her tote.

Her phone screamed for attention inside. It probably hadn't stopped since they left the parking garage—she just hadn't been able to hear it.

The urgency of her return to work crashed into their moment like a wrecking ball, and she tore herself away.

"Thanks for the ride," she said, and tossed his helmet at him. She removed the backpack and handed it over.

He resumed the devastating smile, cheeks flushed this time, and gave her a wave. "Good luck, Birthday Girl!"

CHAPTER

10

When she arrived at her building, Lucy managed to text Oliver that she was on her way up, all the while running across the lobby reading emails and recovering from the scene on the sidewalk.

She smiled at the thought of Adam's kiss as she opened the first email.

Dear All,

Allegations of misconduct have been brought to our attention, and we aim to take prompt action. J&J Public strives to foster a safe and inclusive work environment, and any threat to that standard will be investigated in a timely and thorough manner. We take all allegations seriously and have determined after careful consideration that pursuing greater understanding of these claims is necessary.

Please be prepared to meet with an HR member this afternoon if it is requested of you.

—Amanda C. Wiles

  Director of Human Resources, J&J Public

Her smile was gone. Reading *allegations of misconduct* again made her knees weak, and not in the way kissing Adam had. Even without the other emails, she knew what the allegations were, who made them, and who they were directed at.

She skipped to the email Annie sent to just her before reading the one she knew was the worst of the bunch.

> Hi Lucy,
> I thought about what we talked about and wanted to give you a heads-up. I'm going to expose Jonathan. You're right, I don't have to take this from him, and I've seen enough in this industry to know filing complaints with HR won't be enough. I have to go public. Fuck that guy, right? I don't want to harm you in any way, but I can't promise you won't get pulled into this. I just hope that you'll stand with me when the time comes.
> —Annie

A mix of emotion tore at her while she read Annie's personal email: pride for Annie for taking a stand; worry over what her role in it would be, by choice or necessity; but most of all, sheer terror over what she meant by *I have to go public.*

How public? Lucy wondered as she dove into the lobby elevator. She chewed her lip to a pulp while she read the final email.

> In my ten months with J&J I have experienced mistreatment at the hands of Jonathan Jenkins. I have been solicited sexually, touched inappropriately, and made to feel unsafe both inside his office and at various locations related to my

*job's duties, including Mr. Jenkins's personal hotel rooms
and home. I have done everything in my power to maintain
professional boundaries despite his advances.*

*I want to be clear that these claims are not retaliation for a
consensual relationship that has ended. I have never
engaged in willful sexual acts with Mr. Jenkins. My only
goal is to expose his misconduct so that it may be
addressed and prevented from continuing. I know from
personal conversation that at least one other woman within
the company has experienced similar mistreatment, and I
hope that she will come forward as well.*

*I have seen this scenario play out time and again without
consequence for those responsible for inappropriate
behavior, and I am hoping my choice to share my
experience in this manner will inspire change.*

—Annie Ferguson

She arrived at J&J. Oliver waited by the elevator door, tap-
ping his phone and chewing his lip. "Oh my god, where have
you been?! And what happened to your hair?"

"What *hasn't* happened to my hair today?" she mumbled as
she swept past him. She wanted to get to her office as quickly
as possible to take cover. She felt like she had *other woman
within the company* tattooed on her forehead, maybe a neon
sign flashing on her back. Everyone had seen her dramatic exit
from Jonathan's office that morning. Not to mention, she'd
told Joanna what happened in there.

Lucy suddenly realized why Joanna hadn't told her at lunch
what was going on. She must have found out what Annie was
going to do—maybe Annie threatened Jonathan, and he told

his sister while they were out—and if Joanna had dropped that bomb at the Palm, it would have ruined lunch.

"Did you read them?" Oliver demanded as they moved down the hall. Mikayla sat at the reception desk, phone glued to her ear and typing. She looked out of breath sitting still. And like she wanted to cry.

"Yes."

Oliver sucked air through his teeth, and Lucy's stomach flipped, knowing they were thinking the same thing.

They arrived at her office. Tension hung over the cubicles like an electrical storm. More than one person stared at her. Both of the Js had their office doors shut.

"Do you have a second?" she asked.

"Yeah. Joanna's locked in her office; I have no idea what's going on."

"Come in," she said, and pushed him inside. She shut the door behind them and pulled up Annie's personal email on her phone. She handed it to Oliver without a word and started chewing her thumb.

"What is this . . . ?" His eyes scanned, and his face paled. "Oh. Shit."

"Yeah." She started pacing like a mouse in a very small cage. The vision of her bigger office and promotion was shrinking away by the second. "Remember this morning when I told you Jonathan propositioned me, and I ran to the bathroom? Well, I ran into Annie in there, and . . ." She was afraid to admit her involvement in case it somehow implicated her in the collapse of her own company, but she didn't have a choice seeing that the truth kept spilling out. "I told her about Jonathan, and she implied he'd mistreated her too—which we now know is true—and I told her she didn't have to stand for it." She exhaled a heavy breath and looked to Oliver for advice.

His already magnified eyes grew larger behind his glasses. He pointed at her phone balanced in his hand, mouth open in shock. "You told her to—?"

"No! Of course not! I just told her to stand up for herself. I didn't think she was going to email the entire company about it!"

Oliver grimaced.

"And it gets worse. That second meeting with Jonathan this morning? He tried to fire me with an obscenely large *severance package* that was nothing but hush money for being harassed. I called him out and then went to Joanna about it. So, secret's out that I'm the other woman in Annie's email."

Oliver stared at her, jaw slack. "What? Why didn't you tell me any of this?"

"Well, I've been a little busy. Joanna left lunch early to deal with *this*"—she pointed at her phone still in his hand—"and I had to get a ride back. Luckily, Adam was there, and he—"

"Adam?"

"Yes. The bartender. We ran into each other, and he gave me a ride. Then I kind of tripped, and he caught me and we kissed, and—"

He stumbled back and waved his hands in the shape of a big, swooping rainbow. "Wait. He caught you? With his lips?"

"Yes, and I don't have time to properly freak out about it because *Annie* decided to email the whole company our *very* private business, and I feel like it's all my fault for telling her to stand up for herself!" Her breath quickened, and she felt her chest tightening. She threw her hands over her face.

Oliver's cool fingers gently gripped her wrist. "Hey, Luce. We're definitely going to circle back to the bartender catching you with his lips because that sounds like the universe saying *yes*, but regarding the matter at hand, this is not your fault. You can't control anyone else's behavior, and as far as I'm concerned, Jonathan deserved this. After the way he treated you, and apparently Annie, he should be exposed."

"Yes, but . . ."

She did her best to breathe through all the doubt and fear trying to drown her. She knew the beats, the plotline, and the always disappointing ending to this story. She and Annie would be asked *why now?*; why come forward only now if it had been going on for months and years? They'd have to relive humiliating details, risk losing their jobs, and possibly be exiled from the industry, all to be labeled as victims. Their identities would be centered on Jonathan forevermore because of what he did to them, and all he'd get was a slap on the wrist. He got to hurt them multiple times: the abuse and the public consequences. The injustice was sickening.

But something had awoken in her, and she could not lie about it. The fury she had kept quiet for years was suddenly screaming. She heard it as loudly as she had in the bathroom with Annie that morning, moments after Jonathan put her in the position of choosing between her career and her integrity.

Why the hell couldn't she have both?

Things may have been happening much more quickly than she expected them to, but Annie and Oliver were right: the time for silence was over.

She stood up straight and looked Oliver right in the eye. "Fuck that guy."

Oliver grinned like he was ready to ride into battle with her.

"Now we're talking. Whatever you want to do, I'm here for it."
He handed her phone back just as a new email pinged.

> Lucy,
> We'd like to discuss what you may know about the
> allegations that have been made. We're working with an
> external third-party mediation service, and they are on-site
> this afternoon. Please come to my office in ten minutes.
> Thanks.
> —Amanda C. Wiles
>   Director of Human Resources, J&J Public

Lucy and Oliver met eyes over her phone, and she smiled.
"Perfect."

Lucy gathered herself and headed for Amanda's office. With every step she took she felt eyes on her, probing. The fact that they all knew she was the *other woman within the company* didn't seem to matter anymore. Yes, she was taking a huge risk, but she had no choice—and *not* just because she couldn't lie. It was the right thing to do, and she finally had the courage to do it.

Despite her conviction, when she turned the corner and saw the last person she wanted to share a waiting room with, she almost changed her mind.

"Hey," Chase said, with something reserved in his voice. Lucy was wary of sitting in the chair beside him, but it was either that, stand, or sit on the floor.

She was early, and it would be a few minutes, so she opted for the chair. But she sat as far to one side as she could, the rigid rectangular arm digging into her hip.

"Hello." Her greeting was lukewarm at best.

"I got an email that they want to talk to me."

"Same." Lucy wasn't surprised they wanted to talk to him given the universal knowledge that Chase jumped at every opportunity to please Jonathan, and he had probably witnessed something worth discussing with HR.

They sat in silence, staring at the wall across the hall. Lucy had never paid attention to the abstract oil painting. The blue and purple haze reminded her of the deep sea, or maybe outer space, and she wondered if it was meant to be soothing. After all, anyone who stared at the painting was on their way to meet with HR, and that was rarely a pleasant experience.

She studied the layers of color blended into one another like it was her job because the alternative was making conversation with Chase McMillan.

He quietly cleared his throat, enduring the palpable discomfort as best he could. Lucy would normally have enjoyed watching him squirm, but when the squirming was mutual, it wasn't so great. He folded his arms and crossed his ankles out in front of him. Lucy noticed a sharp scuff in his shoe's pale leather toe about the size and shape of the block heel on her flats.

"Did I do that to your shoe?"

He snorted something close to a laugh and angled his foot to see. "Yep. Nothing a cobbler can't fix though."

A real laugh burst from her mouth. She flinched at how loud it was in the quiet hall. "You have a *cobbler*?"

He squared his shoulders and tilted his chin like she'd offended him. "Of course I do."

"Why, you get your feet stomped on by angry women a lot?"

"Oh, so that *was* on purpose."

She glared at his smug face.

He glared back, but it didn't carry his usual zeal. "How was your lunch with Lily?"

"I totally killed it. She's going to sign with us. How was your lunch with Shawn?"

"Same. He got me courtside tickets for the game tonight."

"Hmm."

"Hmm."

They returned to staring at the oil painting, at an impasse. Lucy strained to hear what was going on behind the closed doors beside them, but she couldn't make out anything other than a muffled hum.

Chase opened his mouth like he was going to say something and then closed it again. He did it twice more, and Lucy couldn't stand it.

"If you're going to say something, say it."

He caught the edge of a breath and sighed. He let his arms fall and rested his hands on his thighs. "Look, you don't have to tell me anything you don't want to, but . . . I'm sorry if . . . if Jonathan did anything inappropriate to you."

She gaped at him, unable to stop herself, because while she felt vulnerable and exposed, she also couldn't believe he'd said something so . . . considerate.

"I'm not the total asshole you think I am, Lucy."

She managed to close her mouth and form words. "I don't think you're an asshole."

And that was perhaps the most stunning revelation of the day.

She balked at her own admission as Chase laughed.

"Yeah you do. And I can't deny that I fit the mold. But it's just—" He cut himself off and flexed his hands like he was struggling to find the words. "It's just that you're so . . . *good* at what you do, that I feel like I have to, I don't know, compensate."

Again, she was floored. He was either an excellent liar or her compulsive truth-telling was contagious.

He frowned at what must have been bewilderment on her face. "Don't look so shocked. You know you kick ass at your job. I feel like I can hardly compete most of the time." He mumbled the last part and ran a hand through his hair.

"Is that why you're mean to me?"

He looked affronted. "I'm not *mean* to you. I just try to find ways to get an advantage. I've never done anything malicious."

"The thing you said about my outfit this morning wasn't mean?"

"I— Okay, that was a little harsh."

"Mm-hmm. And planning your lunch date with Shawn on the same day, at the same place, at the same *time* as my lunch with Lily—a lunch literally everyone knew about, so don't you dare call it a coincidence—wasn't malicious?"

He smirked. "It kept you on your toes, didn't it? You said yourself that you killed it."

She scoffed, suddenly indignant. "So now I'm supposed to thank you? *God.* This is so typical of men: doing something they think is helpful and then expecting gratitude when the act wasn't even necessary—*or asked for*—in the first place."

He leaned back and blinked, looking a little frightened. He seemed to gather himself before speaking. "Okay, fine. I did it on purpose to mess with you. I wasn't trying to keep you on your toes; I was trying to give myself an advantage."

A spark popped inside her like a firecracker. "An *advantage*? Are you kidding me? Chase, you already have all the advantages."

He opened his mouth to argue, but she silenced him with a glare, knowing anything he said wouldn't hold water.

And then, her own words came flooding out.

"You realize I have to work twice as hard for things that are handed to you, and I get paid less for doing it—and women of color get paid even less than me. I can't behave like you can and not be punished for it. You've probably never been called bossy or had to seriously consider how you phrased something before speaking so you weren't dismissed. I bet you've never put an exclamation point or a smiley face in an email to sound friendly for fear of coming across harsh. You haven't been conditioned to apologize when you interrupt someone. No one has ever patronized you with *ladies first* as if they are relinquishing right of way because they own it. When you get mad, you can just be mad. You can raise your voice in a meeting; you can storm out of a room. If I do any of those things, I'm hysterical and over-reacting. No one second-guesses you, doubts you, asks if you're sure you know what you're talking about. They just believe anything you say. Why do you think we're sitting outside HR right now, preparing to be interrogated about Annie's *allegations* rather than watching Jonathan get dragged out of here? And these might all seem like small things, but trust me, they add up, and it's fucking exhausting."

He stared at her, silent. His mouth didn't fall open in shock, but he also didn't try to disagree. He, for once, looked like he truly heard what she had said.

Lucy exhaled a tired breath, feeling the weight of her words and worry and honesty lift off. Though she'd had those thoughts since she joined the professional workforce, she'd never voiced them. She'd never fully considered them, turned them over and saw them for what they were, and thought about the toll they took.

And there she was, opening her heart to Chase McMillan.

She expected a snide remark; something sharp-tongued that would cut her up and reinforce the notion she was *too sensitive* or *overreacting*. But instead, Chase looked at her and simply nodded.

"You're right. I don't have to deal with any of that. And it's not fair."

The Chase-shaped knot in her chest loosened, and she found herself softening toward him. "It's not fair. And I'm not asking you to go easy on me—because you *do* keep me on my toes; you kick ass at your job too—I'm just asking that you please don't go out of your way to make mine harder because you think you need an advantage."

He considered her with a steady gaze, and she wondered if a Lucy-shaped knot in his chest was loosening too. "Yeah, I can do that."

"Thank you."

They settled into silence again, but it was comfortable. She couldn't believe she was getting along with Chase McMillan and she had confessed he kept her on her toes by being good at his job. What had gotten into her?

The truth, obviously.

And she realized she'd rather have Chase around, making her better at her job—as long as he wasn't sabotaging her on purpose—than not have him at all, even if he did drive her nuts.

"You're not so bad, Chase." Her admission embarrassed her, but the words were out without her consent.

Chase smiled. "Yeah, I guess you're all right too, Lucy. Truce?"

He held out his hand, and she slipped hers into it, returning his smile and shaking.

"Truce."

And then she remembered where they were sitting, and an ugly thought struck her.

"Wait. Are you saying all this to me because you feel badly that I've been harassed?"

Color filled his face, and he rolled his lips inward, looking guilty but unsure about it. "Maybe?"

Lucy grumbled, feeling that Chase-knot harden up again. "I'm going to give you the benefit of the doubt because this is a difficult situation, but don't make me regret being honest with you. And I don't want your pity. I want things to change. And *you* have to be part of it. It can't only be women screaming and pounding our fists. We need men on the inside to enact change. To stand up for us. To make a difference. Got it?"

He looked at her, suddenly sober, and swallowed.

"People like Jonathan keep people like me out of the ring by fostering unsafe work environments, and you've admitted that you need me, so it's time for you to stand up."

She watched her words settle over him and hoped they were sinking in.

"You know, you're awfully brazen when you want to be."

She shrugged. "Maybe I'm tired of fighting by myself."

"Well, maybe it's time you had some help."

The door to their right opened and interrupted them.

Annie walked out, eyes puffy and pink as if she'd been crying, but also looking self-satisfied. Her face flushed when she saw Lucy, and Lucy tried to look reassuring, but she was suddenly hit with a wave of nerves.

"Lucy?" Amanda said from her doorway as Annie passed. "We're ready for you."

Lucy looked at Chase as if he might be coming in with her for some unknown reason, and he pointed his thumb at the door to the left. He'd been summoned by Brian, the assistant director of HR, and Lucy realized, as she probably should have earlier, that Annie's actions had put all hands on deck.

"Good luck," he said quietly, and gave her a soft smile.

Lucy took a breath and headed for Amanda's office.

Amanda's office, normally neutral and calm, had been overtaken with stacks of file folders, binders, coffee cups, and takeout containers.

The disorder set Lucy on edge.

As did the unknown man with a bushy mustache at the far end of the table.

Amanda's office was almost as big as each of the Js', since she needed room for confidential conversations that sometimes involved more than one person. A small conference table took up half the space, and in the wake of the Annie bomb, it was buried under the flotsam and jetsam of harassment allegations.

"Lucy, this is Robert Ericsson. He's with the mediation team helping us investigate these claims. He'll be joining us to take your statement today."

He nodded. "Ms. Green."

Amanda took her seat across from Lucy and adjacent to Mr. Ericsson. She was as good at chaos management as any of the publicists at J&J—maybe better, and the fact that Lucy could see worry creasing her dark complexion, bending her brow, spoke to just how bad the situation was.

Lucy had known Amanda for as long as she worked at J&J. In fact, she helped her fill out her hiring paperwork when she first started, back when Amanda worked in the lower ranks of HR. Just as Lucy had climbed the ladder, Amanda had graduated to the top of the HR chain. She reminded Lucy of her favorite high school counselor, who was there to listen and always gave solid advice. She'd always liked Amanda both professionally and personally, and she knew Amanda liked her too. And because of that fact, Lucy couldn't help noting the despair on her face, perhaps that she hadn't come to her sooner about Jonathan.

"Lucy, with your permission, we're going to record this meeting. The audio will only be used to review statements needed to build a case against Mr. Jenkins. Do you agree to be recorded?"

Build a case?

Lucy took a breath, realizing the sharp turn they'd taken into reality. Not for the first time that day, she remembered that telling the truth being the right thing to do didn't automatically make it an easy thing to do. "Yes." Her voice came out a whisper. She cleared her throat and tried to sound more confident. "Yes, I agree."

"Thank you. Mr. Ericsson is going to lead taking your statement so that we obtain an impartial record. Please provide the most accurate information that you can."

"Okay," she said, and internally laughed at the fact that she couldn't provide inaccurate information even if she tried.

Mr. Ericsson clicked on a digital recorder Lucy only just

noticed sitting on the table. He picked up a notepad and pen and flipped open a manila folder. "Thank you, Ms. Green. Now, while we will take measures to maintain confidentiality to the best of our ability, we cannot guarantee complete confidentiality. Over the course of this investigation, certain information may be revealed to the alleged harasser and potential witnesses; however, information will only be shared with those who need to know about it."

"I understand."

"Excellent. With that in mind, we have called you in today based on information we received from Annie Ferguson as well as witness statements that you were seen leaving Mr. Jenkins's office looking upset this morning. Can you tell us in your own words what happened?"

She began to sweat. She'd never been interrogated by the police, but she wondered if this was what it felt like.

It was time for the whole truth, no matter the consequences. "Jonathan invited me into his office to talk about my promotion. He suggestively asked how committed I am to advancing my career, and he squeezed my knee. I shoved him away. I left his office and ran into Annie in the bathroom right after. I told her what happened, and she implied she'd been harassed too. I told her to stand up for herself, and now here we are."

Neither of them looked surprised, though they were professionals at taking shocking news in stride. Lucy had to assume Annie told them everything about their bathroom run-in, but Annie didn't know what came after.

"And then Jonathan called me into his office later this morning and tried to fire me with what he called a severance package but was really just a thinly veiled bribe to keep quiet."

Amanda startled. "He what?"

Lucy nodded. "He said that after our discussion this morning, he felt it best that our paths diverge. Then he offered me payment that I refused to take."

Clearly, Amanda hadn't expected the story to take such a turn. She visibly reeled as Mr. Ericsson pushed forward.

"Did you report this interaction to anyone, Ms. Green?"

"I did, yes. I went to Joanna and told her what happened."

"I see. Have there been other instances with Mr. Jenkins like what you experienced today?"

"Yes." She squeezed her fists in an effort to ease her discomfort. Her face heated.

"I see." He kept repeating what must have been deemed a neutral response by the mediation service training guide. "Have you shared information about those experiences with anyone here at J&J prior to today?"

"Just my friend Oliver."

Mr. Ericsson scratched his notepad with his pen. "Oliver's last name?"

"Bradley," she said, sure that she'd just earned one of her best friends a trip to HR.

"And why haven't you come forward in formally reporting Mr. Jenkins's behavior earlier, Ms. Green?"

The million-dollar and most infuriating question, and Lucy had to answer it.

"Because I was honestly afraid of what would happen. In case you haven't noticed, people don't generally believe women when they come out against powerful men. Case in point, this meeting." She folded her arms and frowned.

Mr. Ericsson sat back in his chair. His mustache twitched.

Amanda leaned forward and pressed her hands into the table. "Lucy, we are following the necessary protocol given the allegations. That doesn't mean we don't believe Annie—or you. There is just a system in place—"

"To protect Jonathan," Lucy finished for her. "He gets all the benefits of the doubt. And yes, I know we live in a due-process world where you're innocent until proven guilty, but his behavior is the kind that evades evidence. The touching and the comments and the private meetings don't leave physical marks, so it comes down to he said, she said, and forgive me for having lost faith in the chances of being believed as a she."

Amanda sat back in her chair. Her hand slowly curled into a fist, and Lucy knew she agreed with her but wasn't in a posi-tion to say so.

Mr. Ericsson's mustache twitched again, and she wondered how accustomed he was to hostile witnesses. He'd surely had plenty of work since the MeToo movement swept Hollywood. Someone must have lost their cool on him during all of that; she couldn't have been the first. "We're just trying to gauge if the behavior spread beyond the individual who reported it, Ms. Green."

"Well, I've confirmed for you that it had."

"Indeed you have, and we thank you for that. Now, you said that you have previous experience with Mr. Jenkins behaving in a similar way. Can you please describe these experiences?"

Lucy took a long, deep breath. She worried she'd have to construct a complicated and exhausting account of it all, but the honesty curse—that maybe wasn't a curse in this case?—took over for her. "Over the years, Jonathan—Mr. Jenkins—has made me feel uncomfortable on multiple occasions. He has invaded my private space, touched me inappropriately, and made suggestive comments."

"Has he ever solicited you sexually?"

Lucy's face warmed, and she thought of all those closed-door meetings in Jonathan's office, of all the opportunities he had to pull one of the vulgar stunts she'd read so many headlines about. What he said that morning was the closest he'd ever come, and even that could be argued as ambiguous.

"Not explicitly, no."

Mr. Ericsson nodded. "Has he ever performed sexual acts in your presence?"

"No," Lucy said, and wondered what Annie had told them. She couldn't fight the guilt roiling inside her over not having spoken up earlier.

"When you say Mr. Jenkins touched you inappropriately, what does that entail?" Mr. Ericsson asked.

A rush of rage filled her like a hot balloon. She wanted to forget the details, but there she was explaining them to a stranger.

"I mean that he frequently touched my shoulder or knee during private meetings like he did today. He sometimes asked for hugs at holiday parties."

"Did you ever ask him to stop?"

Mr. Ericsson carried on like he was reading from a list—he probably was—and it felt so dehumanizing. His question stripped the context out of every encounter and left her answer sounding inadequate.

"Until today, no."

He nodded and scribbled on his notepad. "Ms. Green, do you have any evidence of these interactions with Mr. Jenkins? Perhaps text messages or emails? A photograph even?"

"Of course not. Jonathan is entitled, not stupid."

Her sharp tone appeared to pop him. He let out a deflated breath. "Look, Ms. Green. I'm just trying to do my job.

I appreciate your cooperation so far, and I understand this is not easy."

She calmly folded her hands and leveled him with her gaze. "Mr. Ericsson, I appreciate that you are just trying to do your job, but I just try to do my job every day here. I try to do my job to the best of my ability, and I've had to do that in the shadow of Jonathan Jenkins for years. I don't think you understand what it's like to come to work worried every day; dreading being called into a private meeting; feeling unsafe and unable to speak up about it. Wondering if your outfit or makeup will be deemed too suggestive. Or if today's the day he locks the door and fully crosses the line. If you can promise to do *your* job in a way that removes those factors from *my* job and the jobs of others in a way that is safe for us, then I'm happy to be forthcoming."

Her words hung heavy in the air, and she was glad it was all on record because that was quite the speech.

"Lucy, the company will not permit any form of retaliation for having made a complaint, and we ask that you immediately report anything of the sort should you experience it," Amanda chimed in.

Sure, she thought. They could handle retaliation on paper, but what could they do about Jonathan trashing her name? He had a hundred times the network reach she did.

"What's going to happen now?" she asked.

Mr. Ericsson flipped his manila folder shut. "Well, if you're finished sharing all the information you have, we will compile it with what else we've obtained and continue with our investigation."

Lucy chewed her lip, worried it was all in vain. "And then?"

Mr. Ericsson cast his eyes toward Amanda.

"Disciplinary measures are considered confidential, but we will take appropriate action pending the outcome of the investigation," Amanda said.

"That's an annoyingly vague answer," Lucy blurted. "I think you should fire him."

Mr. Ericsson quietly laughed and tried to cover it with a cough. Amanda's lips twitched at the corners, and Lucy had to imagine she thought the same thing.

"Such a decision would ultimately lie with J&J's board of directors, but you should know that in the state of California, supervisors who harass employees can be held personally liable in addition to the employer's legal responsibility for the misconduct." Amanda left the words hanging like a hint.

Lucy made a mental note to Google *how to sue your boss for harassment* when she got back to her desk. If things went the way she expected and Jonathan only got a slap on the wrist, at least she could gouge out a chunk of his retirement before it was all said and done.

"And what about me? And Annie?"

Amanda frowned like she'd tasted something bitter. "Annie has already decided to make her experience public, but as Mr. Ericsson said, we will do our best to keep what you've shared confidential to the extent possible during the investigation, though we cannot guarantee it."

Lucy couldn't help noticing that she said nothing about *her* keeping things confidential. Whether it was oversight or another hint, Lucy wasn't sure, but she felt a very bold idea take root and sprout blossoms in her head.

When she'd read *I have to go public* in Annie's email, she'd worried what it meant, but it was clear she meant public within the company.

Well. Lucy could do way better than that.

She was a rising star at the biggest publicity firm in Hollywood. She had contacts at every major entertainment news outlet, and they'd kill for an exclusive story sure to rock the industry.

She suddenly knew what she had to do.

"Are we done here?" she asked.

"If you have shared all the information you have, yes. We'll be in touch if we need anything else," Mr. Ericsson said.

"Sure," she said, and stood. She smoothed her skirt and caught Amanda's eye. "I'll be in touch too."

She felt their gazes follow her out of the room. In the hall, every door was closed. She wondered what Chase had told HR and if he'd be willing to join her coup.

But first, she needed a key player on her side.

She pulled out her phone and saw a text from Oliver.

Come to the kitchen when you're done.

Curious, she obeyed. She held her head high from one end of the office to the other despite the stares and whispers. *But does it really matter what people assume?* she wondered. To the extent that they pitied her for atrocities that never occurred, maybe. But otherwise the key takeaway was that Jonathan's behavior was unacceptable, and he needed to go.

She risked a glance at each J's door; both were still shut. She wouldn't be surprised if Jonathan had left the building.

When she rounded into the kitchen, a sunny oblong room with windows overlooking a courtyard with palms, what she found made her smile and want to cry at the same time.

"Happy birthday!" Oliver softly sang. He stood with Annie

and Mikayla behind the kitchen island where a sheet cake sat, decorated in curly script and frosting flowers. A bundle of pastel balloons was tied to a communal fruit basket, and the three of them wore little party hats.

"This is the saddest party I've ever seen," she said with a laugh, because it was true. "But thanks."

Oliver held out a fork. "Well, yes. It was supposed to be bigger, but . . ." He shrugged without needing to explain further.

Mikayla looked like she was only halfway there, with one eye on her phone, and Annie looked like she wanted to run. Lucy had to give her serious credit for even hanging around the office after her email. She had been sure she'd have to hunt her down to talk to her about her plan, but there she was at Lucy's sad little office birthday party. Her makeup showed telltale signs of having been dabbed with bathroom tissue; most of it was worn off. She cautiously met Lucy's gaze, as if she expected to be reprimanded.

"Are you okay?" Lucy asked her.

She nearly flinched in surprise. "You're not mad at me?"

"Quite the opposite, actually. I'm indebted to you for speaking up, and I have an idea I want to talk to you about. Do you have ten minutes?"

Annie gaped, causing her to stumble over her words. "I, um . . . HR told me I should take the rest of the day off, but I wanted to make sure you weren't mad at me before I left."

Oliver placed a small plate with a wobbling piece of cake on it in Lucy's hands. She jammed her fork into it and took a bite. "I told you: I'm not mad," she said around a mouthful—white cake with strawberry buttercream filling, her favorite. "We can go to my office, then you can sneak out the back door. I just need you to sign off on something."

Annie's face shifted to half-nervous, half-intrigued.

"This cake is delicious," Lucy complimented, and took another bite.

"Of course it is," Oliver said, scooping his own forkful. "Only the best at my events."

"You planned this?"

"Yes. Why do you sound surprised?"

Lucy shrugged. "It's just that women are always expected to plan office social events. It's nice to see someone else do it for once."

"Amen," Mikayla said through her own mouthful, one eye still on her phone. Annie was the only one not eating, and Lucy couldn't blame her if she'd lost her appetite over the past hour.

Chase materialized at the kitchen entrance and frowned at the scene. "Well, this is a poor turnout."

On another day, Lucy would have wanted to shove her cake plate into his face and watch him pick pink frosting from his eyebrows. But given their truce and the fact that she hoped he'd support her plan when she told him about it, dessert warfare did not tempt her.

He entered the room and helped himself to a piece of cake. She wondered when the last time was that he ate a carb and decided that the cake binge was a sign his visit with HR went much like hers.

Behind Chase's back, Oliver and Lucy had a silent conversation.

Sorry; I had to invite everyone, Oliver said with a roll of his eyes.

Lucy shrugged. *It's fine. We're cool now.*

What?! Oliver's brows shot up. His eyes narrowed. *You better explain later.*

I will, Lucy promised with a nod.

"Chase, can you come by my office in ten minutes? It'll be quick."

He checked his watch with a flip of his wrist. "Yeah, sure."

"Thank you." She dropped her empty plate on the island with a clatter. "And thank you, Oliver, for planning this event."

Oliver's eyes narrowed further with suspicion, having just witnessed the most cordial exchange between Lucy and Chase he'd seen in years.

"Annie? Are you ready?" Lucy asked.

She nervously nodded, and Lucy wasn't sure if she was nervous about their meeting or nervous about walking through the gossip lying in wait on the way to her office. There was only one route to get there, but at least they could face it together.

Lucy held out her arm because she knew if their roles were flipped, she'd want something to hold on to.

Annie looked at her, at first uncertain but then with a swell of relief. She took her arm, and they left the kitchen with their elbows linked.

"Ten minutes, Chase!" Lucy called over her shoulder.

She led Annie down the hall. When they hit the open office belly, eyes found them from every direction.

"What's your favorite kind of cake, Annie?" Lucy asked.

"Um . . ."

"It'll be less awkward if we're having a conversation while everyone is staring," she muttered. "It's a trick I tell my clients: if you're uncomfortable with people watching you, pretend you're talking to someone, even if it's nonsense."

Annie quietly laughed. "Carrot, actually. But I guess it's really just about the cream cheese frosting."

"I can't argue with that." They rounded the bend to the stretch leading to her door. "I think we should eat cake whenever we want it, not only on special occasions, don't you agree?"

Annie shot her a glance like the idea was revolutionary.

They arrived at her office, and Lucy shut the door behind them. Her damp sundress hung from her bookshelf and her makeup pouch still half spilled onto her desk from her prelunch mini makeover. She did not stop to explain either but gestured to the chair her clients used.

"Have a seat."

Annie sat while Lucy took her place behind her desk. She pulled up Annie's email to the whole company and opened a blank document. She folded her hands and looked at the nervous young woman sitting across from her.

"Annie, I have to say, when I told you to stand up for yourself earlier, I didn't expect something this extreme. But I think you're right: we need to go public. You've already set something in motion with your email to the company, and I'm wondering if you're willing to go even more public."

She blinked her big brown eyes. "What do you mean?"

Lucy stared at her and wondered what would have become of her own career if she'd spoken up when she was Annie's age. Annie had the guts to do what Lucy only dreamed of, and the reason Lucy held back was because she feared no one would support her. There would be no net if she took the leap. Losing her job and being blacklisted from the industry was her biggest fear, the biggest barrier. If only there was someone she could trust, someone she knew would have her back if she spoke up.

Sitting in that room with HR, answering all their painful questions and fearing nothing would ever change, made her realize that *she* could be that person for Annie. Not only could she come forward and corroborate Annie's claims, she had the power to amplify them to the world.

Lucy clicked her track pad to bring up her contact list. She angled her computer screen so Annie could see. "This is a list of editors at every publication in the industry. Any of them would kill for this story on Jonathan, and I think it's the only way anything has a chance of changing. With your permission, I want to write a statement and send them your email."

If Annie felt fear, it didn't last long. Her face lit with hope, and Lucy saw it.

"There will be blowback, I guarantee it," she warned. "You'll be criticized and doubted. People will be upset and they'll come after you; you've seen it all happen before. Once we do this, we can't undo it, so I want you to be sure."

Annie sat up straighter, eager. "I'm sure. As long as I'm not alone."

"You're not alone, Annie. I'll back you." She checked the time; she had seven minutes to whip out a statement. She didn't worry; she'd done more with less before. "And I'm pretty sure I can get someone else on board too. Now, let's get started."

The time crunch was self-inflicted but served two purposes: getting Annie out of the office and away from ridicule as soon as possible and beating Jonathan to the punch in case he decided to mount a counterattack in his own defense. They spent the next seven minutes drafting a statement, pulling in pieces of Annie's email to the company and fleshing out details. They set up whomever they chose to champion the piece with a headline that would stop people scrolling in their tracks.

Right on time, Chase knocked on her door.

"Come in!" Lucy called, pleasantly surprised that he didn't just push it open like normal. Such progress.

"It's been ten minutes," he greeted when he opened the door a crack and peeked inside.

"I'm aware. Shut the door, please."

He came all the way inside and gave Annie a soft smile. Lucy couldn't help but note what looked like guilt shading his face. Perhaps for being aware of Jonathan's behavior and not saying anything about it.

"Remember that conversation we had about an hour ago?" Lucy said. "Well, the time has arrived for you to speak up, Chase. Come here and read this." She waved him behind her desk.

He obeyed, looking more than a little wary. He leaned down beside her to look at her screen, and she watched his eyes read over what she had written.

"This is really good."

"I know." Lucy realized how refreshing it was not to deflect a compliment for once. "I want you to back it."

"Sorry?" He stood up straight and smoothed his hand over his tie.

"You heard me. I want you to go on record, with me, in supporting Annie. It's time to stand up, remember?"

He blinked, and his eyes bounced between her and Annie.

Lucy waited, hoping their conversation outside HR wasn't just talk. "I know this is a huge ask, Chase, but it's the right thing to do. You and I are gunning for the same promotion, but do you even want it if it's for a man like Jonathan? I'm doing this with Annie, and we could really use your support."

Tension strained like a balloon about to burst. Lucy found

herself silently begging him, *please please please*, hoping he wouldn't let her down.

Finally, he spoke. "Lucy, I can't do that."

All the air sucked from the room like they were at altitude and someone broke the window. Lucy felt like she was falling even though she was sitting down.

"What?"

Chase backed away, smoothing his tie again and looking nervous. He glanced at Annie. "I'm sorry, but it's too much of a risk."

Lucy didn't want to believe what she was hearing. How could he do this? "So everything you said outside HR was . . . a lie?"

"No! Of course not. It's just . . ." He swiped his hair and took another step toward the door, like he was trying to escape. "Think about what you're doing, okay? Initiating a scandal like this could cost you everything. You haven't even signed Lily Chu yet. Do you really want to jeopardize that?"

Lucy swallowed a surge of worry at the thought that she had nothing in writing from Lily Chu. All they had were two cheeseburgers, each other's phone numbers, and a hug on the sidewalk. The chance that Lily would bail on a publicity agency embroiled in scandal she hadn't even officially signed with was not zero, and Lucy hated the thought of losing her.

But she hated more that Chase wasn't the stand-up guy she'd recently changed her mind to believe that he was.

"I *am* thinking about what I'm doing, Chase." She stood from her desk, anger burning behind her eyes, and walked him toward the door. "Someone has to do something, and I thought I could count on you to help, but it looks like I was wrong."

He gave her a pained look but didn't try to make an excuse.

He'd made his decision, and the disappointed pang in Lucy's chest felt all too familiar.

She shut the door behind him and paused to collect herself. Her grand plan didn't depend on his support, but it would have been stronger with it. She should have known it would be just her and Annie against the tide. What privilege for him to sit this one out while they risked their careers. Her misplaced faith pushed tears into her eyes. She wiped the thread of liquid rimming her eyelids before she turned around.

"We don't need him."

Annie stared up at her like a worried child.

They didn't need him; it was true, and Lucy felt relief that the words were able to come out of her mouth. But the crushing disappointment of being rejected to their faces only reinforced how alone they were.

"Who are you going to send the statement to?" Annie asked, her voice small and soft like she was second-guessing the whole thing.

Lucy couldn't stand the thought of Chase's lack of backbone dousing their fire. She squared her shoulders and returned to her desk. "I was thinking Monica Brown at *Deadline*; she's usually my go-to for feminist-leaning pieces."

Annie's eyes popped wide as if she'd underestimated Lucy's ability to make good on her plan. "Wow. That will be . . . *big*."

"That's the plan," she said, and finished typing out the message. She'd left room for Chase to add comment, but saving space had been in vain.

Annie fidgeted. "Are you sure this is a good idea? I mean, maybe you should give people a heads-up first if . . ."

Lucy stopped typing, hearing the uncertainty in her voice. "Annie, this is up to you. I'll pull the plug if you don't want to do it, but I think that will lower the chances of any change coming out of this." She paused, letting Annie deliberate and thinking of how warning a few people of the pending scandal was actually a great idea. She stood and opened the email draft on her phone. "But you make an excellent point about giving a heads-up; looks like you have a knack for chaos management." She gave her a grateful smile. "I will only hit send with your permission, so do I have it?"

She thought for a silent moment, and Lucy could guess the plot of the story playing forward in her mind, because the same one was in hers.

"Yes."

"Thank you."

But she didn't hit send just yet. She escorted Annie to the back stairwell for an easier escape and then turned to head toward Joanna's office.

Her honesty streak was alive and well, and the day's events perfectly positioned her to say something she had kept silent for years.

CHAPTER

12

Lucy stopped at Joanna's door and gave her the courtesy of two knocks before she shoved it open.

"I need to speak to you!" she blurted. She wasn't even all the way inside.

Joanna looked up from her desk, startled, from the depths of obvious exhaustion. Her jaw was set hard. Her usually sleek bob was pulled half back in a banana clip Lucy was shocked to see she even owned. All her lipstick had rubbed off, and her eyes were bloodshot, from tears or rage, Lucy couldn't be sure.

But the biggest giveaway of her state was her fist clutched around her necklace pendant so tightly her knuckles were white. She had bypassed nerves and gone straight off the deep end into overwhelming emotion, trying to save a sinking ship while she drowned.

Joanna pressed a polished finger into her desk phone to mute the call. "Lucy? I'm on the phone."

Lucy shut the door and crossed the space she usually took

refuge in; the cool, calm colors and distant ocean view. Perhaps it was her own energy, but the room felt hostile.

"Sorry, but I need to talk to you." She thought Joanna was going to scold her, but the confronted confusion on her face softened into fatigue.

"Now's not really the best time," she said over the voice still yammering through the phone. Whomever she was talking to was none the wiser he'd been muted. Lucy heard snippets of *demeaning* and *counterproductive*. Joanna pointed at the phone. "This is someone at *Billboard* asking for a comment on the backlash over Ms. Ma's single being anti-feminist, and honestly, I can't." In an unprecedented move—at least one Lucy had never witnessed from always-had-it-together Joanna—she held her face in her hand and sighed. "Today is impossible."

A surge of sympathy, rage, resolve, and just plain nerve kicked Lucy into gear. She leaned over Joanna's desk, a normally neat glass top that had been scattered with papers. "Let me take it." She jabbed the mute button before Joanna had a chance to respond.

". . . find the lyrics offensive," the male voice on the other end said. "Particularly, we're looking for a comment on the argument that feminists didn't fight for equality only to have women sing hypersexualized songs in lingerie."

Lucy lifted the phone from the receiver both so the caller could hear her clearly and so Joanna couldn't cut her off. "Hi. This is a representative from J&J Public. Our official statement on the controversy surrounding Ms. Ma's new single is that it's an empowering expression of female sexuality, something the industry has no problem with when it comes to male artists. And as far as the concern over the song being counterproductive to the feminist movement, I'll remind you that part of the purpose of the feminist fight for equality is to give women the freedom to do whatever the fuck they want. Quote me."

She hung up with a gratifying slam of the phone.

Joanna blinked at her, and Lucy swore she saw her lips twitch into a smile.

"That should handle it," Lucy said. She pulled out a chair and sat across from Joanna. "Look, I came in here to give you a heads-up. Obviously everything Annie said about Jonathan is true, as I'm sure you've gathered given our conversation this morning. I know this is why you left lunch early, and I get it; you didn't want to make a scene. But you should know I'm the one who told Annie to stand up for herself. I didn't expect her to out herself in such dramatic fashion, but I have a plan to fix it."

Joanna stared at her, guarded, but seemed to be silently encouraging her to go on.

"I don't know if it's fair of me to ask what you knew about what was going on all this time because *I* knew and never said anything but, Joanna, Jonathan is destroying this company. I know he's your brother, and that complicates things more than I can understand, but *you* should be in charge. Everyone knows it." She pulled up her email draft to Monica Brown and aimed the screen at Joanna. Her thumb hovered over the send icon. "I have an email ready to break the story to *Deadline*. It's Annie's allegations with my corroboration. I was hoping to get someone else to speak up, but for now, it's just us. I'm going to send it, but I wanted you to know first."

For the first time, perhaps ever, Joanna looked frightened.

"Who else was going to speak up?"

"Chase, but he backed out." The sting burned anew as she said it. She shook it off. "Joanna," she said sternly, "you gave me a chance with Lily Chu. You've given me all sorts of chances in my career, and now I'm giving you a chance. I send this, and the story blows up. Jonathan loses his position, and you take your rightful place as head of this company. Yes, it is going to be a painful process, but it needs to happen. It's time."

Lucy held up her phone, consciously keeping her thumb off the screen. She wanted to hit send, to set something bigger than herself in motion, but she realized Joanna's approval was important to her.

The silence stretched, but it wasn't uncomfortable. Lucy felt like she stood on top of it looking down. She was in control, and they both knew it.

Joanna pressed her lips together and reached for the pendant on her necklace. Lucy could see the violent struggle playing out in her eyes. She may have been asking her to do something impossible, but it could become possible if it promised the change she deserved—the change they all needed.

Joanna took a breath, and Lucy held hers.

"Sometimes tough love is the most necessary kind." She glanced at Lucy's phone with a subtle nod.

Her heart swelled as she hit send. She imagined a dramatic climax: the symphony striking up something foreboding and victorious at once, cymbals crashing, strings singing. But it was only her, Joanna, and the tense anticipation that followed electronic communication.

Lucy hoped she did not get Monica's out-of-office autoreply.

"Thank you," she said.

Joanna, looking both shocked and liberated by her own actions, bobbed her head. Her eyes traveled to the door. "And, Lucy? You were never in here."

Lucy read her loud and clear. She left without another word, slipping out the door into the hall. She pretended to be on her phone so no one stopped her on her way to her next destination. Her legs shook as she walked. Adrenaline flooded her veins over the serious drama she'd just started.

She rounded the corner to Amanda's office. Again, she knocked, but she didn't bust through the door in case there was something truly confidential going on inside.

Amanda greeted her, looking just as frazzled and exhausted as Joanna had, and Lucy hoped it wasn't only the women doing the emotional labor of navigating the meltdown, but she had a strong feeling it was.

"Lucy," Amanda started. "Is everything all right?"

"I need to talk to you. Alone."

Amanda glanced over her shoulder at Mr. Ericsson, who was poking at the remnants of takeout lunch. The conference table had even more binders and papers than it had when Lucy had left it not long before. The room was in shambles and smelled like balsamic vinaigrette.

"Robert? Do you mind?" Amanda asked.

He took his time wiping his mustache and pushing back from the table. He gave Lucy a weak smile as he passed. "I could use a walk to stretch my legs," he said, like he was thanking her for the excuse. He didn't look nearly as flustered as Amanda, but then, it wasn't his company that was up in flames.

"What can I help you with, Lucy?" Amanda asked once they were alone with the door shut. Lucy noted a takeout container where Amanda had sat during their meeting. The green salad looked untouched, all fresh and crisp with tomatoes and cucumbers.

"I'm here to give you a heads-up. I was probably supposed to keep things confidential, but I couldn't. This Annie thing is about to go external, and I think it's an opportunity."

Amanda recoiled like she'd said something insane.

"What I'm saying is, *everyone* will be watching, and you've got the opportunity to *do* something—to actually make a change. We've seen this story time and again; the headline isn't new. But the reaction can be new. There's a movement gaining momentum, and we need to be part of it. Jonathan—and men like him—have gotten away with too much for too long, and there have to be consequences. Don't just slap him on the wrist. Don't send the message to abusers that they can get away with it. And for the love of god, *don't* validate victims' fear that speaking up won't achieve anything. Listen, do something, and make a difference."

Lucy exhaled, and Amanda stared at her in awe. She heard the echo of her own words like thunder.

"Please," she tacked on politely.

Amanda closed her mouth, which had fallen open, and nodded. "Yes. Yes, I'm doing my best to do . . . all that."

"Good," Lucy said a bit awkwardly. She came in spitting fire and was happy to see Amanda agree with everything she said. No need for a fight. "Thank you." She turned to go.

"Lucy? Before you go, I just want to say . . ."

The dismay on her face surprised Lucy. "What is it?"

Amanda sighed like her nerves were frayed. "I just want to say I'm sorry you didn't feel safe coming to me, or anyone, about Jonathan. You should have been able to report him without fear of repercussion, and I take responsibility for it."

That was perhaps the last thing Lucy had expected her to say.

"Amanda, it's not your fault, personally, that I didn't report him. You're part of a system that works against women in these situations."

"Yes, I know, but . . . We've just known each other for a long time, and I hope that you will forgive me for not providing the resources or seeing the need for them."

It dawned on Lucy that the weary look she had seen on Amanda's face during their earlier meeting was disappointment directed internally at herself, not at anything Lucy had done.

A soft smile tugged at her lips. "I'll forgive you as long as you promise to do everything in your power to make sure there are real consequences this time."

Amanda softly smiled back and gave her a determined nod. "I'm working on it."

"Good." She turned to go and thought of one more thing. "Oh, and you should order something else for lunch instead of your salad. Get a sandwich or pizza or a burger or a giant burrito because you *want* it, not because we're only allowed to eat things like that when we're cheating on a diet or stressed or convincing ourselves it somehow doesn't count. And there's cake in the kitchen."

Amanda blankly stared at her, probably unused to another woman supporting her choice to eat whatever she wanted. Lucy had to admit, it was unusual. She was guilty of qualifying delicious things as cheat meals or stress eating because it was against the norm to allow herself to enjoy them otherwise— and she held other women to the same standard. She indulged Nina when she said she was being bad when she wanted a cupcake, and she held her accountable for the number of pizza slices they shared on days they ate carbs. All of it was plainly absurd, she realized. And the look on Amanda's face, the slow, scandalous smile, made her sad that they lived by such rules when they were happy to see them broken.

Lucy left Amanda's office hoping she ordered carne asada fries to gorge while she waged war against the injustice of workplace harassment. She checked for a response from Monica, but nothing yet; it had only been ten minutes or so. Once the story broke, she would have to triage the fallout. She'd be in her office on the phone with her clients for the rest of the day, but when the actual bomb went off, she wanted to be nowhere in sight. She'd go for some fresh air, she decided, as soon as she dropped in on Oliver to warn him of the pending scandal.

She found him at his desk, editing some behind-the-scenes footage of a photoshoot with one of Joanna's clients. Brazilian supermodel Alma Pereira posed in the surf during her shoot in Tahiti last month. J&J's social media manager liked to tease behind-the-scenes photos of upcoming magazine issues, major Hollywood events, movie premieres. Lucy had a folder of similar footage on her phone she could sell to a tabloid for half a million dollars if she wanted. Of course, that would violate the NDA she signed and was guaranteed to get her fired and probably blacklisted from every publicity-related outlet in the country, except for perhaps the tabloids.

Alma posed in powder white sand with a shock of teal sea behind her. She stood in the surf up to her thighs, wet like she'd gone for a swim and wearing a sheer white dress that plastered to the yellow bikini and her bronzed skin beneath. Her hair was wet, though Lucy was fairly certain she hadn't actually dunked her head in the ocean; someone had spritzed her down with salt water. She gripped the hem of her dress in her fists, suggestively pulling it high enough to reveal her bikini bottom on her left hip, and shifted her weight side to side, tossing her hair, pouting, tilting her head, and only holding still long enough for the photographer to snap a few hundred rapid-fire images between poses.

She suddenly paused and peeled the wet dress over her head. The video had no sound that she could hear, but Lucy was sure someone had just ordered the next set of photos in only the itsy-bitsy bikini.

Aides rushed in to help. Someone lifted layers of Alma's hair and sprayed an aerosol cloud to reinvigorate the volume, which confirmed what Lucy assumed about the wet look being sleight of hand. Someone else came at her with a makeup brush. Alma held still as the artist powdered her face, removing a sheen in a move that made no sense if she was supposed to be wet. They retouched her lips with a rosy gloss and made her look, in Lucy's opinion, nothing like someone who had just taken a dip in the ocean.

Oliver would edit it down to Alma's toes in the sand, her back, an angle that was mostly her crew primping her and hardly any of her face. All things Instagram followers would fawn over because *look how glamorous*, but also, *she's so normal*. Alma tilted her head back in a laugh that would get the BTS photos twenty thousand likes when they were strategically released days after the official photos hit the web. She looked like she was having such fun.

Lucy wondered if she was cold. And hungry. And sore from having every hair in her nether region ripped out so she could wear triangles of fabric without worry and still be airbrushed in postproduction.

"Do you know how much that fucking hurts?" Lucy muttered.

Oliver jumped with a gasp. He threw his hand to his chest and swiveled in his chair. *"Lucy!* Oh my god. You scared me! How long have you been there? And what hurts?"

She stepped into his cubicle and lowered her voice. *"That.* Having your bits waxed so you can wear a swimsuit because heaven forbid anyone know your body grows hair down there."

A weary look crossed his face, not unlike the one when she earlier accused him of being ignorant of pee string. But Oliver was Oliver and, bless him, braced to be the stand-in for the patriarchy while she expressed her discontent.

"It's really awful, you know. Lying there or bending over or pretzeling into whatever position so they can smear you in hot wax and then *rip* it all out." She pounced on the word, and Oliver jumped. "And then they do it again an inch over to make sure they got it all. And if you don't have time or money—or pain tolerance—for a wax, then you're left with razor burn up to your hips because no one has invented anything to fix that, don't believe the lies. So then we're walking around in our little V-cut suits with skin waxed raw or riddled with burning bumps, all for what? To look like some bizarre prepubescent versions of ourselves, but only between our belly buttons and knees? Meanwhile, *your* body hair is a celebration of masculinity. You get to *manscape* at home and leave it all over the bathroom like goddamned glitter that can't be cleaned up, and I have to go spread my legs for the hot waxer, just so *you* can look at me in a bikini and like what you see." She poked him in the chest and glared at him with the fire of every excruciating wax strip she'd told herself was necessary. For every time she'd laid her intimate region bare for a stranger to let them tear out parts of her body. The injustice of it all had her fired up. "And don't even get me started on the gynecologist!"

Oliver held up a hand, begging for mercy. "I've seen *The Vagina Monologues*; I know all about the cold duck lips. And I agree, they should warm them up."

The honest plea in his voice and the reminder of one of her favorite stage plays suddenly made her laugh. Or maybe it was the cumulative revelation of just how much nonsense women put up with.

Oliver grinned at her. "I'm a little busy screening Joanna's calls while she freaks out and prepping these photos for social media because even an in-house scandal doesn't stop publicity. Did you stop by to smash yet another pillar of the patriarchy, or are you here to chat?"

She playfully stuck her tongue out at him. She checked her phone again for a response from Monica. Still nothing yet.

"I'm here to give you a heads-up." She cast her eyes around to see who was listening. The office belly was ripe for overhearing gossip. "I mentioned your name to HR, so they're probably going to talk to you about what you know about my experience with Jonathan."

His brow flicked up in the most serious arch Lucy had ever seen on his face. "Good," he said with a cold resolution that filled her with warmth.

"Also"—she cast another glance over her shoulder—"I just talked to my friend Monica about Annie, so this afternoon might get a little busy . . ." She spoke in code, knowing Oliver would understand and hoping he'd keep a lid on his reaction.

True to form, he did understand, and his reaction was not subtle.

His eyes jumped wide. "Monica Brown from *Dead*—"

"*Yes*, Oliver. *That* friend Monica." She hushed him with a glare then checked her phone again. "I'm waiting to hear back.

I'm going to take a walk; I need some fresh air after the last hour."

"Yeah, you better get out of here if you're gonna . . . If you . . . If you're expecting to hear from your friend Monica."

She gave him an approving nod as she stepped away.

He waved. "I'll be here, making sure unrealistic images of women keep permeating mainstream media!"

Lucy rolled her eyes but realized he made an excellent point.

She would be remiss not to acknowledge the blood on her own hands when it came to reinforcing the beauty standards she had been resenting all day. She worked in an industry centered on physical appearance, one that blatantly emphasized an impossible standard for women in particular. She was guilty of perpetuating expectations with every statement she wrote, every story she spun, and every airbrushed, photoshopped photo she promoted. The hypocrisy suddenly seemed very circular; she was part of the system that reinforced at least some of the expectations she placed on herself every day.

How did it get this way? she wondered.

The expectations' origins were difficult to pinpoint, she realized. She enjoyed things like pretty clothes and wearing makeup; she wouldn't advocate against either as long as it was a choice. But where was the line between what she wanted for herself and what society pressured her to have, whether it was beauty standards, a relationship status, or something as life-altering as children? Somewhere, somehow, those expectations seeped into her brain like fact, and she lost track of where they ended and she began.

Maybe it was time to figure it out, she thought as she rode the elevator down to the lobby. But not at that exact moment. As with the other deep thoughts she'd had that day, she decided to save them for later since the reason she was headed outside was *not* to think as she waited for Monica to get back to her. She also had to initiate emergency triage protocol for her clients, starting with warning her greatest flight risk, Lily Chu. She couldn't stand the thought of losing her after all her hard work.

She fired off a text. Hi Lily! I need to fill you in on something. Do you have a few minutes to talk?

She didn't get an immediate response. She pressed her thumb into her volume button even though the ringer was already all the way up in anticipation of Monica's email.

She reached the lobby and passed outside into the afternoon sun. The day had grown warm. Sunlight bent between the buildings and splashed the pavement with pockets of heat. She headed for the small park with shady trees and benches two blocks away; far enough to feel like she left but close enough to be able to run back to the office if she had to. Midafternoon on a weekday, the park, which was really a glorified strip of lawn squished between an apartment complex and a brick of medical offices, stirred with late lunch breaks, dogs on leashes, toddlers running circles around their nannies. A few enthusiasts stretched in the shade after a jog, or perhaps before; Lucy couldn't see from a distance if they were sweaty yet.

She found a bench and let the sun warm her skin. Standing on the precipice of self-inflicted chaos—even if it was necessary—did a number on the nerves. She closed her eyes and took a few yoga breaths; she pictured the ocean.

Then she heard a voice that snapped her eyes open.

"Okay, I have to ask: Are you following me, Birthday Girl?"

She looked up to find a very pleasant surprise.

"Adam!"

He stood in front of her looking like he was ready for a jog. Forget the jeans and tee; he wore pleasantly short running shorts and a tank that showed off arms Lucy suddenly couldn't stop staring at. She thought she might be dreaming. The thought of their kiss came rushing back like a rogue wave. So much had happened since they parted, but she could feel it on her lips like it had just happened. She was glad she was sitting down.

Adam pulled earbuds from his ears and sat on the bench next to her. "So?" he said with a grin. "Are you following me or what?"

Lucy laughed, wondering if they were going to carry on like their lips hadn't been pressed against each other not long before. "I think it's more appropriate for me to ask you that, seeing that you know I work right around the corner."

He craned his neck to look where she had pointed, and she studied the line of his jaw. The thick stubble was soft, she'd learned from their little mishap earlier. She wondered what the divot at the base of his throat would smell like if she dipped her nose into it.

"That's right; we are in your neighborhood, aren't we? But in all fairness, *you* also know that *I* work right around that corner." He hooked a thumb over his shoulder in the other direction from her office.

He made a fair point, and she wondered if it was a subconscious choice that she had moved herself closer to where he was, though she had had no idea they would run into each other yet again.

Or, perhaps it was like Oliver said, and their chance encounter was the universe saying *yes.*

"So, what do you do in these parts?" he casually asked, and

Lucy realized they were indeed going to skirt the elephant sitting between them. He was flirty and cute, and Lucy was up for it, of course she was, but she couldn't deny the need to know where she stood with this handsome stranger who had caught her with his lips.

"I'm sorry," she said, holding out a hand like she was confirming she wasn't misremembering, "but we kissed earlier."

Adam shyly laughed, and his face turned the sweetest shade of pink. He bit his lip. "Uh, yeah. Yeah, we did."

Despite having been in a committed relationship for the past two years, Lucy remembered what it was like when things were fresh at the beginning. The insecurity and second-guessing wrapped up in all the butterflies. *Did I do something wrong? What did he mean by that? Is he not into me?* The questions she'd dissect with Nina while they replayed every conversation and reread every text, pouring mental and emotional labor into distilling meaning from ultimately trivial social cues.

Frankly, it was exhausting.

And there on that bench, staring at Adam the hot bartender, whom she'd known for less than a day, kissed by accident, and would like to kiss again, Lucy did not have the energy.

"And?" she asked. "Now what?"

For a second, Adam looked startled by her candor, but he scooted an inch closer. "Well, that first time seemed like it was a bit of an accident. How's your ankle, by the way? You looked like you caught that curb."

"My ankle is fine," Lucy said, inching her way toward him and growing less interested in small talk.

"Good," he said on an exhale Lucy was close enough to feel against her skin. "I'm glad I was there to catch you. I wouldn't want you to get hurt or anything."

"Me neither."

She didn't know if her response made any sense, but she knew his lips were very close to hers, and the sunlight was picking up tiny flecks of gold in his eyes. She felt his gaze studying her mouth and wondered if his heart was beating as hard as hers.

"So, what are we going to do?" she said breathily.

She watched him blink. His lashes fanned in that enviable way typical of so many men when women were always the ones gluing on falsies. "Well," he said slowly, "I suppose we could do it again, if you want—"

The end of his sentence disappeared into Lucy's lips. She turned and leaned forward, gripping the back of the bench for leverage. Where the first kiss was all awkward positioning and capitalizing on a lucky stumble, this one was straight on target and completely on purpose.

They sat close enough that their knees pressed together, but that was it. The kiss was just lips; a sample. An experiment. Lucy liked the outcome very much.

Very, very much.

So much that she hungrily leaned into it, embracing the thrill of her own desire. It felt *good*. Adam felt *good*—like something she'd been missing long enough to not even realize it wasn't there, and nothing like kissing Caleb. She let herself go, breathing him in and feeling the heat of his mouth, and the freedom was intoxicating.

When they stopped, she realized she had completely disarmed him. The handsome, charming, hell-of-a-kisser stranger stared at her, face flushed and lips shining, at a loss for words.

"I like kissing you," she said, her own head in the clouds but honesty still capable of traveling from her brain to her mouth.

It wasn't the most eloquent or sexy thing to say, but it was the truth.

The bashfulness that overtook him made Lucy melt. He rolled his lips inward, perhaps to rein in his smile, and looked at their knees. Where the smooth guy from the bar and the motorcycle had gone, she didn't know, but this shy, swooning Adam was adorable. "Well, I know you're telling me the truth."

"I am."

"I like kissing you too, it's just . . . Well, I thought—" he stammered, flapping his hands, "that first one seemed like an accident, so I wasn't sure— *Oh!* Okay," he mumbled against Lucy's mouth when she leaned in again.

Kissing Adam felt like a key in a lock. Or perhaps a truth in a sequence of lies. She hardly knew him, yes, but she trusted whatever force kept bringing them together. And she trusted the warmth unfurling into her limbs and the feel of his hand on her cheek. Most of all, she trusted that she *wanted* to kiss him. Kissing a near stranger on a bench in a community park was not something well-behaved women did—her mother would scold her if she saw—but dropping the oppressive charade and embracing her desire right there in public was not only thrilling, it was liberating.

When they parted, she didn't apologize for being forward or dissolve into a blushing fluster like she may have on another day. She smiled and enjoyed the leftover tingle on her lips. She pressed her fingertips to her mouth as if to stamp it in place.

"Wow," Adam said, dazed. "Uh, what were we talking about?"

Lucy laughed, trying to gather her thoughts. "I think you asked me what I do."

The reminder of her job brought her back to earth and made her check her phone for anything from Monica.

Still nothing.

"I'm a publicist."

He bobbed his head like this made perfect sense.

"What?"

"I guess I should have known by the power lunch in Beverly Hills and the fact that I've yet to see you without your phone in your hand," he said with a grin.

"Is that a bad thing?" she asked, realizing his opinion mattered to her.

"Not if it's what you like doing. I've just known people who act like they're curing cancer by making movies. But who am I to talk? I make overpriced cocktails for Westsiders who can only afford them because they're in your industry." His smile was genuine and knowing, and it made Lucy lean closer.

"Don't undersell yourself; they're life-changing cocktails, remember?"

"Ah, yes. How's that going, by the way? Did whatever emergency that sent you running back to work get sorted out?"

"*That* is a long story you probably don't have time or energy for."

Adam looked up and down the street as if to indicate his open schedule. "Well, I'll take an excuse to skip my run, and I don't have to be at the bar until four for happy hour, so." His hazel eyes were warm and sincere, interested.

Lucy may have trusted whatever force brought them together, but she was starting to second-guess how this charming, helpful, sincere, willing-to-listen-to-her-problems guy even existed in the first place.

A terrifying thought struck her that suddenly shifted her whole insane day into a new perspective.

Could it be possible that she had . . . made him up?

While the truth-telling could be chalked up to some inexplicable cosmic intervention, it could also be a symptom of her having lost her mind. Maybe she had snapped and he was a hallucination.

In that moment, she wanted to believe in the impracticality of the universe teaching her a lesson more than the much more logical chance that her brain might have gone haywire and she needed professional help.

She swallowed hard and looked at Adam. "Are you real?"

He stared back at her for a sobering second that made her sure she was insane before he burst out laughing. "What does that mean?"

Embarrassment hit her hard, and she wanted to duck under the bench and hide, but she needed to know. She found his gaze, determined, and held it. "I mean I didn't make you up, right? Very strange things keep happening to me today, and then there's *you*, and you're *good*, like too good to be true, and you keep showing up, and I just want to know that you're real and I don't need to be committed."

His brow furrowed at her fluster, and she was sure he regretted everything and was about to run away because her honesty had gone from charming to terrifying. But then his eyes softened, and she realized just how honest she'd been. "You think you made me up because I'm too good to be true?"

Her blood was aflame with embarrassment, but she nodded fervently because he still hadn't confirmed he wasn't a figment of her imagination.

"That might be the nicest thing anyone's ever said to me." He softly smiled. "But flattery aside, I can see you are sincerely distressed by this, so I can assure you that, yes, I am real." He reached for her hand and placed it on his half-bare chest, right over his heart, which she could feel beating under his skin. "See? Real."

She stared in his eyes and knew with every cell in her body that he was real and she wasn't crazy. At least not on a psychotic-break level. But the electricity passing between their skin and the weightless thrill it sent coursing through her again was pretty crazy.

She pulled her hand back before she caught fire. "Thanks."

"Anytime."

She wondered if that was invitation to touch him anytime or to ask him outrageous questions anytime.

She hoped for both.

"So, do you want to talk about it?" he asked.

"Do you want to hear about it?"

"I do."

She took a big breath, bracing herself. "Well, there's been a bit of a scandal at my office, and pending an email any minute now, I've shoved it into overdrive on purpose."

"Oh?" His brows rose like he was not expecting anything of the sort. "I didn't have you pegged as the scandal type."

"I'm a publicist; my job revolves around scandal."

"Tell me more." He leaned back and kicked an ankle on his knee.

"So, the CEO of my company is a jerk who has been harassing me for years. I've never told anyone for fear of jeopardizing my career—and it was never that bad, so don't get carried away thinking of the worst headlines you've read," she clarified when his face shifted to shock with a hint of feral rage on her behalf that made her heart flutter.

He stared down at the sidewalk, looking like he was plotting Jonathan's punishment despite not even knowing who he was. He composed himself, and his face grew serious. "I respect the fact that you experienced it and know better than I do, but I don't think that any kind of harassment should be downplayed or dismissed."

His tone made her wonder if he, or perhaps someone he cared about, had history with harassment or abuse.

"Noted and appreciated. So, another woman in the company came forward today—his assistant, to be exact. I'm the one who told her to stand up for herself, but I didn't think she'd interpret that to mean email the entire company about it. That's what sent me running at lunch." Adam stared at her, riveted, like he was watching reality TV. "She also identified *one other woman within the company* who'd been harassed, and everyone knows it's me."

His eyes shot wide enough for her to see all the gold flecks. "Yikes."

She smiled, though she had to admit she felt like she was standing on a ledge about to leap, praying there'd be a net below. "That's what I thought too at first. But then I realized it's an opportunity. If we want things to change, we have to do something about it, because nothing will ever get better on its own."

He looked at her with bald admiration. His lip curled up like he wanted in on whatever she was up to. "So, what did you do?"

Lucy's lip curled to match his. "Sent the story to *Deadline*."

"Damn!" He laughed a warm, impressed sound. "You don't mess around."

"I do not. At least not anymore, thanks to this truth-curse thing." She waved a hand.

"You so sure it's a curse? Like I said earlier: maybe it's a gift."

She was glad they circled back to their earlier conversation because she had honestly thought she was never going to see him again and wouldn't get the chance to talk about it. "You did say that, and I've been thinking about it. I *have* been trying to fix this—whatever is going on, I still don't know—and I'm wondering if you're right. If this thing is causing more solutions than problems."

He encouraged her to continue with an interested gaze.

"I mean, since this morning, I've done a bunch of things I wouldn't have otherwise."

"Like?"

"Like, standing up for myself, admitting my relationship was over, and outing my boss for harassment."

Not to mention eating what she wanted, wearing comfortable clothes, ditching makeup sweat, and telling her mother she may not get grandkids and she'd just have to deal with it. But that seemed a bit much to dump on him after only a day.

"What about kissing hot bartenders you met the night before? Is that out of the ordinary?"

"Oh, most definitely. And I noticed you slipped *hot* in there again."

As much as she liked the sweet, swooning Adam, she enjoyed the playful, cheeky version of him as well.

He gave her a sly grin. "You have no one to blame for that label but yourself, Birthday Girl." He reached out and gently tucked her hair behind her ear as if he were proving he could be sweet and sassy at the same time. "And I'm honored to be counted among your revolutionary acts, assuming kissing a hot bartender is in fact a good thing."

"It is."

"Excellent." He gave her a dimple-popping smile that turned her belly weightless. "All those other things sound like they're in the win column to me, even if they may have initially sucked."

She snorted. "Yes, some of them did suck big-time. I'm waiting to hear back from *Deadline* about the outing-of-the-boss thing, and I can guarantee the fallout won't be pretty."

"I think you're brave, and I'm sorry you have to deal with it at all, especially on your birthday, but I hope for the best outcome."

"Thank you."

"Of course. And if things go awry, I've got an uncle in Calabasas who'll bust this guy's kneecaps if you want."

Lucy burst out laughing. "Don't tell me you're in the mafia or something; I'll have to revoke the *too good to be true* thing. What's your last name, Gambino?"

"De Luca, but don't hold it against me. *I've* never busted any kneecaps; I just know guys who will."

"Hmm. Can we send them after my ex-boyfriend too?"

"It would be my pleasure. Just say the word." He held out his arms with a chuckle, and Lucy couldn't help thinking of a face-off between him or anyone in his family and Caleb going in a very obvious direction.

"That won't be necessary, but thanks for the offer."

"Sure. So, what's your last name?"

She coyly eyed him like she was keeping secrets. He was clever, slipping it into their playful conversation like that.

"It's only fair. We've run into each other what, three times now? Not counting the time you came to my bar looking for me. You've coerced my whole name out of me, as well as a free ride, *and* you know my place of work."

"You know my place of work too, thanks to the free ride," she countered with a smug tilt of her chin.

"Not true. I know the building you work in, but that's it."

"Fair. But I assume you're smart enough to deduce which company based on our conversation and find my office."

"Fair assumption. But I would never do that unless you invited me to. I find the whole showing up at your place of work uninvited like the dudes in supposedly romantic movies a little creepy, don't you? I mean, it's essentially stalking."

She considered it and realized he made an excellent point, but that she wouldn't mind if he showed up at her office unannounced.

"Green."

"What?"

"My last name. My name is Lucy Green."

He gave her a knowing grin and couldn't hide his happiness. "You just wait, Lucy Green. Next time we run into each other, I'm gonna get a phone number too."

"We'll see," she said with a laugh.

Just then, her phone let out two sounds in such quick succession, she couldn't tell which came first: the ding from Lily's text message or the chime from Monica's email.

The text was shorter so she read it first.

Hey! I'm in the makeup chair on set and we're behind schedule. Come to the studio if you need to talk. Or call Francine.

She texted Lucy the studio name and stage 6.

Lucy would go to Mars if an A-lister summoned her. And she didn't want to talk to Lily's agent; it was too important to risk anything getting lost in translation. She knew she had to go.

But first she had to make sure the reason for her visit was greenlit.

She opened Monica's email with her breath high in her throat.

Lucy,
This is incredible. Thank you for trusting me with it. I had to
get internal sign-off, but I drafted a full piece, and we're
ready to publish today if you're still in.
Talk soon.
—M
<attachment>

Lucy jumped up from the bench. Her hands shook. She was used to being on the initiating side of breaking news, but the news never concerned her. The situation suddenly pressed down on her with the weight of seven years. Ever since the day she walked into J&J and Jonathan's smile was a tad too friendly. The reckoning, she hoped, was now just on the other side of an email.

She clicked Monica's attachment and scanned her additions. It was perfect.

"Good news?" Adam asked.

Her heart pounded and her thumbs trembled as she typed, I'm in, and hit send.

"Yes. Very good news. That scandal I mentioned is about to

blow sky-high, but in a very good way." Her voice shook. A sharp memory of the moment before she walked onstage to sing "Somewhere Over the Rainbow" as a ten-year-old at her class recital pierced through her. Same as then, the exposure terrified her. And she hoped, like back then, that her courage would blow everyone away. "I have to go."

Adam had stood up from the bench. If she hadn't been so preoccupied with texting Lily, On my way! Lucy would have noticed the anxious look on his face that she was about to slip out of his hands.

"Do you need another ride?" he asked, hopeful.

The thought was tempting, Lucy had to admit. The idea of pressing herself up against him again made her dizzy. But getting to where Lily was involved freeways, and she did *not* have the guts for that on a motorcycle. She would know that even on a day she wasn't forced to tell the truth.

"Thanks for the offer, but I don't think I can handle the 405 on my first day on a bike. And it's not a matter of trusting *you*"—she pressed her hand to his chest because she couldn't completely cheat herself out of touching him again if the offer was on the table—"it's one hundred percent the fact that I would pass out or throw up. Maybe both."

His chest bounced with a laugh just as her phone let out another *ding!* She pulled away at the same time he reached for her hand. He reeled her in like a dancer until her whole body pressed up against his. What little breath it didn't knock out of her he stole when he pulled her into a full kiss.

It was very, very real, and her mind went blank. His tongue slipped warmly against hers, and if he hadn't wrapped his arms around her, she may have fallen over. The shape of him was new and different; the pattern of his breath against her face distinct. She wanted to memorize it all right there on that sunny sidewalk.

He pulled back after a dizzying moment that was equally eternal and brief, and smiled. "Just in case we don't run into each other again. Good luck with your scandal, Lucy Green."

Most people who had never been to L.A. held the glamorous view that movies and TV were made in Hollywood and that the Sunset Strip was actually a desirable place to hang out.

Most people were wrong.

Many of the film studios were in and around Burbank, on the backside of the Hollywood Hills, which meant Lucy had to haul it up the 405 and pray she didn't get stuck in traffic. She threw her faith in midafternoon on a Thursday being an open window, pending any brake-slamming fender benders clogging up the highway. She passed the Getty, Mulholland, Ventura Boulevard; all the storied landmarks of the greater Los Angeles area. By the time she hit the 101, Ms. Ma's song came on her satellite radio, and she blared it as loud as her stock speakers could handle, singing along with every *inappropriate* and *vulgar* lyric. She hadn't had time to check if her official statement on behalf of J&J had hit the web yet, but she was sure it was only a matter of time. And she was just as sure that Ms. Ma wouldn't give one damn that she'd said something so blunt on her behalf because all the controversy would only lead to more streams, downloads, and purchases anyway. Ms. Ma had probably been saying the same thing she had said all day anyway.

She used the song and the drive to distract herself from thoughts of Adam. She needed to focus on her job, and the scene on the sidewalk kept looping through her head like a rerun binge on Netflix. She allowed herself another heart-fluttering smile and indulgent memory of his kiss before she stored it away for later.

Her nerves sparked like live wires the closer she got to the studio lot. Begging Lily Chu not to fire her before she even hired her felt like calling after a first date and proposing marriage. It was risky and desperate, but she wanted to clear the air and make sure Lily knew which side of the scandal she was on. And she was working against the clock seeing that Monica was going to drop the story any second. Maybe she already had.

She made it to the studio lot and told the man at the gate she was with J&J Public and had a meeting with Lily Chu on stage 6. She tried to read his reaction to see if the news had already broken; he probably spent a fair amount of time on his phone while he sat waiting in his booth, so he could have seen it on the internet. He gave nothing away, but that may have just been conditioned numbness to yet another industry meltdown, she couldn't say.

She drove toward stage 6, passing by outdoor sets, people in costume whizzing by in golf carts, trucks full of props. The land of make-believe was in full swing despite yet another scandal imploding in its midst.

Sure enough, by the time she parked and checked her phone, she had a notification from *Deadline*, posted two minutes earlier. "Hollywood Publicity Agency Exposed in Sexual

Harassment Scandal." She swiped it and watched Monica's article fill her screen. She saw her own words and felt a swell of pride crash into one of fear.

No turning back now.

The news would spread like wildfire, she knew. To see just how far it had already gone, she opened Twitter. She went to search the trending hashtags, but the algorithms blessed her with a smack in the face.

Right at the top of her feed was a tweet from her favorite rock star and problem client, @LeoAshOfficial. He quote-tweeted the *Deadline* story with a note declaring, "Zero tolerance for this shit." The tweet went out to his thirty-five million followers and already had two hundred thousand hearts and counting.

Definitely no turning back now.

Lucy knew there wasn't a risk of Leo parting with J&J; she was the only one who would tolerate him, and they both knew it. But she also knew the tweet would land Leo in trouble one way or another, and she would have to clean it up.

She'd get to that after she talked to Lily.

She entered the soundstage through a side door and stepped into another world.

Her job rarely entailed visiting actual movie sets, and every time she got to, she felt a little like Dorothy looking behind the curtain. Cables and cords ran across the floor, powering the cameras and lights. A huge green screen covered the main stage's back wall. The set looked like a city street after a bomb went off. Large pieces of concrete were placed like fallen boulders; rubble filled the ground. Lucy spotted Lily in the middle of it wearing a skintight black outfit that looked suited for the apocalypse with a chest plate and shoulder pads. She had two swords strapped to her back. She had just started filming the lead role in a sci-fi franchise based on a series of novels that would haul in an obscene amount of money over the next three years. They were mid-scene, which gave Lucy hope Lily had no idea of the news yet.

A large man—much larger than Lily—dressed in shiny black nylon from head to toe with a collection of motion-capture balls glued to his arms, legs, and face stood opposite Lily. For the moment, he just looked like a guy in a wetsuit with pom-pom polka dots, but Lucy knew movie magic would turn him into the terrifying alien Lily's character was battling. He and Lily were sharing a laugh before the next shot. Lily's hair had been twisted into complicated braids that tucked and dove around her head; a practical hairstyle for the apocalyptic warrior on the go. She had a small, fake scrape on her cheek courtesy of the makeup department. A man with huge arms and a tight tee shirt approached her, explaining something Lucy couldn't hear. He pointed to the floor like he was blocking out dance moves. Then he spun around and turned his back to the alien actor and held his arms in an X over his head before driving his hands down toward his hips. Lily nodded along.

The director called for places, and Lucy's heart kicked up that she was about to see something spectacular, even if it was green-screened and void of postproduction edits. Lily backed way up on one side of the stage, and the alien actor stayed put. The man in the tee shirt hopped down to watch.

When the director called action, the alien crouched into a fighting stance. Lily let out a battle cry and ran full bore at him, dodging the fallen concrete blocks and looking like a woman on a mission. About five feet in front of him, she planted her feet right where the man in the tee shirt had pointed, hitting each mark and reaching back for her swords at the same time. She looked like the most terrifying little ballerina as she drew the blades, spun, stopped with her back to the alien man, lifted her arms in a perfect X over her head, and drove both swords backward into what would be a gruesome death once all the CGI was incorporated.

"Cut!" the director called. "Beautiful. I think that's the take."

Lily smiled, and a few people clapped.

"Let's take five," someone hollered, and the crowd disintegrated into muffled chatter.

Lucy waited for the stage to clear before she waved at Lily. She caught her eye, and Lily jumped down, alien-slaying swords replaced on her back and looking like she was ready to slash the patriarchy to pieces herself.

"Hey, you made it." She smiled as she approached. Someone called her name, causing her to turn around and ask for a minute. When she turned, Lucy saw up close that the swords were just well-made props and not actual blades. She let go of the niggling worry that Lily might turn them on her when she delivered her news. "What's up?" Lily asked, slightly out of breath from the climax of her battle scene.

Lucy studied the intricacy of her costume: the rubbery shoulder pads, the loops and twists of her hair, the fake dirt smudged on her face along with the fake abrasion. Lily's bright smile was positively out of place in the midst of it all. And just as Lucy thought about her smile, it dropped.

"What's wrong?"

Lily had no idea, and that was exactly what Lucy wanted.

She knew the main reason people were looking at her was because she was talking to the star of the movie, but she couldn't shake the feeling everyone knew about the scandal. Even though it had only broke minutes before, Hollywood was an endless party line of gossip. And normally, on any day other than her day of honesty, Lucy would hold her chin high and assure her client that everything was fine, but she knew by the look on Lily's face that the look on *her* face said otherwise. She had to tell Lily the truth—it was the reason she came, and of course she had no choice. As she prepared to do so, she felt the strain of every time she lied about everything being *fine* evaporate in the way that the grating discomfort of white noise only became noticeable when it stopped. The relief was instant and so profound, her ears almost rang.

"Can we go somewhere more private to talk?" she asked.

Lily's brow flattened, and her lips bent down. She looked over her shoulder at the stage being reset. "I don't have much time, but sure."

Lucy almost laughed. Lily was so fresh and green and so sincerely sweet; she had no idea the power she held. Another truth—one Lucy had learned from hanging around more seasoned stars—tumbled from her lips. "Lily, I don't think they're going to start without you."

A flush curled into her cheeks, and she rolled her eyes at herself, embarrassed, as if she forgot she was the star of the show. "Right."

She led Lucy back to the makeup trailer, where a man with bleached white hair and piercings dancing up his ears let them take over the space. It looked like a Sephora exploded inside of a creepy old attic. Wigs and props and shelves of prosthetics lined the narrow walls; bins of makeup sat on the countertops.

Lily didn't bother removing her swords before she sat on a

countertop. She pulled one leg up beneath her and looked like a kid playing dress-up. "So, what's going on?"

Lucy knew they were on borrowed time and that someone would surely come looking for the star if she went missing for more than ten minutes, even if they weren't going to film without her. She got to the point.

"Look, this story just broke minutes ago, and I wanted to be the one to tell you: J&J is in trouble."

Lily's eyes narrowed and she patted her hips in an ingrained reflex to reach for her phone. She nodded like she remembered it wasn't stashed in her apocalypse suit but probably in a trailer or some assistant's pocket. "Trouble? What do you mean?"

Lucy leaned against the counter opposite her, brushing against a dangling arm of alien skin. "An employee within the company came forward with sexual harassment allegations, and we're under investigation."

If Lucy expected bewildered naivety to cross Lily's face, she didn't see it. Her eyes did flash at first, but her expression easily settled into a disappointed fatigue that looked eons too old on her face.

"Are they true?"

Part of Lucy's job was protecting clients from bad news. When *Us Weekly* printed pictures of their cellulite or Rotten Tomatoes slaughtered their new movie, she acted as a shield. She spun stories and mounted counterattacks. She turned bad press into good press like water into wine—actually, more like stagnant pond scum into Dom Pérignon. But this felt different. If Lily was going to last more than five minutes in Hollywood—or any male-dominated industry—she needed to know the ugly truth. She needed to be prepared. Shielding her from it would do her no favors.

Lucy thought about herself at the start of her career. If she had known what was in store, would she have given up before she even started? Or would the knowledge have sparked a flame and motivated her to stand up for herself from the very beginning?

Looking at Lily, she couldn't help but think that being honest with her would lead to the latter, so when the truth spilled from her lips this time, it was by choice.

"Yes, they're true. I know from personal experience. And I'm here telling you about it because I want you to know I am standing up for myself now. I didn't before, and I should have. I don't know what's going to happen, but I wanted you to hear this from me instead of reading it online."

As Lily stared at her, Lucy saw the je ne sais quoi that would make every director in Hollywood want to work with her. Something to do with eyes wise beyond their years in a face as fresh as the morning sun. The combination couldn't be taught, and Lily Chu was born with it. She could play a precocious teenager for the next six years, easily. And then a college kid; then a twentysomething; a young wife; a young mother. The roles would shift, but the common thread would be young, young, young. She'd be twenty-one on-screen until she was thirty. And all the while, she'd bring a maturity to her parts, a professional ethic uncommon in someone her real or portrayed age. One that would make her irresistible to watch and coveted as a coworker. She would have her pick of projects and shelves of golden statues engraved with the words *best* and *outstanding*. Her career would be a joy to behold, and Lucy wanted more than anything to be part of it.

She hoped Lily wasn't so wise beyond her years that she fired her on the spot.

"I'm sorry for what happened to you, Lucy," she said. "And I appreciate you coming and telling me about it."

"Of course. And thank you. I'm sorry all this has come out right now, when we're just getting to know each other. It's obviously not ideal, and if it's not obvious, the main reason I'm here is to convince you not to give up on me. I think we could do great things together, and I don't want to lose that opportunity over some scandal." She watched her with hopeful eyes and tried not to make it too noticeable she was gnawing at her bottom lip.

Lily looked down at her hands, contemplative. Lucy couldn't be sure what she was thinking. "You know the book this movie is based on?"

She caught Lucy off guard, but she quickly scanned her brain for the information. Because of her job, she knew more about the business side of it: the film deal, the studio backing it, the director, the cast list. But the actual book, she came up short. It was the first in a young adult sci-fi trilogy that had first been released some five years before, she knew that much. Lucy had bought the first book with intentions to read it but never cracked the cover.

On another day, she would tell Lily it was her favorite series of all time and she'd read each book cover-to-cover twice. But because she hadn't and she couldn't, she just said, "I'm familiar with it, yes."

Lily's lips quirked. "Then you know that the girl in the book is white." Her eyes cast down, and she shook her head. "I was *so* excited when I got this part. I called my parents and cried. I ran around the house screaming. I *love* these books. I met the author, and she was thrilled to have me in the lead role. And getting to work with this director and cast; it's all a dream come true. But then people had opinions. I don't know if I was too optimistic, but I didn't think that people would get upset over *me* playing the lead character. I was attacked on social media; people sent me literal hate mail. I didn't leave my house for two days because I was afraid of what would happen when I went out."

Lucy remembered the backlash the previous year. The argument that an Asian American actress couldn't portray a character originally written as white. Cruel hashtags casually circulated racism around the internet, calling the casting *wrong* and *unfaithful to the source material*. The author of the book had to make a statement giving her blessing to actors of any race or ethnicity portraying her characters. But still, some people were married to the image in the book and refused to accept Lily.

Lucy pitied all those bigoted naysayers because they would never get to see the badass alien-slaying scene she just saw filmed in all its glory. Despite that, she wasn't sure why Lily was sharing the story with her.

"When all that happened," Lily went on, "it really hurt, and I just wanted to hide from it. But I knew that hiding from it would only make it worse. Nothing changes that way."

Lucy heard the truth she had been awakened to echoing in her words. She had never walked the world in Lily's shoes and couldn't relate on every level, but she did know that the time for silence was over. "I'm sorry that happened to you, Lily. And I agree that speaking up even when it's hard is the right thing to do."

Lily's lips curled into a sly grin. "I know you agree. That's why I'm not firing you. Look, I know there's a lot of bullshit out there, and most people pretend it doesn't exist, but you confront it. That speech you gave at lunch about this town being tough? And the fact that you're here telling me the truth about this scandal? I don't know what went on in the past, but you're speaking up about it now, and that's what matters. And that's the kind of person I want in my corner. I want people on my team who are going to say something when they see something."

She hopped down off the counter and held out her hand. She wore fingerless gloves, and Lucy noted that her ruby red nail polish from lunch had been removed. Manicures probably weren't standard during the apocalypse. "After all that backlash, I vowed to be the best in this role that I possibly can be just to show them all. I'm here to fucking fight. You with me?"

Even though she looked like a soldier, and Lucy had seen her slay an alien, she knew she was talking to the young woman under the costume. The fearless one ready to take aim at whatever came her way. But it shouldn't have been only Lily and others like her fighting, Lucy realized. The disadvantaged shouldn't be responsible for dismantling what held them back. The same as she had told Chase they needed men on the inside helping fight for workplace equality, those on the other side of Lily's struggle—like Lucy and the vast majority of the entertainment industry who looked like her—needed to help structure the system that favored themselves over everyone else.

Lucy took her hand and shook it with a smile. "Yes. I am."

"Good. Then go do whatever you need to do to blow up this harassment thing, and don't worry about me. I'll back you, and if anyone has a problem with it, remember I've got swords and I know how to use them." She smiled a mischievous little grin that made Lucy want to hug her.

Instead, she threw caution to the wind and blurted her true desire in that moment.

"Do you want to come to my birthday party tonight?"

In another situation, she would have laughed at herself for inviting a college kid to her thirtieth birthday party, but things were different when the kid was a movie star. She'd hung out with plenty of stars before—literally in her job description—but Lily felt different. It was like asking the coolest girl in school to come to her party.

And the coolest thing was, Lily was looking at her like *she* was the coolest girl in school.

"Really? That'd be fun. What time?"

Lucy beamed. "It's at Perch at eight."

"Cool," Lily said, just as someone knocked on the trailer's door. "Looks like time's up. Thanks for stopping by. And good luck with everything. I'll see you tonight." She waved and scooted past, turning sideways so she didn't whack her with a sword hilt.

She left Lucy standing in the trailer next to the limp alien skin feeling accomplished and a little giddy that she'd have a movie star at her birthday party.

Lucy checked her phone on the way back to her car. She was a pro at triaging scandal, but rarely did she start fires herself. She took a quick inventory.

First, there was the *Deadline* story about J&J that had been retweeted a few thousand times. #Herewegoagain was trending on Twitter, with post after post calling Hollywood a cesspit of harassment and scandal.

No news there, really.

And then there was the Ms. Ma story, which had unsurprisingly blended with the *Deadline* story because some internet sleuth figured out that J&J represented Ms. Ma. The hot take centered on the hypocrisy of an artist supposedly pushing a feminist agenda being represented by a publicity agency embroiled in a sexual harassment scandal. Reluctantly, Lucy had to agree that wasn't a good look.

Then, in a mutated union of the *Deadline* story, Ms. Ma, and her own brash behavior, *Billboard* posted an official statement on behalf of J&J Public with regards to Ms. Ma, noting that a representative from the *disgraced agency* gave comment. The post included the colorful language Lucy used in Joanna's office, and she thanked the stars her name did not appear in the piece, because there was no way she was going to deal with misogynistic internet rage aimed at her for speaking up on that front as well as the *Deadline* story front. She had more important things to do.

Like sort out the fourth and final leg of her mutant scandal monster on the way back to the office.

Leo Ash's *zero tolerance* tweet had gained a lot of traction. A scroll of his feed showed what was basically an impulsive argument with the internet, just as Lucy expected. And even if he was on the right side of the argument, his uncensored posts were going to land him in hot water, again, just as Lucy expected. And of course anyone armed with Google was quick to unearth past scandals that did not paint Leo as the most progressive feminist: girlfriends he'd cheated on; music videos featuring him buried under piles of nearly naked women; a quote about female pop stars from an old interview that sounded demeaning when taken out of context.

Lucy felt a sharp burning sensation deep in her belly and wondered if thirty would be the age she developed an ulcer.

She made it to her car and waited until she was off the lot to dial his number. The sound of a ringing outbound call on speaker filled her little cocoon. She hoped he answered because she was not about to drive out to Malibu and kick down his front door like she did that time no one could get ahold of him and she drew the short straw to go check on him in person. She found him floating on a unicorn raft in his pool, snoozing off a bender. He had been fine though very, *very* hungover. He swore he was never drinking again and then offered to fix her a highball at one o'clock in the afternoon.

"Lucy?" he answered in his raspy voice on the fifth and final ring before she would have been sent to voicemail.

"Leo, hi."

Muffled music pulsed in the background. Given the time of day and the fact that his last tweet was timestamped for two minutes earlier, she decided he was brooding in his mansion, probably in a hoodie and slippers rather than in a bar, a grungy underground show in London because he skipped town without notice, or backstage somewhere else entirely. Keeping tabs on Leo was high on Lucy's list of exhausting babysitting duties, but the noise leaking through his phone usually gave away his whereabouts.

"Listen, if you're calling about Twitter, these assholes are—"

"Shut up, Leo!" she snapped. Her outburst did not startle her because that was something she had wanted to say for a long, *long* time.

Leo, on the other hand, was stunned. "Um . . . what?"

She accelerated onto the freeway onramp and felt a surge of courage. "You heard me. For once, stop talking and just *listen* or so help me god, I will tell everyone your real name is Leonard and not Leonardo like you have them believe. I get what you're doing with the tweets, and it's great you're speaking out against harassment, but you're going to get yourself in trouble, not only by arguing with everyone, but it's also no secret you don't have the shiniest penny of a past with women. And then I'm going to have to step in and save you—*again*—so I'm calling to tell you to actually *do* something rather than just tweet about it! Most people *have* to take to Twitter to scream into the void because that's the only way they can feel heard. But you—*you*—have piles of money; you have a voice, a platform that millions of people follow and listen to, so use it, goddamn it! Donate to survivors' funds, women's rights groups, workplace sensitivity training—I don't care, just use your power for good instead of making another mess I have to clean up!"

Her hands were white on the steering wheel and her arms shook, but *oh*, did she feel righteous. She sped around slow traffic, bobbing and weaving like a true Southern California jerk, and she was living for it.

The silence booming through her speakerphone spoke volumes. She was probably the only person on the planet aside from his mother who dared talk to Leo Ash like that, and she'd stunned him speechless.

An inkling of fear fizzled deep in her brain. Worry that she'd gone too far, and he was going to fire her and add yet another leg to the scandal beast.

"Please," she added.

"I—" he started but didn't finish.

Lucy felt the many years of their relationship stretch between them. She'd done more than her share of cleaning up his messes: tabloid breakups, radio show scandals, Twitter rampages. That was all in her job description though, so she couldn't hold it against him. But then there were some literal messes—trashed hotel rooms, bloody noses—that fell outside the scope. And that time she invited him to Christmas at her parents' house in Orange County the year his parents flew to Barbados and he broke off his engagement to a British TV star, because she couldn't stand to think of him so lonely. Even if she was fond of him, it was about time he repaid the favors.

She waited for him to finish his thought, fully anticipating a snarky remark, some megastar egotistical sass, but he kept quiet.

Was he actually . . . *listening?*

Feeling victorious that she got through to him, she wanted to pump her arms in celebration. But at the same time, she worried that she had just torched one of her most important relationships. Due to the latter, she blurted, "Oh, and you're invited to my birthday party tonight. Perch at eight," before she jabbed the button to end the call.

She had a solid twenty minutes of peace while she drove. She kept the radio low and pictured the *Deadline* story leap-frogging its way across the industry. It would infect social media and spread around the web. Other outlets would pick it up, reprinting excerpts and adding voices to the cry. If it got big enough in the next few hours, it might even make the six-o'clock news. And all of it was exactly what she wanted. They had broken the silence, and now they needed all the noise they could make.

But for the moment, Lucy was enjoying the relative quiet of her car. The office would be anarchy when she returned; full-scale publicist meltdown. With Lily secured, Lucy needed to get back to her desk and assure the rest of her client list that the situation was being handled. She planned to enjoy the next ten minutes alone in her car before her skills were in high demand. She might already have emails from clients; she hadn't been able to check while she drove. She was at least respecting the laws of the road by having her phone in her lap and not in her hand. She smiled at the thought of what Adam said about her phone never leaving her hand and had the urge to tell him he was wrong. But she needed his number for that, and that was something she did not have. And anyway, calling him to say she didn't have her phone in her hand seemed counter to the point. Maybe she would drive by the bar later.

The thought made her smile bigger as she pulled off the freeway. The rushing whir of high-speed traffic softened right as her phone rang.

Her mother was calling.

She swore the woman had radar for the moments Lucy most wanted to be left alone.

She pressed the accept call button on her steering wheel because the phone would ring all the way back to work if she didn't. "Hi, Mom."

"Lucy! What on earth is going on? Your company is all over the news! They're saying employees have been harassed and are coming forward with allegations? I see your name in the article! It says your boss tried to pay you off?"

She sighed, already exhausted by where she knew the conversation was going.

"It's true, Mom. I helped write that article."

"You *what*?!" she shrieked. Lucy heard no knitting needles in the background. She imagined her mother instead scrolling *Deadline* on her iPad, wearing her reading glasses that bugged her eyes to 3× zoom. "What does that mean, Lucy?" The question was accusatory, and she couldn't take an interrogation by her own mother after everything else.

"It means exactly what you think it means, Mom."

Her mother sounded flustered, and Lucy knew it was because she was in denial. "Well, I don't—"

"It means that *I* was one of the employees being harassed, Mom. And I never told anyone because I didn't want to lose my job."

Maryellen sputtered again, unsure where to place her anger. "Well, you could have told *me*, Lucy!"

Lucy hit her brakes hard at a yellow stoplight and summoned an angry honk from the driver behind her. "Why, Mom? So you could lecture me about it? So you could tell me to *do* something about it when I didn't have any options I felt safe doing?"

Maryellen scoffed. "That's not what—"

"That's *exactly* what you would have done, Mom. You would have told me I wasn't handling the situation right, that there was more I could have done, like you *always* tell me. I never do enough for you! Or I do the wrong thing!"

And suddenly, a dam busted loose.

"You never give me space, Mom. I know you care, but I'm not your project. I have my own life, and I'm living it how *I* want to live it. I love my job, despite its faults. I want to build my career before I focus on a family. I actually don't even know if I want kids! And that's just something you're going to have to deal with. And I guess now is a good time to tell you Caleb and I broke up, so I won't be getting married anytime soon anyway. And I don't know what's going to happen with this scandal, but I finally spoke up because it was the right thing to do and I was ready. The point is, this is *my* life, and *I* will figure it all out!"

She was a few blocks from her office and her mother was speechless.

Of all the bridges she could light on fire, that one had the greatest chance of not burning down. And she felt justified in being so honest because those words had been caged up in her mind easily since high school.

In the silence, Lucy heard a news alert chime from her mother's iPad as she was in fact reading it. Maryellen's interests ranged wide; it could have been anything from a new knitting pattern to world politics to a sea turtle rescue in Hawaii.

"Oh," Maryellen said. "Well, isn't that interesting."

Lucy was not in the mood for a guessing game. "What is it?"

"They say there's going to be a press conference about your company. Right now."

"What?!"

Of all the remote possibilities, that one hadn't even entered Lucy's mind.

"Yes. It says, 'Jonathan Jenkins, CEO of J&J Public, to give statement on harassment allegations. Stream live here.' Oh! That's the link to the video. I see . . ."

"Oh my god." Lucy listened to her mother read the headline and navigate whatever website sent her news as her heart lurched up into her throat. *A press conference?* She needed to get back to her office immediately. "Mom, I have to go. Will you send me that link?"

"Sure. How do I . . . ? Oh, it's starting. They are showing the podium with all the microphones. Whoops! I shrunk it."

"Mom! I've told you this before. It's the icon with the arrow."

Once she stopped driving, Lucy could easily search *J&J press conference* and find the video herself, but if it was livestreaming, she didn't want to miss the beginning if she could help it. The fact that Jonathan was giving a press conference and not Joanna to say he had been fired left her sick with dread. She had a very strong feeling she knew what he was going to say.

She pulled into her building's parking garage and heard a *whoop* then a *ding!* as her mother successfully sent the link and she received it.

"Did it go through?" Maryellen asked, her voice crackling as the phone signal ran into the concrete walls. The underground garage was notoriously reliable for cutting out service.

"Yes, thank you!" Lucy shouted. She pulled into a parking spot and the call dropped.

She threw herself from the car and hurried toward the elevator, desperate not to miss the show. She opened the link her mother sent, and her screen offered up a loading ring futilely circling around and around over a block of gray.

"*No!*" she growled.

She growled again when she got in the elevator and it stopped on the lobby floor instead of taking her all the way to the sixth and back to the safety of her own office. A man in a sharp suit waited to step inside, and over his shoulder Lucy saw a display that solved her problem of missing the show but left her stunned with nerves.

She didn't need her phone to load the livestream because the press conference was happening live, right there in the building lobby.

CHAPTER

14

Lights and a panel backdrop converted a corner of the marble-and-glass lobby into an impromptu stage. Hollywood moved fast when something needed filming.

The pace of how quickly the press conference came together put a bitter taste in Lucy's mouth. Jonathan had resources, sure he did, but it had only been a little over an hour since the news went public outside of the company, and if it had stayed internal, why would he plan to expose himself with a press conference? It was like he knew it was coming and wanted to retaliate.

Now that she had cleared the garage and elevator, Lucy's phone burst with a flurry of new messages. She unlocked her screen as she scanned the crowd clustered into the corner. Familiar faces popped out at her, journalists she worked with on the regular with phones and notepads at the ready. TV cameras aimed at the podium where Jonathan stood flanked by people Lucy could only assume were his lawyers.

She looked down at her phone and saw a text from Oliver:

OMG presser in 5. Where are you?

One from her mother:

Is the link working?

One from Annie:

I'm so nervous. What is he going to say??

And one from someone Lucy looked up to see hurrying toward her as soon as she finished reading it.

Shit. Should have seen this coming. I'm on my way.

Monica Brown squeaked to a stop beside Lucy, flushed in the face and wearing sneakers with her tunic dress. The smell of her perfume and a hint of sweat hit Lucy like a summer garden party. Hair slipped from the haphazard brunette bun atop her head. She was a good six inches shorter than Lucy and fantastically curvy.

"Did you run here?" Lucy greeted.

"Yeah," she said, out of breath. "I keep sneakers in my desk for emergencies. Luckily this emergency was right down the street. Has he said anything yet?" She stood up on her tiptoes to peer over the crowd.

"Not yet."

"Well, I can almost guarantee I know what he's going to say . . ." Monica tsked in dismay. She stomped her foot and grumbled. "How did he pull this together so fast? Did he know about the story?"

"He shouldn't have. I only told—"

Lucy's response stopped dead in its tracks when she found the answer to the timing mystery standing at the crowd's edge. Chase.

Besides Annie, Joanna, Oliver, and Amanda, Chase was the only one who knew to anticipate the story going public, and no one else on that list would have sabotaged her. Chase knew because Lucy asked him for help, and *this* was how he repaid her. By warning Jonathan.

Lucy muttered something so unkind that Monica turned her head in alarm. A raging fire roared up inside her, and before she could stop herself, she was shoving her way through the crowd.

"*You,*" she seethed at Chase, pointing a finger in his face when she stopped in front of him. "You did this, didn't you?"

He took a step back and smoothed a hand over his tie. He had little room to move, what with the crowd pressing in on them from the front and the wall close behind. His composure slipped as he glanced side to side. "Lucy, I—"

"*Don't* lie to me, Chase. You are the only one who would tell Jonathan about the article, and there's no way he would have had time to pull all this together without some kind of warning."

Chase let out a nervous *ahem*. "Lucy, please. You're making a scene."

Curious glances came at them from all directions. Monica appeared behind Lucy, likely sensing there was more to the story. Over her shoulder, Lucy noticed Oliver spill from the elevator right on Joanna's heels. While he was flustered and anxiously scanning the room, she glided across the marble, stone-faced and composed.

Joanna's poise reminded Lucy that there were cameras

present, and while she was largely anonymous at the back of the gathering, it wouldn't take much for someone to recognize her, link her to the article, and make an actual scene.

The conference was seconds from starting. Jonathan sipped a glass of water and looked down at the podium, likely at a statement his legal team had prepared on his behalf.

Lucy's blood hit an uncomfortable boiling point, and thankfully she made eye contact with Oliver, bless him, because it stopped her from screaming.

He bugged out his eyes in an *I've been looking for you* glare that was more comforting than accusatory and hurried over.

Lucy turned back to Chase and lowered her voice in the final seconds before Jonathan began speaking. "You betrayed me, Chase. I know sometimes we have to do extreme things to get ahead in this industry, but you're on the wrong side this time."

He gave her a solemn look and said nothing.

Oliver arrived and squeezed himself between them, firmly bumping Chase aside with his shoulder and discreetly slipping his hand into Lucy's.

The show was starting, and everyone knew it would be unpleasant to watch.

"Thank you all for gathering on such short notice," Jonathan opened.

Lucy swallowed a fiery ball of rage and Oliver scoffed. Joanna lingered at the back of the crowd. Lucy couldn't catch her eye.

"J&J Public has been a Hollywood institution since its founding by my father more than four decades ago. When he retired and handed over leadership to me, I vowed to run the company with the integrity he himself instilled in me as both an upstanding man and as the head of a respected business." He paused and looked at his notes.

Oliver's hand tightened around Lucy's in anticipation. So far, nothing Jonathan said was blatantly false. The company was a respected institution, and Lucy had met Jonathan Jenkins Sr. on multiple occasions; he was a lovely albeit traditional man. The odds were not in his favor, but Lucy allowed a fleeting moment of hope that Jonathan was positioning himself to admit his fault and take responsibility for his actions. She felt the room holding its breath with her.

"I'm here today to state definitively that the accusations made against me by employees of J&J Public are false."

The room exhaled. Cameras clicked, and pens scratched. The rage boiling beneath Lucy's surface found its way into her eyes and sent them awash with silent tears. She began to tremble. Oliver squeezed her hand and muttered expletives to match the ones coming from Monica. Chase stood like a pillar.

"I have never engaged in inappropriate behavior with an employee. I take pride in how I conduct myself, and quite honestly it pains me to see these promising young women influenced by social politics. Annie Ferguson has been my assistant for most of the past year, and Lucy Green is one of the most promising publicists at our firm. I know each of them personally, and I have to assume that the motivation behind these baseless and false accusations derives from the larger movement aimed at discrediting men like myself in positions of power. My colleagues will tell you that I am one to champion women in the workplace. I am a father to a daughter and a loving husband. It may not have been their intention, but the false accusations brought forth by these two women will have harmful consequences beyond just myself."

"Oh boo hoo, now he's the victim?" Oliver hissed.

Lucy was too furious to see straight. Any hope she had of Jonathan admitting fault was dashed deader than roadkill. Every word out of his mouth was a lie. On the day she was bound by the truth, Jonathan was blatantly deceiving a room full of people—plus whoever was watching the livestream.

But the lies Lucy told, she realized in that moment, really only harmed herself. Her appearance, her diet, her relationship. She needed to stop, she'd learned that, but she didn't run around spouting dishonesty that damaged lives. Jonathan lied freely. He could say whatever he wanted, and people would believe him. And if they didn't believe him, they wouldn't speak up about it because there would never be consequences if they did.

Just like there would be no consequence now.

Lucy's efforts with the article—the risk she convinced Annie to take—suddenly felt in vain. For how big of a platform Monica gave her, Jonathan had just called her a liar on live TV. She may have been the strategist behind some of the biggest names in entertainment, but that was exactly where she stayed—*behind* them. Compared to Jonathan, industry mogul, she was no one. She'd tried to raise her voice, and he silenced it with a single sentence.

A tear spilled over her lid and burned down her cheek. She dashed it away.

"I'm so sorry, Luce," Oliver whispered.

She felt Chase's eyes and refused to look at him. She would not give him the satisfaction of her tears.

"I thought it important to gather here today and make a formal statement in an effort to curtail the spread of these allegations as much as possible," Jonathan said, and then added with a stern gaze at the crowd, "before any other publications irresponsibly spread misinformation without proof."

"Two women coming forward isn't proof?" Monica shouted.

Heads turned, and murmurs rippled through the crowd. Jonathan put his hand to his brow as if he were shielding the sun and gazed deep into the room. Many eyes searching for the brave soul who spoke up landed on Lucy, seeing that she was a head taller than Monica.

Jonathan tittered a vile laugh. "Well, I guess we do have some time for a few questions. Where should we start?" He pointed into the crowd.

"I already started!" Monica called, her voice ringing off the vaulted ceiling. "Two women have come out against you, one with allegations dating back years. How do you explain that, if these allegations are false as you claim?"

Nervous tension blanketed the room like a thick quilt. Lucy began to sweat. Jonathan cleared his throat and leaned toward the man in the suit beside him, who whispered in his ear.

"Talk yourself out of this one, asshole," Oliver muttered with a malice that Lucy felt in her bones. She also felt an unease because she had little doubt that he would in fact talk himself out of it.

"I can only credit that to some kind of collaborative and active imagination. Next question." He waved a hand and pointed to someone in the front row.

"You're saying they made it all up?" Monica was a dog with a bone. She would not give up. "What incentive do they have to do that?"

A frustrated breath slipped from Jonathan's mouth. "Tarnishing my reputation; threatening my status; jumping on the bandwagon because accusing men in positions of power is on-trend right now. Perhaps they are suffering from some form of mental or emotional instability and have targeted me. The reasons run many, but I can't say. Perhaps you should ask them."

Sadness stabbed through Lucy like a blade. She ached for Annie and for herself. Not only were they liars; now they were crazy ones. Making up stories to get the boss in trouble. More unhinged women with an agenda.

She had known it was all coming—she had even warned Annie about it in her office before they decided to publish the article—but hearing it all live in person hurt more than she expected.

She was at least thankful Annie wasn't present in the room.

"What about the allegations that you attempted to pay off an employee to keep quiet?" a faceless voice asked from the front of the room.

Lucy kept her eyes down. What good would calling out the lie she knew was about to spew from Jonathan's mouth do anyway? Her losing her cool with an audience would only serve his unhinged-woman narrative.

Just another way to silence her, she realized.

The injustice burned at her like she was tied to a stake. Aflame in a room full of people and no one could see.

"That too is a baseless accusation," Jonathan said. "I have made no monetary offers to employees for any purpose, especially not in the context I'm accused of doing here."

His shift in story was almost comical. The adamant cruelty in his office when he tried to fire her was nowhere to be found. It was as if none of it had happened because it no longer served his purpose. She was a *promising publicist* gone rogue, and he was the victim.

The conversation turned to static buzz in her ears. Like a

million mosquitoes trapped in a tube. Perhaps it was self-preservation sparing her hearing more lies. Or maybe it was just rage. She didn't realize the press conference had ended until Oliver nudged her and said, "It's over."

The crowd dispersed in a dull hum of chatter. Jonathan was whisked off by his legal escorts, going who knew where. Perhaps to hide behind the gated driveway at his house in Laurel Canyon, where he'd be safe from anyone begging him for more comments.

Lucy looked around at her colleagues in a daze. Oliver's face twisted into a combination of disgruntled contempt and soft support that only he could pull off. Chase met Lucy's eye and opened his mouth like he had something to say, but she didn't want to hear it. She turned away to see Joanna approaching, neutral-faced and extending a folded piece of paper to Monica.

"Not here," she said with a subtle shake of her head as she handed it over. "I'd like to see you in my office, if you're available. Both of you." She nodded at Lucy and headed toward the elevators.

Lucy and Monica swapped a confused look as Monica swiftly stuffed the folded paper in her bra.

"What's that about?" Oliver whispered.

"I don't know; you're her assistant," Lucy said, and dutifully followed.

"I know nothing."

They wound their way to the elevator and rode up to the sixth floor in an anxious silence. Most everyone inside J&J was staring at their phone or gathered around someone's computer screen, surely to watch the press conference and ogle the fallout on social media. Lucy felt like a pariah being paraded down the hall. Eyes peeled from screens to watch her go by, the *promising publicist* just publicly called a liar. She could almost see the camps dividing as she passed: Team Jonathan versus Team Lucy and Annie. Loyalty bent with the wind, it seemed.

"Oliver, there will be a company-wide briefing in twenty minutes; send an invite, please. And notify the board we'll be meeting later," Joanna said ominously.

Oliver exited at his cubicle with a nod, and Lucy and Monica continued on. On her third visit to Joanna's office that day, Lucy still took no comfort in the normally soothing view.

As if nothing were amiss, Joanna swanned over to the sideboard under her TV and grabbed three crystal tumblers and a bottle of amber-colored liquid. She set the glasses on her desk and twisted the cork free with a squeaking pop. Lucy had never seen Joanna drink in her office; the sideboard usually held only fresh flowers.

"Are we celebrating something?" Monica asked, sounding as dubious as Lucy felt.

Joanna splashed two fingers into each glass and lifted one. She took a sip and exhaled a long breath. "Yes. I just watched my arrogant, condescending *ass* of a brother hang himself on live TV. Cheers." She nodded at the two remaining glasses.

Clearly, they were supposed to join in what appeared to be a victory dance.

Lucy lifted her glass. The sharp smell of an oak barrel having been lit on fire watered her eyes.

They all three sipped and shuddered.

"I don't know why men pride themselves on drinking such foul things during working hours." Joanna studied her glass as if it would tell her the answer. "I stole this from Jonathan's office while he was preparing for his press conference; I think it's at least eighteen years old."

Lucy set her glass down, deciding one sip was enough. On another day, she would not have insulted the drink offered to her, but since Joanna had just done it—and it really was awful—she felt no remorse. "This is terrible, and what do you mean, *hang himself*? Everyone believed him when he just stood up there and lied for five minutes."

"*Exactly.*" Joanna grinned. She pointed to Monica's chest with drink in hand then took another sip. "Read it."

Monica looked down as if Joanna told her she had a stain on her clothes. Her face lit with understanding when she remembered the piece of paper shoved in her bra. She dug down her dress, rooting around like she was adjusting her underwire, and pulled it out. "What is this?"

Lucy recognized it immediately. She snatched it from Monica's hand and unfolded it.

"Proof," Joanna said.

The dollar amount Jonathan tried to buy her silence with stared her in the face, unmistakably in his handwriting and on his personal letterhead.

"You kept it," Lucy said. A smile lifted her face, out of surprise, gratitude, and, most of all, hope. In that moment, she was immensely thankful she hadn't torn it to shreds as soon as he handed it to her that morning.

"I don't understand." Monica frowned. "What am I looking at?"

Joanna drained her glass with a determined gulp. "*That* is the bribe Jonathan passed to Lucy this morning when he tried to fire her and then pay her to keep quiet. She brought it to me after the fact, and I thought holding on to it might work in our favor. Turns out, yes. See, when I confronted him about what

Lucy told me, he denied it. I know Lucy would never lie to me, and I told him as much. I didn't tell him I had proof of his offer though. You'll see that number is written on his personal letterhead, which he commissioned from a stationery firm in Brentwood for an obscene price. I know my brother, and I know he doesn't let that ridiculous paper out of his sight. There is no denying he wrote it. I gave him a final chance to confess, and he didn't, so here we are."

Lucy's mouth burned with oaky scotch and her head still swam from the revelation, but the pieces came together with a sharp snap that made her smile again.

"And we're going to share it as proof that everything he just said during the press conference was a lie."

"Indeed." Joanna smiled. She uncorked the bottle for another pour. "I have to say, Lucy, I'm glad you didn't include it as evidence in the article. He would have discredited it along with everything else."

The oversight struck her as wildly fortunate. "I didn't even think of it, but I'm glad you did."

Joanna tipped the bottle toward her like a toast.

"What's going to stop him from discrediting it now?" Monica asked. She braved another sip of the scotch, perhaps embracing the moment.

"Nothing," Joanna said. "But it's going to look pretty bad for him when it goes public, seeing that he just lied about it on live TV."

Lucy had to agree, the sequence of events would not work in Jonathan's favor. She marveled at Joanna's ability to think one step ahead. A good publicist always had at least one backup plan, and sometimes those backup plans were forward plans.

A startling thought struck her like a smack in the face.

"It was you," she said, stunned. "*You* told Jonathan about the article before it was published."

Joanna hummed with a knowing smile. "Like I said, I know my brother. If he knew it was coming, I knew he'd try to nip it in the bud and, in doing so, expose himself as a liar. I'm really sorry for everything he said. I had a moment of hope that decency would get the best of him and he'd come clean, but my faith was misplaced."

Lucy shook her head in disbelief, smiling, but at the same time realized she had made a terrible mistake. "It wasn't Chase."

"Sorry?" Joanna asked.

Lucy pressed her hand to her forehead, feeling remorseful. Chase may not have been there when she needed him, but at least he hadn't actively sabotaged her. Not this time anyway. "I thought Chase warned Jonathan about the article so he'd have the chance to defend himself with the press conference. He was one of the only other people who knew about it; I asked him to back the piece, but he said it was too risky. I accused him of helping Jonathan."

Joanna pursed her lips in consideration, and Lucy noted how she didn't needlessly apologize for the misunderstanding she had nothing to do with. "I know you and Chase have your differences, but perhaps your faith isn't as misplaced as you thought. What you did was incredibly brave, Lucy—and a huge personal risk. Some people might just need time to catch up. He may still surprise you."

Lucy sat with the odd emotion of owing someone she was mad at an apology.

"So now what happens?" Monica asked.

"Now," Joanna said, "you write a follow-up piece with the

offer as evidence and post it on every channel you can. I will call an emergency board meeting for later to discuss Jonathan's replacement and a company briefing for now to reassure everyone things are okay. You're right, Lucy: I should be in charge. And if staging a coup is the way I have to get what's rightfully mine, then so be it."

Lucy admired the woman a whole hell of a lot already, but never more than she did in that moment.

"And what do I do?" Lucy asked.

"After the briefing, take the rest of the day off. You've been through hell."

She couldn't argue the latter point, but she needed to contact all her clients given that they'd surely heard the news by then. Some of them were probably wondering if she'd been fired and if they were still represented.

But then she could take the day off. Maybe she'd go home and take a bubble bath before her party.

"Well, this is going to be fun," Monica said into her glass before draining it. "I'll be in touch before I make anything live." She pivoted for the exit.

"Thanks, Monica," Joanna called after her.

"Never a dull moment in this town," she said, throwing her arms in the air as she slipped out the door.

Lucy and Joanna were left alone, standing on either side of Joanna's desk. As if to offset the symbolism, Joanna rounded to the same side as Lucy and leaned back. "Lucy, before I go out there and address everyone, I want a word with you. We both know that you deserve your promotion, and I want to be transparent with you that I'm not sure what's going to happen with the board meeting, but I will do my best to ensure an outcome that favors us both. You have excelled with obstacles in your way, and I'm both incredibly remorseful about and amazed by that."

The compliment warmed Lucy's face. "Thank you. But I learned it all from you. How to handle difficult situations, I mean. You're the best I've ever seen at it."

It was Joanna's turn for modesty. She shook her head. "If I were any good at it, none of this would have happened." She stared at the floor, and Lucy couldn't be sure what she was thinking. When she looked back up, her face twisted with remorse. "Why didn't you tell me?"

The heavy question sat between them, prickled with shame on both the asking and receiving ends: Joanna for even needing to ask, and Lucy for staying silent for so long. But Lucy had to tell the truth. And she had already said it, if not in so many words, earlier that day anyway.

"Because I was afraid. Not only is he your brother, I didn't want to jeopardize my career by accusing the CEO of harassment. You've probably noticed that things don't usually work out too well for people who do that."

Joanna's mouth hardened like expecting the response did not lessen the pain of it. "I'm sorry, Lucy. I know I can't undo time, but I hope my actions now show you where I stand on the matter."

Lucy couldn't fight a smile. "You mean how you sabotaged him?"

The grin that bent Joanna's lips looked positively wicked. "Like you said: he is my brother. It's best to keep such matters within the family."

Having no siblings of her own, Lucy could not understand the dynamic making Joanna grin like the Cheshire cat, but she did not take issue with the much-needed support. In fact, it made her swell with gratitude.

"Do you want to come to my birthday party tonight?"

Joanna looked genuinely surprised. "Do you want me to come?"

Lucy laughed. "Yes, that's why I invited you. Today has been crazy, and I'm sure after the board meeting you will need something better than that to drink." She nodded at the glass still in Joanna's hand.

A warm, soft laugh hummed from Joanna's throat. It was a rare sound, and Lucy reveled in it. "I can't make any promises, but that would be a lovely way to end this nightmare day."

"Great. Perch at eight."

Lucy hoped she was talking to the future CEO of her company, but she also felt like she was talking to a friend. How fortunate to have those be one and the same thing, if all went well.

"Sounds great. Now if you'll please excuse me for a moment. I have to attempt the impossible."

Lucy watched her drain her glass in a single gulp. "Which is . . . ?"

Joanna set the glass down with significant force and the most *I am not entertained* face Lucy had ever seen. "Convince my father I'm capable of running this company."

Oh.

Lucy didn't know the current intricacies of the Jenkins family dynamics, or what power Joanna's father held over company ownership and decision-making, but it didn't surprise her to learn he still had a say.

"Want me to tell him like I told that guy at *Billboard*?"

Joanna laughed a full, throaty sound that made Lucy smile—and assured her she wasn't in trouble for her colorful commentary on the Ms. Ma debacle. "As much as I would enjoy that, this is something I need to do on my own. Finally." Determination, coupled with a bit of weariness, filled her face.

"Well," Lucy said, "I wish you the best. And if it counts for anything, you know where I stand on the matter."

"It counts for a lot, Lucy. Thank you."

Lucy shrugged a shoulder as if her life-changing day of honesty were no big deal. Her brief conversation with Annie in the bathroom that morning had snowballed into, hopefully, Joanna taking her rightful place as CEO of the company, but far be it from her to take credit for the butterfly effect. "You deserve it."

"Thank you. Oh, how did lunch end with Lily?"

"Couldn't have gone better, actually. She agreed to sign with us, and then I went to talk to her in person about the *Deadline* story before it broke so it wouldn't scare her away before she actually signed."

"That's exactly what I would have done."

"I know."

They smiled at each other, two women highly competent at their jobs and not afraid to say it.

"Good luck with everything," Lucy said. "I hope to see you tonight."

Ten minutes later, the whole company was gathered for the second time that day. Lucy didn't doubt a few colleagues wanted her head since she was the driving force behind the *Deadline* story and consequent mayhem, but so be it. She had done the right thing and no amount of coworker shade would convince her otherwise.

She made her way to Oliver's cubicle, where he interrogated her in quiet hisses.

"What happened? Is everything okay? Joanna is being insanely vague. Her email said Jonathan is temporarily on leave. Do you know what's going on?"

She gave him a silent nod, not feeling the need to explain since Joanna emerged from her office to do just that.

Everyone's routine positioning had changed since that morning in ways that spoke volumes. Jonathan was of course not at his door; Chase had abandoned post as well, standing across the room and pointedly avoiding Lucy's gaze; and, most notably, Joanna was not in her office doorway but at the front of the room right in the center where she had always belonged.

"Good afternoon, everyone," she began. Lucy couldn't help noting the change in her posture. Instead of leaning into the building like she was keeping it from falling over, she stood solidly on the floor, head high.

"Thank you for making time to meet," Joanna continued. "I know everyone is very busy in light of the recent news and events, but I wanted to share an update." She cast eyes in the direction of Jonathan's office, and her composure floored Lucy. She could gloat, she could taunt, she could maybe even scream because he was her brother, but all she did was nod at the vacancy and continue talking. "As you know, allegations of misconduct have been made against our CEO. Mr. Jenkins has publicly denied these allegations. Some of you have already been involved in working with our mediation service, and I thank you for your effort. As the investigation is ongoing, the board of directors has called an emergency meeting for later today to better understand what has transpired and decide what action is most suitable."

Lucy didn't miss the hint of an upward inflection, of hope, in Joanna's last sentence. She made no direct mention of herself taking over as CEO, but the implied succession was obvious.

And it struck her how unfair it was that Joanna was only getting her dues because her brother had messed up. After years of deserving it, she could only assume the position because a man had lost it.

"So unfair," she muttered.

Oliver looked at her, signifying she had muttered louder than she realized.

She shook her head so as not to distract from Joanna speaking.

"Though things are chaotic today, I want you to rest assured that we will persevere. Our public reputation may suffer as these allegations are investigated, but I personally vow to bring this company up to the standard where it belongs— above where it was before. You are all incredibly talented, and I count myself fortunate to work with you. I know you are all capable of great success individually and as a team, and I sincerely apologize for anything that has ever stood in the way of you reaching that potential." Her eyes found Lucy's and lingered for a moment. It was a public apology for all intents and purposes, and Joanna wasn't even the one who owed it.

Lucy decided to take it anyway because she honestly hoped she'd never have to see Jonathan again.

"You will be briefed tomorrow morning on the board's decision regarding our company's leadership. In the meantime, please continue cooperating with HR if a request is made of you. I trust you are in contact with your clients as necessary. Thank you." She finished with a nod and turned for her office.

Murmurs broke out like ripples, at first quietly, until they all ran into one another and filled the room with overlapping chatter.

"I hope he gets fired," Oliver said, swiveling in his chair as Lucy tried to catch Chase's eye. She owed him an apology, and she would rather give it to his face than email it.

She stepped out into the walkway to block his path as he made his way toward his office.

"Chase, I—"

But he stepped around her, brushing past and mumbling something about needing to get to Shawn's pregame press conference.

His indifference stung like a slap to the face. She regretted further investing her faith in him and snapped.

"Fine! I was going to apologize for what I said earlier, but forget it! You don't deserve it. Your silence is as good as standing with him."

He whirled around, and she realized they were standing in the exact spot they had been earlier when she told him to choke on his steak. A similar sentiment surged in her veins.

Chase, rarely one to lose his composure, suddenly flushed the deepest red Lucy had ever seen on him. He looked angry and trapped and like he wanted to hurl an insult right back at her, but people were staring, and he had places to be. He clenched his jaw and turned down the hall.

Lucy huffed a frustrated grumble and stomped her foot, mad at herself. "I don't know why I keep hoping he'll change."

Oliver snorted. "Most people will find a way to disappoint you, no matter how much you want them not to. So what's going on? Joanna sounded pretty confident up there for what went down in the lobby. Is there something she's not saying?" He eyed her with the same glinting temptation as he did when she earlier asked for his help testing her theory that she couldn't lie. He knew there was more to the story, and he knew Lucy would have to tell him if he asked.

She glared at him and nodded at her door. "Come to my office."

"Ooh, there *is* a secret," he quietly cheered behind her.

When they arrived, she shut her door and figured she could kill two birds with one stone.

She reached for her phone and saw a staggering number of messages and missed calls. After the press conference, she had put it on silent and killed the vibration so her hand wouldn't go numb. She had messages from her contacts at every publication she worked with: *Vanity Fair*, *Variety*, *Rolling Stone*, *People*, the *Los Angeles Times*, everyone asking for an update and a call. *She* was usually the one begging for their attention to get her clients in their pages, and they were absolutely bombarding her.

She bypassed all the notifications and texts to dial instead. Oliver suspiciously watched her as he made himself comfortable in her chair.

"Hello?" Annie answered sounding nervous and relived at once.

"Hi—"

"Who's that?" a deep voice cut in. "Another reporter?"

There was a shuffle like Annie put her hand over the phone. Her voice shrank away to a muffle.

"It's fine, Dad. It's Lucy from work. I want to talk to her."

"Lucy? The one who—"

"*Yes*, Dad. It's fine."

The muted muffle disappeared, and Annie came back full volume. "Sorry. I'm at my parents' house just in case someone put my address online or something. My dad is being a little overprotective."

The thought of Annie feeling the need to hide irritated Lucy. How backward that the accuser was more at risk than the accused. At least Jonathan wasn't still roosting in his office like nothing had happened.

"How are you doing?" she asked.

Annie let out a big breath. "As well as I can be, I guess. I'm getting a lot of phone calls."

"You don't have to answer any of them if you don't want to."

"I know. I answered one and started crying. Then my dad took the phone and yelled at someone from *People*." She quietly laughed.

"If it was Vince Garret, he deserved it. I've worked with that guy, and he sucks."

Annie laughed louder. "I don't know who it was, but my dad let him have it."

"Good." She paused, searching for words to express her feelings. "Annie, I'm sorry for what Jonathan said at the press conference."

A thick pause filled the line, and Lucy listened to Annie's stuttered breath. They'd known the risk, but that didn't mean it didn't hurt.

"What do you think is going to happen now?"

Oliver eyed Lucy like he was getting impatient listening to only her half of the conversation. She nodded at him, letting him know she was getting to the good part.

"Well, Joanna just briefed the company here at the office, and they've called an emergency board meeting to discuss what to do. Hopefully Joanna is going to be CEO by the end of the day."

Oliver sat straight up, and Annie sucked in a sharp breath.

"What? How? After he publicly denied everything, we've got no chance—"

"We do have a chance. Joanna kept the written offer Jonathan gave me in his office this morning when he tried to bribe me. Monica is going to run a second story this afternoon exposing the evidence and invalidating Jonathan's public denial."

A grin spread across Lucy's face, and Oliver's mouth fell open. Annie remained quiet.

"Are you sure that's going to work?" Annie asked.

A bit of wind left Lucy's sails, because in truth, she wasn't sure. She was hoping—really, *really* hard—but there was no guarantee. And the doubt in Annie's voice faltered her faith.

"It's not a slam dunk, but it's something," she offered. "If we can expose him as having lied about that, then there's doubt about all of his denial."

Another heavy silence weighed the line. Lucy had not expected gleeful cheering given what they were up against, and she couldn't blame Annie for being nervous. The optimism she had felt in Joanna's office, she realized, was mostly due to knowing she had someone in her corner. Someone willing to risk it all to stand beside her.

"You've very brave, Annie. I hope you know that, no matter what happens."

Annie sniffled. "Thanks for saying that, because I'm starting to question if this was too much."

"Most brave things involve risk, otherwise they wouldn't require bravery to do them."

She heard Annie smile. "You're very wise, Lucy."

"Well, I am older now, so." She grinned into her phone, impressed by her own enlightened words. "And speaking of being old, I wasn't calling just to be flattered. I wanted to check on you and to invite you to my birthday party tonight."

"Really?"

"Yes. I know all this seems like I did you a favor, but really, it's the other way around. I needed your help and I didn't even know it until it happened, so thank you. My party is at Perch at eight. I hope I see you there. I have to go."

She ended the call before Annie could protest or come up with some nonsense self-deprecating reason she didn't deserve to come to the party. Her invitation made her realize there was someone else she wanted to invite to her party as well, someone else who had helped her in a way she didn't even know she needed until it happened.

And that invitation would have to be delivered in person because she was still without a phone number for a particular attractive bartender she couldn't seem to stop running into.

"So, Joanna is in on all this? She's taking down her own brother?" Oliver asked, bringing Lucy back to the moment.

"She's doing her best to," Lucy said optimistically while still being aware that it could all go wrong.

"And you are . . . ?" Oliver watched her circle her desk to sit at her computer.

"I'm doing my best too."

He heaved a sigh. "Don't worry; it'll all be fine. Everything is fine."

She opened her email to draft a damage-control message to her clients, and his words rang around her head like church bells on an empty street.

Everything is fine.

Her mantra, her gospel. The thing she said to her clients and to herself ten times a day. It struck her, profoundly, in that moment that she had not said it once since waking that day.

Because nothing was fine.

"I'm not okay," she said.

Oliver snorted, busy with his phone. "Join the club."

She stood up and felt the tension of honesty she'd been fighting all day stubbornly settle into place. And she didn't resist it. "I," she started with more conviction, "am not fine. Nothing is fine right now."

For all the times she convinced herself *she* was fine, and *everything* was fine, when in fact neither were true, she was surprised her mouth could even form the words. That her brain allowed her to admit it when she'd been trained to bury discomfort and pretend everything was okay. In place of the fear she expected, the panic that would push her carefully balanced world into unrest, she felt strength in admitting the truth.

"I'm not fine," she said again. "I haven't been fine for a long time."

Whether it was her tone or her admission or something else altogether, Oliver stopped thumbing his phone and looked up at her. It was written all over his face, clear as day that this wasn't news to him, and it struck her that convincing herself she was happy was the biggest lie of them all.

She wasn't fine. And in admitting it, she felt something slide into place. A missing piece that was equal parts terrifying and gratifying.

Is this my lesson? she wondered. Was *this* what the universe had been trying to show her all day?

She'd become complacent in so many aspects of her life—

her appearance, her relationship, her job—following routine and expectation because that was easier than admitting she was unhappy. She'd tortured her body, settled for a partner she shared no real connection with, tolerated mistreatment at work, and for what? Because confronting her unhappiness meant going against the grain, maybe being alone, and standing up for herself?

To hell with that.

"I'm not fine!" she declared, and Oliver jumped. The look on her face told him not to even consider telling her to calm down. "Oliver, I get it now. All day long—all *life* long—I've been telling myself everything is fine when it's not. I'm so conditioned as a woman—brainwashed!—to keep quiet about it, to pretend that everything is okay and not make a scene, that I went along with it. I *always* go along with it, but not today! *That's* what this is about!"

And suddenly, it all made perfect sense.

"I wished for a perfect day, and this *is* a perfect day! This is the day I needed!" She gasped as the brunt of the truth hit her.

And then she laughed hysterically.

"My wish *did* come true."

Oliver stared at her with equal parts skepticism and belief. It was an odd look, but Lucy understood it since she was feeling the same way.

"Well, I don't know what genie was on the receiving end of that wish, but they've got a warped sense of humor."

Lucy laughed because it was all absurd but made so much sense at the same time.

Her perfect day.

CHAPTER

15

After a round of emails and phone calls with clients—and many ignored messages from contacts wanting a statement—Monica's follow-up article dropped, exposing the bribe. Lucy lingered online long enough to watch it blaze across social media and news outlets, leaving an angry streak of demands for justice. She didn't have the emotional bandwidth to watch the rage surge and recede as everyone with an opinion weighed in.

There goes reasonable doubt.

It's fake.

Why didn't she bring this up before?

Can she be arrested for withholding evidence?

Though expected, the comments were tiring. Instead of reading them, Lucy took Joanna's offer to take the rest of the day off.

With work as under control as it could be and her promotion pending the board meeting, she needed to get on to another arena: her love life. It had managed to completely combust and spark anew in the span of six hours—twenty, if she counted the time since she met Adam the night before.

She grabbed her bag and slipped out of the office. The short commute to Adam's bar was the precise reason she had gone there for drinks the night before. If Caleb had shown up, who knew what would have happened.

Actually, she did know. She would have lived out the exact night she anticipated, right down to listening to Caleb grind his teeth as they fell asleep, and remained resolutely yet ignorantly unhappy. But Caleb hadn't shown up, which led her to the drink and the wish and to Adam. And that, well, that felt a little bit like fate.

By some miracle, she found parking on the street in front of his bar. She took it as a sign she was following the right path and not about to do something she'd regret. She also took a moment to think about how much had changed since she entered the bar the night before. How Adam had made such an obvious observation that took her a day of cosmic intervention to recognize for herself. She was the same person but saw life—and herself—through open eyes now.

It occurred to her that Adam had seen the truth from the moment they met. He had even seen her without makeup, in weekend clothes, and in a fit of inexplicable and highly illogical-sounding distress. And yet.

He still smiled at her when she walked into the bar.

"Hey. Here for another birthday cocktail?" He flipped his rag over his shoulder, his eyes sparkled, his dimple popped; the whole works. Lucy couldn't have hidden her swoon if she tried.

"Not exactly." She glanced around at happy hour in full swing: people in suits and skirts who escaped the office early, tourists from the beach, locals wearing athleisure like badges of honor from an afternoon workout. The atmosphere was light and airy, fun, but she wanted privacy. "Can I talk to you?"

He took the hint and turned toward the end of the bar. "Sure. Give me a minute."

She stood by as he said something to the other bartender, an attractive woman with a sleeve tattoo and enormous hoop earrings. As Lucy wondered if they had some kind of history, she realized she knew nothing about Adam's relationship status. She was only guessing he was single based on how disappointed he had been when she told him she had a boyfriend earlier, how he had jumped on the opportunity to give her a ride when she needed one, and the whole kissing thing.

Her lips tingled at the memory, and she hoped her plan wasn't about to destroy any opportunity of getting to kiss him again.

He nodded toward the far end of the bar. It wasn't as private as she hoped for, but she had just shown up during happy hour rush and demanded his attention. She would take what she could get.

First order of business, she needed to know: "Do you have a girlfriend?"

His brows bounced in surprise. "Uh, not what I was expecting"—he chuckled—"but no, I don't have a girlfriend."

She eyed the woman with the sleeve tattoo and mulled his answer. She needed to cover all bases. "Wife? Fiancée? Boyfriend? Husband?"

Adam laughed like he found her amusing. "None of the above. Is this what you came here to talk about? My relationship status?"

"No!" Her face warmed. The honesty train she'd been

riding all day charged ahead, and for the first time, she felt like she was being dragged behind it. Maybe it was his eyes, or his smile, or the way he leaned on the bar with a casual and open comfort, like he wanted to hear whatever she had to say, no matter how wild it was. She took a breath. "I mean, yes. Well, kind of. Depending."

He propped himself on his hands and leaned toward her. She hadn't minded the jogging outfit one bit—in fact, it may have been her favorite thing she'd seen him wearing, but the button-down with rolled sleeves he'd swapped it for was only working in his favor. "Depending on what?"

His gaze unnerved her, and she realized it was because she wanted a certain outcome very much, and she wasn't sure if her honest tongue was going to get her there. "Depending on how this conversation goes."

She saw a spark in his eye and hoped that he too wanted a certain outcome.

"Well, you've certainly got me intrigued, birthday girl Lucy Green. I am ready to talk."

"Good. But, um, well, I guess I need you to listen first." She had one hand on the train now, still running to keep up, but moving forward.

He bowed his head. "The floor is yours."

Why is he so nice? she wondered, and realized that if she was going to pour her heart out to a near stranger, she'd prefer it be a nice stranger.

But then, they weren't really strangers anymore. The universe had made sure of that.

She took a breath.

"Okay. I made a wish that today would be perfect, and it came true, but not in the way I expected. Being unable to lie *is* my perfect day. You were right about this honesty problem actually being a solution. Telling the truth all day has made me realize that I lie a lot, mostly to myself. Last night when you told me I was unhappy, you were right about that too, I just didn't know it. But today has shown me in dozens of ways. By being honest, I've completely blown up my personal and professional lives, but both were for the better."

She paused, and he didn't interject. He also didn't run away, so she kept going.

"And then there's you. I'm sure you've noticed we seem to keep running into each other. I think you might also be right about this being a twenty-four-hour thing, so I'm here in case the honesty mandate expires, because I don't know if I'll have the guts to do this otherwise."

He looked at her with the same intrigued wonder that he had before. As if he might be on the verge of laughing but desperately wanted to hear what she had to say at the same time.

She threw her faith in the power of her perfect-day wish, which had landed her standing in front of him once again, and spilled her heart.

"Today has been the strangest day of my life, but meeting you has been the best part. Even if I wasn't being forced to be honest, I'd still want you to know that I just got out of a two-year relationship about four hours ago. I thought we were going to get married, but he was on a completely different page, and it made me realize the five-year plan I was living by was a lie—my own lie. I'm not ready to settle down and have kids and all the trappings of the life society tells women my age they're supposed to want and have. Maybe someday, but not today. And all of that made me realize how much I've lost sight of what *I* want in a relationship. What I *really* want; not what is convenient or expected. Women are taught to put themselves second, to be the caregiver and bear the emotional labor with no complaint. And that's not fair."

She was fired up, now fully on board the train with no stops in sight.

"It's like I'm not allowed to express what I want because that would make me *needy* or *demanding*, and I'm sick of the degrading language used to describe women when all we're doing is standing up for ourselves. I want flowers for no reason, not because you're sorry or it's an occasion, spontaneous backrubs, weekends in bed, emotional availability. I want to be kissed in the rain, great sex—no, *amazing* sex. I want you to remember my mom's birthday without me telling you, to make dinner when I'm too tired. I want you to listen to my problems without trying to solve them all. I don't want you to read my mind; I want you to ask me what's on my mind and care when I tell you. I want to know what's on *your* mind. I want to make up as fiercely as we fight. I want to not be afraid of making mistakes because I know you'll be there to help me fix them. I don't want to take what's between us for granted, but to treat it like it's alive and needs tending. And I want a partner who wants all that too."

She inhaled deeply after her long list and realized she didn't even know she wanted most of those things. She also realized that somewhere along the line, she slipped into using *you* and *we*, and by some miracle, Adam didn't look horrified.

She decided to quit while she was ahead.

"I don't know if this will frighten you or welcome you, but it's the truth, so I'm telling you. I really like you. And you've already seen more of me in one day than I showed the guy I thought I was going to marry in two years." She dug in her tote for a pen and snatched a napkin off the bar. "This is my phone number," she said, and scribbled it next to the time and place of her party. "I know it's only been a day, and if I haven't completely scared you away, I'd love it if you came to my birthday party tonight." She slid the napkin across the bar, hoping he didn't wad it up and throw it away.

He gave no indication that he was going to, but she didn't stick around long enough to give him the opportunity to do it in front of her.

She shot him a quick smile, feeling more vulnerable and exposed than she had all day, and turned on her heel. In her mind, he followed her, pulled her into his arms, and kissed her in front of everyone like in the last scene of a movie. But she knew she'd given him an emotional buffet to digest—a literal list of demands after knowing him for under twenty-four hours—so he needed time. And he knew how to reach her and where to find her.

She stepped back into the afternoon sunlight and took a deep breath of Westside air.

What have I just done? she wondered as she climbed back into her car. Was that level of honesty a crime in the dating world? She was probably never going to see him again. Her napkin was probably already in the trash under a gutted lemon rind.

But at least she knew what she wanted. Maybe everyone should be that straightforward from the start when it came to dating, she thought. That would at least spare everyone the stress of pretending in order to get the other person to like them. And if you didn't like what you saw, move along. She could get women to rally behind her cause, she was sure. But convincing the rest of the population to discuss such details before the first date would not go over well, she knew.

It was a good thing she wasn't personally responsible for revolutionizing modern dating.

She slumped into the driver's seat and felt the weight of the afternoon. She'd run around L.A. putting out and starting fires; yelling at and forming friendships with celebrities. She'd exposed a major scandal and hung her heart on the line. It felt like more work than she'd done in the past year combined. She would never make it through her own party without a serious recharge beforehand. All she wanted was to go home and sink into a hot bath until she pruned.

Lucy's apartment looked the same as it had when she left that morning, but everything had changed. She entered the small space feeling like a new person. Maybe not entirely new, but much more in tune and aware. She set her bag on the dining table and considered what to do with Caleb's apology flowers. She didn't want them, but throwing them away felt like a waste. She decided to walk them down to the mail room for everyone in the complex to enjoy.

When she returned, she looked around at all the moving boxes that would need to be emptied and decided to save it for another day. She slipped off her flats and passed into her bedroom. There, she swapped her dress for her bathrobe and noted the absence of relief she normally felt when removing her uncomfortable undergarments because the undergarments she was wearing were in fact comfortable for once.

She plugged her phone in to charge on her nightstand then

entered the bathroom where she quickly showered to wash the day from her hair. She then filled the tub for a bath, and for good measure, she dropped a lavender bath bomb in the water and left the room to steam. She made her way into her small kitchen to collect a glass of wine.

Her vision for pre-party prep had involved happy hour drinks and redoing her hair and makeup to some peppy soundtrack with a play-by-play for her Instagram Story. But maybe, she realized, that was how someone in her twenties prepared for a night out. Now that she had turned the page into her thirties, she wanted nothing more than to slip into a hot bath with a glass of wine and be alone for a few hours.

She laughed to herself that perhaps the bath and the wine and the candles she would surely light were signs she was in fact gracefully ascending into the next decade as she set out to do that morning, and she had to admit, she didn't mind the shift.

She returned to a room swirling with steam and the smell of lavender. When she slipped into the water, her skin tingled and she instantly relaxed.

What a day.

And it wasn't over. The scandal was still unfolding; she didn't know what would become of her promotion; she'd yelled at her mother twice, which was sure to have consequences. And then there was Adam.

She could not convince herself the investment was minimal and that if she never saw him again it would be no great loss. She wanted to see him again. She had wanted to see him again from the moment he made her that drink—she just hadn't admitted it to herself. She had always believed someone like Caleb was her type: reserved, practical. She never saw herself with

a motorcycle-riding, kiss-her-in-public-after-a-day charmer like
Adam. But maybe she had never seen it because she hadn't allowed herself to look.

What power the truth holds, she thought as she slipped her
ears below the waterline. One day. Just one day of telling only
the truth, and so much had changed. She listened to her heart
beat a slow *wha-whomp* under the hot pool like it was saying *I
told you so*. So much had been held back or held in place just
because she was dishonest: With others, with the world. With
herself.

Change was never easy, but her day of honesty set things in
motion that had needed to move for a long, *long* time.

She took quiet inventory of her to-do list for the day as she
stared at the ceiling.

1. Lock down Lily Chu.
2. Secure promotion.
3. Gracefully ascend into the divine decade of her thirties.
4. Have one hell of a birthday bash on a rooftop in
    downtown L.A. where her boyfriend would finally
    propose to her.

She'd signed Lily Chu with everything but the actual signature, which, pending whatever happened with the rest of the
list, was a huge deal. She couldn't say much about securing her
promotion other than she knew that Joanna was fighting for
her. And despite the layers upon layers of drama and sometimes
getting burned by the fires she was constantly putting out, she
loved her job. Her big day of honesty had assured her of that.
She had done nothing remotely resembling graceful all day

other than indulging in her hot bath, but that wasn't too surprising, all things considered. Perhaps the biggest change, and
maybe the most unexpected, was that she was single. But the
fact that marriage hadn't been the first item on her list told her
where it ranked in her priorities. Granted, she'd made that list
in chronological order of her day, but even if it was out of order,
she wouldn't have put her relationship above her career, and
that told her everything she needed to know about her decision
to end things with Caleb.

She marveled at how she started the day with such high as-
pirations, a clear path, and by late afternoon, so much of it had
diverged.

The truth had changed her life.

She finished her bath, relaxed and pruned like she hoped,
and curled on her bed in her bathrobe. As a gift to herself, she
switched her phone to silent and closed her eyes.

When she woke in her dark bedroom refreshed but disori-
ented, she realized she had an hour to make it to her party.

She grabbed her phone with that just-woke-up panicky urge
of needing to know if she received any messages while she
slept and saw she had indeed missed many messages, but one
stuck out.

Chase McMillan had texted her two minutes earlier.

I want to be on the right side, his message said above a link to
the Lakers' Twitter account.

Intrigued, Lucy clicked the link and watched her app load a
live video of a long table with a microphone and a backdrop
behind it dotted in NBA logos like a monogrammed handbag.
Shawn Stevens sat at the table, his massive shoulders hunched
forward as he leaned toward the microphone. Off-screen

cameras clicked and flashed, punctuating the dull murmur of questions coming from the crowd and Shawn's deep baritone responses.

Lucy frowned, having no idea why Chase sent her a link to the pregame press conference.

She watched Shawn give a few answers that could use some polish, in her professional opinion, but he was a rookie and still learning how to present himself publicly. When he took his final question, Lucy was about to text Chase, Why am I watching this?, but something at the corner of the screen caught her eye.

Shawn stood, unfolding himself from the chair, and out of nowhere, Chase came rushing into the shot, still wearing his suit from the office and flushed in the face.

Lucy almost dropped her phone.

Shawn backed up out of the way, not having much room to move with the monogrammed wall right behind him, and Chase dove on the microphone.

"Wait! Wait just one more second; I have something to add," Chase blurted. His tie swung forward, and he gripped the little microphone stand tightly enough to turn his hands white. His face flushed all over again, as if he suddenly realized he had an audience staring at him.

Lucy wondered if she was still asleep and it was all a dream.

"Hi," Chase went on. "I'm probably going to get fired over this, but I don't know how else I'll get a platform this big. My name is Chase McMillan, and I work at J&J Public. I want to go on record and say the allegations against CEO Jonathan Jenkins that came out today are all true, and I fully support the women coming forward. I should have spoken up much earlier, and I'm truly sorry if my silence has hurt anyone. You all deserve better." He paused and stared out at what had to be a room full of shocked, gaping faces. "That's, um . . . That's what I wanted to say. Thanks."

He gave the camera one last horrified look and dashed off-screen.

Shawn still stood behind the chair, hands raised like he might get run over for being in the way. "Gotta love live TV," he said with a chuckle.

A few more cameras clicked, reporters murmured in confusion, and then the screen cut to a silent image of the Lakers logo with *Please stand by* scrawled across the bottom.

A full, sincere laugh burst from Lucy's lips. She wasn't sure it was an appropriate reaction, but it was an honest one.

Did he really just do that?

Warmth filled her chest as she thought of what Joanna said about Chase needing time to catch up and maybe surprising her. And what a personal risk he had taken. She smiled as she pulled up his number to call him, realizing he *would* pull a stunt as outlandish as stealing the microphone on live TV. He was always needing to one-up her in some way, and this time, she didn't mind.

"Hey," he said when he answered, clearly out of breath from running. He must not have stopped once he dropped the microphone.

"You're insane. You're not running from the cops or anything, are you?"

"No, but I am in a dark hallway somewhere under the Staples Center right now, so if you never hear from me again, send a search party."

"Oh my god, Chase." Lucy laughed, still unable to believe what she'd just seen.

He laughed back, and it sounded like the guy she had been friendly with years before. "I ran through the first door I saw and kept going."

"Shawn knew that was coming, right?"

His footsteps echoed off the concrete tunnels Lucy had visited herself. He could definitely get lost down there. "Of course he did. What kind of publicist do you think I am?"

She smiled, despite all her anger from earlier in the day. "One on the right side of things. Finally."

She heard the smile in his voice. "I was hoping you'd say that. Sorry about earlier. I was a dick. I should have stood up for you."

An apology from Chase McMillan. A real one. If she hadn't had such an unbelievable day already, she wouldn't have believed it.

"It's not only me, Chase. What you did will make a difference for a lot of people. Thank you."

His footsteps and labored breathing filled another few seconds, and Lucy found her gratitude getting the best of her.

"Do you want to come to my birthday party tonight? I mean, I know you have courtside tickets, but you probably—"

"Yeah, I definitely shouldn't stick around here after that," he finished for her. And then, "Yeah, sure, that would be great."

"Great. Perch at eight," she said, repeating the same invitation she'd been extending all day.

Chase laughed again, the end pinching up into honest concern. "I'll be there if I can find my way out of here by then."

Lucy dropped her phone in her lap, still bouncing with laughter.

Chase McMillan: *not* a supervillain after all.

She rose from her bed, damp hair still smushed in her towel

wrap, and walked to her bathroom mirror. She let her hair down and stared at her reflection.

It may have been a trick of lighting, or some self-fulfilling conviction, but she swore she looked wiser. Wise enough to know that she didn't need to plaster her face in makeup or stuff herself into the dress and heels she had planned to wear to her party. She would go low-maintenance and classy, and it would be perfect.

Lucy Green stood on a precipice.

Really, she waited at the rooftop bar of her favorite restaurant, sipping a crisp chardonnay and wondering who was going to show up to her birthday party after her big day of honesty. The hostess told her no one else had arrived when she claimed her reservation. Nonetheless, she led Lucy to her banquet table dressed in sparkling stemware stretched between squat palms and serving stunning views of downtown L.A. from the very heart of it. Instead of announcing her solitude by sitting alone at the table, she decided to wait at the bar.

It was, technically, early yet; her phone showed 7:58 p.m. And how desperate to show up early to her own party, but thanks to her low-maintenance look, she hadn't needed that full hour to get ready. She'd blow dried her hair into soft waves and put on a pink party dress that didn't restrict or dig or require assistance to zip. Her feet were comfortable in slides with festive bows on their toes.

As she waited at the bar, taking tiny sips of wine, she checked in on the media circus she had helped create. Thanks to Chase's stunt, the internet had gone wild. J&J Public had single-handedly created a scandal worthy of reality TV. The *Deadline* story breaking the allegations, the press conference denying the allegations, the second *Deadline* story confirming the allegations, and then Chase reconfirming the allegations in front of a few million NBA fans made for quite the spectacle. Thankfully, the masses were capable of keeping score, and it was currently three to one, Team Lucy and Annie. Though not fully defeated—yet—Jonathan was losing by all public accounts. The reluctant criticism and benefit of the doubt from earlier in the day turned sharply into accusations of certainty and demands for justice. Twitter was one trending hashtag away from torches and pitchforks. But public opinion only counted for so much. The final score would be tallied by Joanna and the board members, and the thought of their meeting that was perhaps still ongoing made Lucy take bigger sips of wine.

She had not deliberately tried to tell a lie all afternoon, and as the hour approached what she was sure would be the midnight expiration of her wish, she wondered if she even wanted her capacity for dishonesty restored.

But honesty had always been a choice. She had the power to do and say what she wanted and needed all along; she was just led to believe by personal, professional, and profound social expectation that she did not. Perhaps the day's greatest gift was simply awareness of the choice.

Nonetheless, having an actual wish come true was positively the strangest thing that had ever happened to her. Though her inability to lie was bizarre and at times frightening, she survived and came out better for the experience on the other side. And she had only described the insanity to three people, two of whom would bury a body for her and didn't care if she sounded crazy, and the third had the most enlightened understanding of them all. Whatever source had sought to teach her a lesson had succeeded, and she was content to say thank you and carry on.

She checked her phone again to see that it was eight p.m. sharp. She scanned the rooftop and felt her heart swell when she saw two familiar faces. The body buriers themselves: Oliver and Nina. She had known they would come, but still, she couldn't stop her relief from spilling over.

Oliver looked sharp in a suit jacket, though a little peaky from scandal aftershocks. He had probably come straight from the office. He carried a bottle of champagne with a garish pink ribbon tied at the neck and gave Lucy a warm but tired smile.

Nina carried a gift bag spurting with tissue. She wore a short black dress and flats because anything suggesting a heel put her over six feet tall, and being a woman at that altitude presented a host of challenges Lucy could not relate to. She had heard Nina speak of shrinking herself in public spaces and feeling gigantic in dressing rooms and bathroom stalls and wishing she could wear the cute heels Lucy sometimes abhorred without intimidating everyone within a mile radius. Lucy was used to seeing her friend in flats when they went out, but the injustices of female footwear had never felt so apparent. She considered offering to go buy Nina some heels, or maybe suggesting they both pitch their shoes off the roof and go barefoot to make a statement.

Instead, she greeted her friends with a welcoming smile. "You made it."

Nina gave her a fragrant hug, and Oliver air-kissed her

cheek. "Of course. And before you ask, I don't know anything about the board meeting. Joanna told me I could go home, and they were all still at the office when I left. Why do you sound surprised we're here?"

She absorbed the board meeting comment with another sip of wine. A big one. "Honestly? I thought I may have scared everyone away today with all the truth-telling."

Oliver tugged at her lacey cap sleeve. "Well, you did try to convince me you were cursed, and when that didn't send me running, I came to the rescue when you got pooped on by a bird and fell in a fountain."

"I didn't get pooped on." She glared at him, but as she said it, she realized she could not say without a doubt that there was no bird poop involved in the fountain incident. Given the rest of the day, it suddenly felt plausible, and she was thankful she had washed her hair twice before the party.

Nina laughed, warm and sincere. "Yes, I heard about that. And if anyone should be ghosting out of embarrassment, it should be me over the whole bloody-nose incident. *Sorry*," she sang like the word had ten *Y*s and held out the gift bag.

Lucy took it, feeling something solid and heavy inside.

"What we're saying," Oliver said, "is *of course* we're here. We love you, Lucy. Even if you go temporarily insane on us."

"Hey, insane or not, you witnessed it yourself, so . . ." She smiled.

"Well, then I guess we're all crazy." He shrugged with a laugh. "But really, I'm happy you learned a lot today, even if the source of the lesson is questionable."

Nina nodded. "Me too. I'm glad you finally realized what we've been telling you for ages."

Lucy was so caught up in the warmth of unconditional friendship and their praise, it took her a second to realize what Nina had said. "Wait, what?"

They both gave her flat stares but at least had the decency not to roll their eyes.

"Lucy, you've been settling for Caleb all along, and everyone knows you deserve better treatment at work. Not news to us," Nina said.

Lucy gaped at them. "Why didn't you say anything about it?"

Oliver and Nina exchanged a look and matching arched brows.

"I told her," Oliver said. "Did you tell her?"

"Oh, I definitely told her."

"You just weren't listening," Oliver scolded, and poked her arm. "Lucy, you haven't been fine for a long time, and we've done our best to help you see that, but maybe you weren't ready."

She stared at the two people in front of her, profoundly thankful and humbled to have friends who cared about her like they did. What cosmic intervention put them in her life? What did she do to deserve their faith?

Perhaps those were questions that did not need answers, but rather gratitude and a vow to carry on.

"I'm listening now," she promised them.

"Good," Oliver said approvingly. "I'm going to go check out the food situation." He headed toward the table. Nina lingered with a hint of concern in her eyes. Other than a few text messages, they hadn't had the chance to talk during the day.

"You sure you're okay?"

Lucy released a big sigh, thinking she'd rather rehash it all with Nina over brunch that weekend instead of at her birthday party that night. "It's been a day but yeah, I'm good."

"Good." Nina cast a glance over her shoulder. "And Caleb's not coming, right?"

"Definitely not."

"Great. We can totally talk about it if you want to, or we can pretend it didn't happen. Or we can get drunk and do both or neither."

A swell of gratitude lifted Lucy's heart, and she threw her arms around her. Nina stiffened, caught off guard by the sudden burst of affection. Lucy surprised herself, not normally one to pass out hugs until she was a few drinks deep. But she realized as she embraced her friend that the usual reservation was only another form of dishonesty. "Thanks, Nina."

Nina softened into a warm squeeze and patted her back. "Of course."

From over her shoulder, Lucy spotted the arrival of someone she never thought she'd ever invite to her birthday party, yet there he was.

Chase McMillan entered in the same suit he'd been wearing all day, his tie a little loosened now, and Lucy wondered if he came straight from running around under the Staples Center.

Nina noticed Lucy looking over her shoulder and turned to see Chase. "Isn't that the guy you hate?"

Based on her reaction, Lucy knew Nina hadn't seen the news. She came from a shift at the hospital where she probably hadn't even looked up all day. She was none the wiser about Chase's eleventh-hour redemption.

"Yes, but not anymore. We're kind of friends now. Long story for later," she rushed out before blurting, "Chase! Hi. I'm glad to see you made it out of that basement."

"It was looking dicey for a minute, but yeah. Hey, I'm Chase." He greeted Nina with a nod and a handshake.

Nina did her best not to eye him too suspiciously while shaking his hand and gauging if Lucy somehow invited him by accident and needed her to bail her out.

"This is Chase, my colleague," Lucy said to reassure her. "And this is Nina, one of my best friends."

"Nice to meet you," Nina said, loosening her defensive stance and nodding toward the table. She took the gift bag from Lucy. "I'm going to grab some champagne. I'll see you later."

They watched her walk away, and Chase laughed. "Does she not watch the news? Does she not know who I am?"

He made a fair point; his press conference video had gone viral. It had a million views already.

But Nina, rarely one to indulge in celebrity gossip—thank god, because Lucy needed a break once in a while—was not one of them. She used her Instagram to post pictures of food and books she enjoyed and the occasional sunset. She never touched Twitter. In fact, if Nina *had* heard the news, Lucy would have been shocked.

"Contrary to what you think, the world does not revolve around our jobs, Chase."

"Sure it does." He grinned.

She rolled her eyes.

"So," he said. "Any news on this board meeting?"

Lucy leaned back on the bar. "Not yet. Did you get in trouble for the press conference?"

He flagged the bartender down with a friendly wave. "I might owe the Lakers a fine, but I at least made it out of there without getting tackled by security."

She laughed. "I still can't believe you did that. But thank you. I know it was a big risk."

He causally shrugged and ordered a glass of wine. "Sometimes the right thing is risky."

Lucy tipped her glass to him in total agreement. "What about Shawn Stevens?"

The bartender returned with his order. Chase lifted his glass, holding the red wine in his palm, and smiled at her. "Still got Shawn. And it looks like you've still got Lily, unless some other movie star just walked in." He nodded over her shoulder, and Lucy whipped around.

Lily's outfit more resembled what she wore to lunch than her apocalypse warrior costume. Lucy wouldn't have protested if she came in with swords strapped to her back, though building security may have had an opinion, but her burgundy draped dress instead made her look like a Grecian goddess. Lucy wilted for the slightest second over the fact she'd invited such a beautiful person to her party, but then she remembered the thought was a waste of energy and was happy she was there at all.

"Cheers," Chase said, and clinked his glass against hers. He left to join the others at the table as Lily approached.

Other rooftop patrons pretended not to look, since acknowledging the presence of a celebrity in the wild was unbecoming of a local. That was something only tourists and people from San Diego did. Los Angelenos were forbidden to break the facade that they too were part of the glamour. Lily wasn't alone but with another young woman. The pair of them surely got carded in the building lobby and wouldn't have been on the rooftop if they hadn't passed.

"Lucy!" Lily greeted, cheerful and bright. She paid no attention to the fact that half the people on the roof were staring at her. "This is my sister, Jessie. I hope it's okay I brought her."

Same as the comment about filming not starting without her, Lucy bit her tongue so as not to tell Lily Chu she didn't need permission to do anything, including invite plus ones to birthday parties.

"Hi, Jessie. Nice to meet you."

Her handshake was soft and gentle, and Lucy sensed a quiet curiosity in her. Where her sister emanated charisma, Jessie seemed one to hang back and observe. She looked a little struck by the rooftop setting.

Oliver swanned back over, bubbling champagne flute in each hand. Lucy was almost certain he visited the bar and intended the drinks for the two of them, but smooth as if on purpose, he handed them off to Lily and her sister.

"Welcome, Lily. You are in fabulous hands with Lucy. Please do enjoy yourself tonight," he said with the air of a benevolent host.

"Thanks!" Lily chirped, glass in hand, and guided her sister toward the table.

Oliver turned to Lucy, eyes wide. "Did I just serve alcohol to a minor?"

"No."

"Whew!" he said with a playful sweep of his brow. So, it appears that you and Chase made some kind of peace treaty after his little sportsball stunt? I assume that's why he's here."

Lucy sipped the last of her wine, wishing it were bubbles. "Yes, turns out he's not so bad after all."

He narrowed his eyes. "Either your ability to lie is back online or you are having some kind of psychotic break after all. I thought we were Team I Hate Chase McMillan?"

Lucy shrugged. "People can change."

He snorted, though she knew his loyalty would shift in whichever direction she pointed it. "Okay then. Just send me a memo next time so I'm not shocked when the sworn enemy shows up at your birthday party. Speaking of work, Boss Lady coming at you."

Her jolly, buoyant heart suddenly seized. Joanna had actually shown up, and she surely had news from the board meeting, which meant Lucy was poised to learn the fate of her promotion and what happened to Jonathan right then and there at her birthday party.

"Did you invite her?" Oliver asked.

"Yes. And now that she's here, I'm second-guessing."

"It's a little late for that. Order another drink; you'll be fine." He nudged her elbow and floated off toward the table.

CHAPTER
17

Lucy summoned all her professional training as Joanna approached. "Joanna!" she said, bright and pleasant, but even she could hear the nerves riddling her voice.

Despite looking even more exhausted than when Lucy left her at her desk sipping pilfered scotch, a coy smile played at Joanna's lips. She still wore what she wore to work, and Lucy wondered if she was the only one who hadn't come straight from the office.

"Hi, Lucy. Happy birthday."

The stage was set the last time they spoke, and the elephant that stood between them couldn't have been more obvious than Chase staring at them from across the roof. Lucy knew Joanna didn't come to her party just to hang out; she had to have news about the board meeting.

"So?" Lucy asked, her breath tight and shallow.

Joanna leaned into the bar and asked for a martini, dirty. Lucy couldn't stand the suspense. Luckily, Joanna didn't make her wait any longer.

"So, effective immediately, you are speaking to the CEO of J&J Public."

Overcome with relief, Lucy almost doubled over. She couldn't contain her gasp. She slapped her hands over her mouth and felt tears prick her eyes. "*Really?* Oh, Joanna, I am thrilled for you!" She squeezed her own arms in a hug so she didn't throw herself at her boss—her *CEO*.

"Thank you." Joanna beamed, giggling a little, and Lucy had never admired her more. Her voice then slipped back into collected boss-mode. "In light of current events and with major pending contracts on the line, the board was unanimous in their decision in reappointing leadership."

The relief washing over Lucy, the justice, the respect and dues finally paid, was like pure sunshine.

"Joanna, I can't even . . . This is such great news! Congratulations."

The bartender returned with her martini, three olives pierced with a skewer and carefully balanced on top. Joanna lifted the little sword and ate an olive. She then took a healthy sip of her drink and smiled. "So much better than that bottle in Jonathan's office. And thank you; both for the congratulations and for your bravery in setting this all in motion."

"Well, it wasn't just me, but you're welcome. What's going to happen to Jonathan?" Lucy realized that just because he was no longer CEO didn't mean he was gone.

Joanna took another healthy sip. "The board agreed it's best for the company to sever ties with him."

Another wave of relief hit Lucy. He *was* gone. Never again would she have to go to work worried and wondering if it was the day he fully crossed the line. She was free.

"And for the record," Joanna said, "what you told me about

him in my office today, that was the first time I heard it confirmed, but I've had suspicions for some time now. You were right: he was destroying the company. I let it happen for too long, and that's something I'll have to sort out on my own time, but meanwhile, I'm hoping you are still willing to take on more responsibility."

Lucy's heart leapt. *More responsibility.* That could only mean . . .

"There will be some restructuring within the company. As CEO, I am promoting you to senior publicist. You've shown yourself more than capable today, and long before. I'd like to see you in the position for a few years before perhaps moving you to lead a division, if you're up for it."

Lucy's jaw did not drop; she knew how well-deserved the promotion was. On another day, she may have deflected the praise, somehow downplayed that she earned it, but on her perfect day, she stood up straight and proudly smiled. "I am absolutely up for it."

"Fantastic."

And then she squealed and did a little dance because even if she knew she deserved it, that didn't mean she couldn't celebrate.

Joanna laughed. "Congratulations, Lucy."

"Thank you! I'm so excited."

"Me too." Joanna turned her gaze toward the table where the other guests laughed and mingled. Chase was visibly failing at pretending he wasn't trying to read their lips from afar. "I'm happy to see that I was right about that." She nodded toward him.

Of course she knew about the press conference—it probably weighed into the board's decision, having another public allegation against Jonathan like that. And she was the one who told Lucy to keep her faith in Chase. The fact that he was at Lucy's birthday party could only mean they'd overcome their feud.

"I'm glad you were right too. Chase is actually great. I really value him as a colleague."

She wondered at how mature she sounded and silently laughed at how insane she would have found that statement just twenty-four hours earlier.

Joanna cast her a surprised look but didn't argue. "Well, that's good, because after today's events—that basketball press conference stunt was rather bold but speaks volumes to his integrity—I've decided to promote him to senior publicist too."

Lucy couldn't bite back her smile. Never did she think they would *both* get what they deserved in one fell swoop. She gave Chase a discreet nod, doing her best to put him out of his misery, as he was clearly dying to know what they were discussing. She could see a sheen of sweat on his brow from across the rooftop. "I think that is an excellent decision."

"Well," Joanna said, smiling warmly, "then perhaps I'll go tell him."

She left her at the bar, and by the time Lucy turned around and ordered a cosmo because she wanted something ridiculous to celebrate, she saw yet another familiar face enter the rooftop.

She felt like she was trapped in a bad movie where each next guest kept her pinned to the bar, coming to deliver their message like a Ghost of Birthday Present, and she'd never make it to the table now full of appetizers. She saw sliders and skewers and fancy little cheese platters. She was hungry, and the food was sitting right there, taunting her, but Leo Ash was approaching like sex on a stick in ripped skinny jeans, a deep V-neck tee, sunglasses even though it was dark, and a mop of tousled hair that probably hadn't been washed in days. He wore silver rings on all his fingers, chipped black nail polish, and leather boots with a short heel that screamed rock n' roll. He really had no business looking so attractive dressed like a total slob. And yet.

"Leo!" Lucy blurted. "What are you doing here?"

Despite inviting him, she hadn't expected him to show up, not in a million years.

He whipped off his sunglasses and glanced over his shoulder like he might expect the crowd to mob him—which was a completely fair concern. But they played it cool. Another celebrity; no big deal. Lucy caught Oliver's dramatic gape, his splayed palm to chest as if he just couldn't believe his eyes. She casually shrugged and hoped Leo wasn't about to make a huge scene.

"Happy birthday, Luce," he said, and kissed her cheek. He smelled of cigarettes and musky cologne, and she was not surprised at all when he rapped on the bar and ordered a double Johnnie Walker. "You doing okay? You seemed a little . . . stressed when you called earlier."

With everything else that had happened that afternoon, yelling at Leo on the phone felt like an age ago. The memory brought heat to her cheeks. "About that. I'm sorry—"

He shook his head. "No need to apologize. You're right: I'm a total ass. And instead of being an ass, I've decided to do something." He patted his jeans pockets, searching. When he came up empty, he reached into the breast pocket on his V-neck and pulled out a folded piece of paper.

"What's this?" Lucy asked when he handed it to her. She almost dropped it.

A check for one hundred thousand dollars, made out to Lucy Green.

"It's money."

Her hands started sweating, leaving tiny prints on the paper marked with Leo's famous signature. She'd never held so much money in her hands, check or otherwise. "Y-yes, I see that. But . . . why?"

The bartender brought his drink, and Leo swallowed it in a single gulp that would have sent Lucy to the floor retching. He breathed out a flammable breath and grinned at her like a three-year-old proud of a finger painting. "Because you told me to do something, so I'm doing something."

"Yes, but how is handing me a check for a hundred grand doing something?" She used her patient Leo tone, the one she'd honed over years of managing his chaos.

She realized in that moment that she might in fact make a great mother someday because she had been mothering Leo Ash for years.

She sipped her cosmo because she couldn't decide how she felt about that fact.

Leo cupped her face in his big, calloused, guitar-playing hands. His whisky breath burned her nose. "Because, dearest Lucy, you told me to donate to a worthy cause, and I figure *you* know much more about those than I do. I trust your judgment. Use the money as you see fit."

She frowned, her face squished between his hands. "So, you're passing this task to me."

He shrugged and dropped his grip. "At least it's a step in the right direction."

She couldn't fault him that. She looked at the check again and briefly thought of all the immoral things she could do with a hundred grand: buy a boat, take an obscenely luxurious vacation, take a year off from work and backpack through South

America. But she knew the money wasn't for her. She'd do her research and figure out where it could be put to the best use.

Leo leaned sideways on the bar, pushing out his chest and chewing a plastic straw. "Make sure you donate it in your name too; it's my birthday present to you." He waggled his fingers at the check like it was of little significance. In truth, it *was* chump change to him. A fraction of the profit he hauled in off his last show at the Forum.

But Lucy's annoyance with him melted away as she realized he'd buried the lede, probably not on purpose. He wasn't giving her homework; he was giving her money to give to whomever she wanted. And having become a multimillionaire as a teenager, his grasp on financial reality was loose. It was on-brand for him to hand her a hundred-thousand-dollar check not even in an envelope. She was surprised he didn't show up with a bag of cash. "Leo, that's . . . Wow. Thank you."

He casually shrugged and pinched the straw from his mouth. "So, what's up with the firm? Did that fucker Jonathan get fired?"

She blushed at the coarse reference, though she herself had had the same thought many times. "Yes. Joanna is taking over as CEO, and I'm being promoted to senior publicist."

"Badass."

"I know."

He turned serious for a second. "Lucy, I just want to say that we both know you are the best thing that's ever happened to me, and no one else in this town will put up with my shit. You are a saint, and I'd be lost without you. You deserve better than whatever that prick did to you, and I vow to do my part in making your job easier."

She tipped her glass toward him with a smile. "I will gladly accept that vow."

He knocked his knuckles on the bar again, and the bartender materialized another double before Lucy blinked twice. Leo downed it in a gulp as his phone rang from his back pocket. He held up a finger and winked at her, sliding down the bar to take the call.

He left her with a hundred thousand dollars burning a hole in her hand. Her dress, like 99 percent of the ones she owned, didn't have pockets, so she had nowhere to put it. She took a step toward the table and the appetizers watering her mouth from fifteen feet away when yet another person appeared on the rooftop.

Annie approached like a timid deer. Her look was as sensible as Lucy's: a breezy cocktail dress, wedges, and a fishtail braid. It was the first time Lucy had seen her since that morning without the threat of tears in her eyes.

"You made it."

"Yes, well, I figured I could use a night out before anyone *really* knows who I am. My parents weren't too happy about letting me leave the house. God, I feel like I'm in high school again." She weakly smiled, and Lucy was glad to see her.

"What'll you have to drink?"

Annie looked at the pink cocktail swirling in Lucy's hand. "One of those would be nice."

Lucy waved at the bartender and pointed to her drink. She noticed Annie nervously look over at the party table gradually filling with her coworkers. "*Joanna*," she whispered under her breath, as if she was afraid.

"Will be happy you are here," Lucy assured her. "She's officially CEO now. Jonathan is out, and the company is finally in the right hands. Speaking of which, I've been promoted to senior publicist and I will need an assistant."

Annie blinked the big brown eyes she'd been staring at Lucy with all day. Her eager innocence was still there, but the past ten hours had seasoned her. Her lips pulled into a coy grin. "Well, I happen to be in the market for a new boss. Mine recently got fired."

"Is that so? How convenient."

"Sure is."

The bartender delivered her drink, and she lifted it to clink glasses with Lucy. They sipped and silently sealed the deal.

The pivotal role she played in progressing change was not lost on Lucy. In offering her a job, she provided Annie the very support she herself feared being denied should she ever speak up. Annie leaped, and Lucy caught her. And Lucy leaped, and Joanna caught *her*. Not to mention all the other open arms that offered support—Chase, Amanda, Oliver, Leo. For the first time, Lucy felt a swell of hope for the future.

Before she could continue celebrating, she needed to do something with Leo's check. Short on options, and no stranger to undergarment trickery, she whipped around to face the bar and discreetly stuffed it in her bra in a fluid motion that no one even noticed. She turned back just in time to see Jonathan Jenkins charging at her and Annie like a wild boar.

Lucy gasped, and Annie's cosmo slipped from her hand. If the shattering glass didn't turn heads, the fury flying from Jonathan's mouth did.

"Is this a goddamned *party?*" he roared, nearly shoving the poor hostess out of the way. He scanned the rooftop with the humiliated indignation of a guest discovering he'd been left off the invite list. He zeroed in on Lucy and Annie, as they were closest in his path. "*You,*" he seethed. "You've been in this together from the start, and now I'm *ruined!*"

Annie sealed herself to Lucy's side, or maybe Lucy moved first, she wasn't sure. Either way, they stood together like a tower in an earthquake as Jonathan stomped toward them, accusatory finger pointed. Rage contorted his face; spittle flew from his slick lips. "Do you have *any* idea what you've cost me? I—"

"Jonathan!" Joanna stepped in. The cool calm normally custom in her voice was nowhere to be found. "What do you think you are doing here?" she hissed, pointing at the floor like she was telling a bad dog to *sit*.

His face twisted into a deep furrow as he glared at her, contemptuous. "*Joanna.*" He said her name like it was poison. "I followed you from the office after you finished *ruining my life*, not knowing you were coming to her *party*. I should have known! My own fucking *sister*. Does loyalty mean nothing to you?"

Lucy was too stunned to check, but she felt every single eye on the rooftop staring at them.

Joanna stepped closer, lowering her voice to an even more terrifying hiss, doing her best to maintain control. "You don't deserve loyalty when you're hurting people, Jonathan."

"*Hurting?*" he crowed, making no effort to keep his voice down. "Do you want to talk about hurt? Do you know what I've lost because of this? My clients, my career, my *company*, probably my house, my—"

"Those are *things*, Jonathan. *Things!*" Lucy cut in, shocked to hear the sound of her own voice. It came crying out from the outrage rippling inside her, and she could not stop it. "Do you know what *we've* lost because of this—because of *you*? Dignity, self-worth, our sense of security. All because you thought you had some right to—"

"Shut up!" he barked, and Lucy jumped. His usually passive intimidation tactics erupted into action. The reserve he always showed in his office vanished. He stepped toward her like he wanted to strangle her, a vein pulsing in his forehead and his hand like a claw. "This is all your fault. You should have taken the money and *kept your mouth shut*, you little—"

A flying fist cut off his final word. A fist decorated in silver rings and chipped black nail polish.

The rooftop collectively gasped, and if Lucy weren't so shocked, she would have worried about someone pulling out a phone to take a video of Leo Ash's latest scandal that she would have to clean up.

Jonathan stumbled and landed on his backside, arms sprawled to catch himself and an angry red welt in the shape of a signet ring bruising his cheekbone. He blinked in a daze as Leo stood over him. Lucy couldn't tell if he was more shocked that he had been punched in the face or that he had been punched in the face by a rock star.

"Do *not* talk to Lucy like that," Leo spat with an authority Lucy did not know he possessed. His jaw set hard, and his fist stayed clenched. Worry that he had injured his Grammy-winning hand on her behalf flitted through her mind, but she assured herself he could at least still sing if he had to give up the guitar. Though he didn't look fazed at all. "I think it's best that you leave now," he rasped like an unreasonably attractive sheriff in a Western.

Jonathan crab-walked away from them, silent, and slowly got to his feet, holding his face and still looking confused. Watching him scurry away, pride obliterated, was perhaps the best birthday gift Leo could have given her.

Leo's fist didn't unclench until the doorway swallowed

Jonathan inside. He then turned to Lucy with glassy eyes and a lopsided grin that reminded her he'd had four shots of whisky in the past ten minutes. "How's that for doing something, huh?" He threw up his hands like he was going to take a bow.

"Oh my god, Leo" was all Lucy could say. Violence was rarely the answer, but she had to admit that vicariously it felt pretty damn fabulous.

He chuckled. "Listen, I can't hang, but I hope you have a great night. You're a superstar, Lucy Green." He kissed her cheek as if nothing had happened. "Happy birthday. Spend that money wisely." He pointed at her with both hands as he walked away.

"Leo!" she called after him, already worried and envisioning the mess she'd have to clean up not only over the punch but likely another DUI too. "You're not driving, are you?"

He held up his phone without turning around, then pressed it to his ear, she hoped in signal he was calling his driver.

And then he was gone as quickly as he came, took four shots of whisky, and punched out Jonathan Jenkins.

Chatter slowly refilled the rooftop like birds waking at sunrise, one, and then another, until everyone was chirping and singing. Lucy had half a mind to force everyone outside of her party guests to sign an NDA over what they just witnessed, but in truth, news of Leo throwing hands at Jonathan Jenkins would do a lot more for his reputation than giving a hundred grand to a charity—especially since Jonathan had just admitted to the bribe in front of a rooftop of witnesses.

A waiter appeared to sweep up Annie's broken glass. Joanna turned to them, pale and looking nauseous.

"Lucy, I'm so sorry. That was . . . Well, that was mortifying on so many levels. I didn't know he followed me here. I'll go if you want me to."

"It's okay, Joanna. And no, please stay."

Joanna numbly nodded like she was still processing the scene, unable to believe what all had just happened, and went back to the dinner table.

Lucy turned to Annie. "Are you okay?"

The shock on her face gave way to an open-mouthed smile. She laughed. "That was the greatest thing I've ever seen. Holy shit. I need another drink." She stepped over the pink puddle at their feet, and Lucy was left alone.

But only long enough to look up and see another set of unexpected guests at the doorway.

"Mom! Dad!" she blurted.

Lucy's parents approached dressed in their best attempt at a night out. She had last seen her father in a suit jacket at her cousin's wedding three years before, and her mother wore the wrap dress and cardigan she saved for trips to the local theater. They looked positively lost on a glitzy rooftop in downtown L.A. The fact that they were even there sent a warming rush of affection to Lucy's chest. She tried to remember if she invited them or simply let the time and location slip to her mother. Most likely the latter.

Based on their faces, she knew they had, thankfully, missed the drama. Her father would have inflicted twice the damage Leo had if he had witnessed the scene. And her mother . . . Well, Lucy could only imagine.

"Happy birthday, darling," her father said, and kissed her cheek. He held a pink envelope in his hand, no doubt stuffed with a birthday card bursting with glitter or butterflies or flowers and a generic quote about being a beloved daughter. There would be a check inside for one one-thousandth the amount of the one stuffed down her bra, and Lucy would put it toward useful things like groceries or her internet bill even though the card would instruct her to *buy yourself something nice.* The predictable sentiment tightened her throat with emotion.

"Thanks, Dad."

Her father excused himself farther down the bar, leaving Maryellen and Lucy alone for what Lucy knew was the whole reason they had come.

Her mother hesitated, one hand on her purse's strap like someone might steal it. Or like she was nervous.

The thought that she had made her mother nervous twinged Lucy's heart with sadness. "Mom, listen. I didn't mean to upset you earlier. Sorry if what I said sounded harsh."

Maryellen looked like she was fighting to let Lucy finish speaking. Lucy wasn't sure what to make of that, since her mother often cut her off. She took a breath and nodded. "It's okay. I understand why you would feel that way, sweetheart."

Lucy started, expecting to be scolded.

Her mother let go of her purse strap and continued. "I just want what's best for you; both your father and I do. And I'm . . . I'm sorry if I get carried away sometimes, if I may seem perhaps more involved than you would like me to be. You are a remarkable young woman, and we are so proud of everything you do."

Lucy thought she might be dreaming. In fact, she couldn't be sure that her mother had ever told her she was proud of her before. She had shown it in various ways, sure. But saying the words out loud? Lucy had no specific memory of it.

"Thank you," she said. "And thank you for driving all the way up here. You didn't have to do that."

Her mother brushed her off. "Well, I know you've had a

hard day, and we thought it would be special to see you on your birthday. How are things with work?"

The reflex to roll her eyes came on strong but fizzled out given her mother's peace offering. But still, they'd gone from greetings to discussing her career in under a minute.

Lucy realized with a rush of relief that she had good news to report on that front. "Work is excellent. I've been promoted to senior publicist."

Her mother nodded in impressed approval. "That's fantastic. And that man . . . ?"

The way she trailed off, Lucy knew her mother had read everything she could find on the internet. She'd spent the afternoon watching the volley of allegations and denials, and she had just narrowly missed the grand finale. Though if she stuck around the party, she'd surely hear about it.

"I won't have to worry about him anymore."

"That's good to hear. You know, girls your age have so much more support than back when I was working full-time." Something unexpected and dark shaded her voice, and Lucy wondered just what was in her mother's past. What did she not know about the woman who raised her? Maryellen paused and looked down at her feet in sensible pumps. She looked back up and gave Lucy a soft smile. "I'm glad things have changed enough that you can speak up now, even if it is still hard."

Lucy cast eyes toward the table where Annie had joined the crowd. She chatted with Nina and sipped her cosmo. "I had help."

Her mother breathed a contented sigh. "Well, I don't doubt that you know what you're doing and that you are making the best decisions for your career."

The words melted over Lucy like golden light. She basked in the approval.

"And what was that you told me about you and Caleb earlier?"

The golden light snapped out, and Lucy silently swore that if the topic of marriage and children came up, she would drown the rest of the night in tequila shots.

"We broke up."

"Ah, that's what I thought. Unfortunate, but for the best, I presume?"

"Yes." Lucy's face burned, and she looked at her own feet. "He was not the one for me, turns out."

"Well, I wish Caleb the best, but I trust you to follow your heart, Lucy. And I hope I have reason to get to know the very nice young man who was asking about you in the elevator."

She heard the smile in her mother's voice before she saw it. Her head snapped up. "What?"

Maryellen tilted her head toward the door, where none other than Adam stood by, patiently waiting with a bouquet of pink roses in his hand. He gave her a small wave, and the rush of nerves that hit her almost knocked her down.

Her mother squeezed her hand with a smile. "Happy birthday, honey. I'm going to join your father for a drink."

She left Lucy standing alone, and she suddenly had no idea what to do with herself. The one person she most wanted to show up to her party had arrived. He had been there as long as her parents, but he graciously let them go first. Her heart kicked into high gear, and she no longer cared that she was starving and the second round of appetizers was passing by on platters: tuna tartare and truffle fries. She only had thought for the man she met the night before who she already had an enormous crush on, and who was walking straight at her, smiling.

"You lied to me this afternoon, Lucy Green," he greeted.

Warmth coursed through her. One, because he was there at all; two, because he looked hot as hell in jeans and boots and the same button-down from the bar and hair clearly mashed by a motorcycle helmet; and three, because he accused her of lying.

"Hi," she said breathily. "I'm glad you came. And that's impossible. How did I lie to you?"

He stepped closer, and a heady rush hit her. A wave of something light and fresh filled her nose, a scent that reminded her of kissing him on that sunny sidewalk. He set the roses on the bar and leaned on his elbow. "You lied to me because you said you came to the bar to talk, but I only got to listen. You left before I could say anything."

He was right; she had bailed out of self-preservation. She was suddenly embarrassed. "I wasn't sure you'd have anything to say after I . . ." She awkwardly waved her hand. "After all that."

His full lips pulled up into a sly grin. "Oh, but I do have things to say. And thanks to your little fib earlier, I'm here crashing your birthday party out of necessity."

He was a magnet drawing her in. She was sure she had scared him away. And yet, there he was.

"I don't think it's crashing if I invited you."

"Fair point." He reached for the roses. "Now, I know you said you wanted flowers for no reason, but I hope you will make an exception since it is your birthday and there's really nothing I can do about that." He handed them to her, and she realized he was reciting part of her list.

She took the half-dozen pink roses and touched them to her nose, inhaling the signature scent. "Thank you. They're lovely."

"Of course. So, I know we've only known each other for a day, but I feel like I should tell you that my last relationship ended three months ago and lasted just over a year. We weren't planning on getting married, though that is something I see in my future someday. And as for kids, sure, but I could go either way, honestly. I have been known to give a mean backrub on a whim; I don't know how to spend a weekend other than in bed; and I am an emotional 7-Eleven: Pixar movies and airport reunions make me cry. I hardly remember my own birthday, but I will be hard-pressed to ever forget yours, and I will do my best to commit any others you deem vital to memory. I do cook, though most of my culinary skills revolve around appetizers and cocktails, but I am a whiz with a takeout menu. You are without a doubt the most interesting person I've ever met, Lucy Green, and I would be honored to know what's on your mind and to listen to your problems. I'll even help you solve some, if you'd like. Given that I make mistakes, I don't hold anyone to standards of perfection because that's wholly hypocritical. And I've learned that taking things for granted is the best way to lose them. Finally, this is L.A., so I hope I don't have to hold out for rain before I can kiss you again."

She gaped at him and realized he just ran through her whole list. Not only had he listened, he memorized exactly what she wanted. And he'd been every bit as honest with her as she had been with him. He hadn't run away; he was standing right in front of her, open and vulnerable. He didn't make himself perfect either; he made himself real. And he brought her flowers.

Her knees wobbled. She gripped the bar for support.

He stepped even closer—there were only inches between

them. She started babbling mainly because she wondered all over again if he was real. "Um, you . . . you left out the great sex part."

He slowly nodded and gently reached for her face. "I believe it was *amazing* sex, and let's at least get another kiss under our belt first, yeah?" His thumb brushed her cheek, and his face came close enough to see the gold flecks in his eyes.

The magnetism was irresistible. If anyone had told her she would end the night kissing a man she met the day before instead of getting a marriage proposal, she would have laughed hysterically. And yet.

Adam pulled her lips to his, and the warmth that spread over her like the bone-melting sun on an autumn day assured her she was right where she was supposed to be.

The kiss was soft and gentle this time, polite, until Lucy decided she wanted more. After the day she had, the discoveries she'd made, she wanted to be swept off her feet. The welcoming yield of Adam's body said he was more than willing to do the sweeping.

She wrapped her arms around his neck, and he leaned in. His palms spread between her shoulders then he hugged her around her waist, bending her backward enough so that their chests pressed together. Lucy forgot they were in public; her hazy mind drifted to future possibilities if the kiss—the best one so far—was any indication of what was to come.

She moved her hands to his face, knowing they had to reel it in. They were two seconds away from full-on making out in front of her boss—and her parents. She brushed her thumbs over his flushed cheeks and kissed his lips again because they were right there and she just couldn't help herself.

"Whoa," Adam said, dazed, and it sounded so genuine, Lucy laughed. The dopey shine in his eyes made her weak in the knees, and she wondered if they could sneak off without anyone noticing she'd gone missing from her own party.

She heard Nina's laugh ring out over the din, and she knew she wanted to share Adam with her friends as much as she wanted him to herself. Based on the promise in his kiss, there would be plenty of time for privacy later. By some miracle, and despite her most honest efforts, she had all the people she cared about in one place. She had to take advantage.

She pressed her hand to Adam's chest, right on top of his heart. "I didn't think you were going to show up."

He wrapped his fingers around hers and held on. Somehow the contact felt more intimate than their kiss. "Are you kidding? I had to see how the story ended. Has the honesty curse been lifted?"

"I'm no expert, but I think it's going to last until midnight."

"Oh really? Hmm. Well, we could always test it again."

She hesitated, not really sure she wanted to play along.

"Something easy," he offered when he picked up on her nerves.

"Okay, fine."

"Okay. Will you go out with me this weekend?"

A laugh popped from her lips. "Of course I will. Why would I lie about that?"

"I was giving you something easy! All you had to do was say no."

"I don't want to say no."

"I don't think you understand the rules here."

"I understand them perfectly. I've just decided that even if I can lie, I don't want to anymore."

He stroked his chin like he was contemplating her declaration. "Ever?"

She studied the planes and angles of his handsome face. She had only known him for a day, but her heart was already cartwheeling at the thought of where they might go together, what they might become. The rush of opportunity and unfettered *anything could happen* excitement whipped through her veins. The start of something new, something fresh, to go with her new, honest lease on life. She couldn't promise she would never lie to him, even something small and innocent for his benefit, because relationships got messy, she knew that. But the hope in his eyes, the promise, and the feeling of his kiss, she knew deep in her heart that she would never want to lie about the way she felt about him.

"Not to you."

His grin widened into a warm smile, and he kissed her again. He kissed her like a movie ending in the rain. Her head spun; her heart raced. For the first time since she woke that morning, she felt like she was having a truly happy birthday. He released her politely, but she could feel the reluctance in his grip.

Adam leaned on the bar like he needed support. He nodded toward the table. "So, I've already met your parents. Are you going to introduce me to everyone else—is that Lily Chu?" He balked when he recognized her.

Lucy smiled, wondering what he would say if she told him she had a hundred-thousand-dollar check from a rock star in her bra. "It is, and yes, I will. But I just realized this is the first time we've been on the same side of a bar. Let me order you a drink."

He turned to her with a knowing if not slightly wary grin. "You sure that's a good idea, you know, given how this all started?"

He made a fair point, and Lucy could not be sure that the drink he served her the night before had not played a role in her wish coming true. But she did know that the drink and the wish had changed her life, so what was the harm in testing the theory on him?

She gave him a smile and shrugged. "Let's find out."

Lucy studied her reflection in her bathroom mirror, wondering if she needed a touch more Bobbi Brown. She had been a senior publicist for a year and a half, and she had new clients, several major and successful publicity campaigns, and plenty of dark circles under her eyes to show for it.

But she would not trade any of it.

She had hit the ground running after her promotion and Joanna's appointment as CEO. J&J Public underwent changes—all for the better—that left her with miles-long to-do lists. Not to mention the fact that the fallout from the *Deadline* scandal left her and her new assistant with public notoriety that took some time to die down. Nevertheless, she took it in stride, albeit with a little less sleep.

Looking in the mirror, she decided that yes, she did need a touch more concealer given she would not be completely in the shadows at the night's event. She dipped her sponge into a little dollop on her hand and dabbed beneath her lashes. Although she had a professional stylist at her disposal, she opted to do her own hair and makeup, not wanting to end up overdone and looking like someone else. She swiped a finger to smooth out the supple red color on her lips just as her doorbell rang.

"Come in!" she called through her small apartment, not really wanting to abandon her post until she finished her look.

Where she expected a key in the door, a silence followed. She dug her fingers into the sweetheart bodice of her dress one last time, securing her chest in the built-in padding that fit her like a glove and eliminated the need for a bra.

When Lily Chu invited her to her movie premiere—the hotly anticipated first installment of the alien-slaying saga—as a guest and not as her publicist, she offered all the trimmings: hair and makeup, styling, transportation. Lucy took her up on the final two and indulged in not having to wear something off-the-rack. Her buttercup yellow gown hugged and draped like it was custom-made because it was. She'd given strict instructions to prioritize comfort and functionality, and the designer hit every mark while still making a stunning look for her. Red carpet or not, she did not want to be stuck unable to breathe or bend over or even walk with a normal stride all night. The fabric gracefully moved with her, and she could even wear normal underwear beneath the fluttering skirt. She marveled at the fact that it was entirely possible to make something both beautiful and functional when the world told her that was a feat as impossible as finding Atlantis.

To complete her look, she softened her hair into old Hollywood glamour waves and painted her lips ruby. Rarely having an occasion to get so dressed up, she found herself enjoying it.

The doorbell rang again, followed by insistent knocking.

Her driver was due in ten minutes, and she knew that was not who waited at the door; she was expecting someone else first. What she did not know was why Adam was not using his key and instead making her navigate a maze of moving boxes to let him in.

The night of her thirtieth birthday party, when they shared drinks and kissed a dozen more times, no spells were cast. At least, none of the inexplicable, life-changing kind. Well, perhaps a little life-changing, seeing that Lucy was head over heels for her Hot Bartender and counting down the days until they moved in together—for real and 100 percent mutually on purpose this time. On the night of her big day, after she hugged all her guests goodbye and the restaurant closed, she and Adam made it a point to stay out past midnight to test the wish's expiration. He took her to an underground bar—literally; she had no idea the place even existed in downtown L.A.—that ended up being a classy, low-lit lounge where, of course, he knew the bartender. She quickly learned that about Adam: not only did he know all the best places, he knew the owners, chefs, bartenders, and waitstaff at almost every place they went. And he was an incredibly generous tipper.

They sat in that bar, talking, flirting, getting bolder about touching each other, and sipping cocktails until the clock struck midnight. At 12:01, Adam asked her what she was drinking— the question they had earlier agreed would be a harmless test— and she said a martini when it was in fact a Manhattan.

Where she half expected to feel relief, some kind of restraint being lifted, she was surprised to find that her primary emotion was sadness—disappointment, even—that she was no longer bound by the truth.

But then she remembered that honesty had always been a choice; it just hadn't been the one she had been making.

She vowed to follow her newly found morals, Adam as her witness and cocktail as her oath keeper, and had lived her life as if it were her thirtieth birthday since. Mostly. There were times, of course, when she permitted little white lies for the greater good. Like when she told Oliver his experimental vegan cheesecake was delicious or told Nina that she finished the book she lent her. Or when Leo Ash needed to hear that chopping off his signature mop of hair was a good move—which actually turned out not to be a lie when videos of his fans buzzing their heads in solidarity went viral. *Those* untruths were fine. But the ones centered on integrity, self-respect, and injustice had no place in Lucy's life anymore.

The knocking on her front door continued. She put down her makeup and gathered her dress to walk barefoot through her apartment, careful not to snag the silky fabric on any of the moving boxes. Adam had a three-bedroom house in Santa Monica she had slowly been invading over the past year, and they recently decided it was time to take the leap and move in together. Of course the move coincided with Lily's movie premiere—the biggest event on Lucy's fall calendar—but she thrived off the excitement of juggling many tasks at once. She would not survive a single day as a publicist otherwise.

She arrived at the front door, threw the dead bolt, and opened it to Adam standing on her doorstep in a tux.

"Why are you knocking and not using your key?" she asked before the brunt of how goddamned sexy he looked in black and white had the chance to hit her. When it did, her whole body flushed. She bit her lip and pressed her thighs together, twisting her bare feet and swishing her dress.

"Because I wanted this moment." He grinned his dimple-

popping smile. "Of seeing you open the door looking like this."
He stood there staring at her, eyes soft in the way that had
come to make Lucy's heart swell and her blood heat.

They really only had ten minutes until their car came to
take them to the premiere, and she had just spent a good hour
turning herself red-carpet-worthy—and his bow tie and buttons looked complicated and like they would take more than a
few minutes to reassemble should she choose to undo them all
in that moment. But that did not mean she didn't want to for-
sake it all and destroy both of their outfits.

She composed herself with a smile and let him in. "Well, it's
rare I get to attend these events not wearing background black
and accessorized with a lanyard and earpiece; I have to take
advantage. We'll still be invisible next to the actual stars
though."

She turned to resume getting ready, and he reached for her
arm, pulling her back to his front and pressing his lips to the
exact spot on her neck where she liked to be kissed. He knew
where it was because she had told him. He knew where *all* her
preferred spots were because she had told him, and that was a
freedom she never thought she would have the courage to
embrace.

"You will be far from invisible," he mumbled into the hol-
low below her ear, making her dizzy and melt all at once.

Another thing she quickly learned about Adam was that he
was a complete romantic. Once she worked up the nerve, he
took her on motorcycle rides up the coast to Malibu just to kiss
her on the beach as the sun dipped below the sea's horizon and
then turn back home. On her thirty-first birthday and what
was for all intents and purposes their anniversary, he gave her a
cocktail napkin with a list of her relationship wants written on

it; her number and the time and place of her party were on the other side. He told her he had written down everything she said as soon as she walked away that day because he knew, even after one day, that he had to do everything to keep her.

And then he did things like made her answer the door when he had a key just so he could make her feel beautiful.

She leaned back into him. "Adam, I have to finish getting ready. We can't be late."

"Hmm," he hummed, like being punctual was of little concern.

On the day of, it had not occurred to Lucy the extent to which Adam was part of her perfect day. That he was the honest relationship she did not even realize she had been denying herself. Perhaps it had to do with the scandal and her breakup and her promotion all happening that day as well, but in moments like the one they shared there in her living room, his arms wrapped around her like they had always belonged, she wondered how it had not been completely obvious.

She had also overlooked the potential of true love's kiss, chalking it up to fairy-tale magic with no basis in reality. But then she experienced firsthand a wish coming true, so she was no longer so quick to dismiss such possibilities. She should have realized that day when she fell into Adam's arms and landed on his lips that it was a sign, a not-so-gentle hint from the universe setting her on the right path.

Still, a year and a half later, she had no idea what she had done to deserve such fortunate cosmic intervention, but she did not take it—nor what it had gifted her—for granted.

The car was due in ten minutes, but she could take a few minutes to pause the hurry and stand in Adam's embrace, feeling loved and in love.

She turned to face him and gently pressed her lips to his. "You look amazing, by the way."

"Thank you. Is this color good on me?" He touched his fingers to his mouth, testing if her lipstick had transferred.

"It doesn't come off," she said, smiling.

A daring thrill sparked in his eyes, flashing the gold flecks and making Lucy's knees wobble. "Well, in that case . . ."

He pulled her into a movie-ending kiss, and Lucy knew they were going to be more than a few minutes late.

ACKNOWLEDGMENTS

What a dream to write an acknowledgments section. I have been an avid reader my whole life and now I understand, truly, the village it takes to get a book into someone's hands.

My agent, Melissa Edwards: thank you for pulling me out of the slush pile and sticking with me. Thank you for believing in Lucy from the very beginning and helping her story reach its potential.

My editing team at Dutton: Stephanie Kelly, thank you for seeing the spark in this story and for your direction in making it truly shine. Lexy Cassola, thank you for your kind and thoughtful feedback. Janice Barral, thank you for your sharp production edits. Cassidy Sachs, thank you for shepherding me through publication. The Dutton art team, thank you for the cover of my dreams!

The Twitter writing community: thank you for the endless support, the laughs, the commiseration, the information, and the unwavering belief that dreams can come true.

My agent siblings: I could not ask for a kinder, more talented support group to cheer me on and to ask a million questions. Thank you for your wisdom and unconditional encouragement.

The wonderful women of my L.A. writers' group: thank you for your guidance, support, laughter, and friendship. Brunch anytime.

My teachers who played a special part in my pursuit of this dream many, many years in the making: Mrs. D, thank you for reading *Harry Potter* to our fifth-grade class in a British accent and doing all the character voices. You made books magical. Mr. McClanahan, thank you for bringing literature to life for me in high school and reminding me that reading is like breathing. Dr. Amy Clarke, thank you for planting the belief that I was good enough to be published by suggesting I submit to the campus undergraduate writing contest. You scared me to death and gave me courage at the same time. My graduate school professors, thank you for tearing my scientific writing to pieces and giving me the backbone to grow from criticism. You influenced my art in unexpected ways that I am eternally grateful for.

My friends and family: thank you for always answering my no-context questions without blinking, for fact-checking, and for cheering me on. Special thanks to all the women who allowed me to infuse data into my fiction by answering my poll on the many things that we put up with but never talk about. Our conversations were incredibly validating, and I hope I did them justice.

My grandparents: thank you for teaching me how to tell stories, and for always listening.

My parents: thank you for never once doubting my dreams, no matter what shape they take or how enormous they grow.

Stella: thank you for taking me on walks to fix all the plot holes. Good dog.

My husband, James: thank you for your endless support through this journey, starting with that conversation we had on the beach in Hawaii in 2015. Thank you for believing in me even when I don't. Thank you for our life.

This story came to me in the late summer of 2020 during a year that was for me, as for many others, tremendously difficult. Lucy was a bright spot, and though her story is drawn from real-life experiences—my own and those of women close to me and many I've never met—exploring those experiences through a fictional lens was cathartic. The pandemic changed my perspective on the expectations the world has for me and those I have for myself. If Lucy's story can make anyone relate, laugh, reflect, or find a voice they didn't know they have, I will count myself extraordinarily fortunate. Thank you, sincerely, for reading.